KU-786-686

CHILD WONDER

1961: Finn lives with his mother in a working-class suburb of Oslo. Life is a constant struggle to make ends meet, and eventually they must advertise for a lodger. But when Ingrid Olaussen turns up, she is not there to rent the room, but to bring tumultuous news — Finn has a six-year-old half-sister, who is now coming to live with them . . . Soon, both half-sister Linda and lodger Kristian are ensconced within the flat. Irritated by Linda's strangeness, and enthralled by Kristian's bad language and Bakelite television, Finn must strive to find his place within this new family arrangement.

ROY JACOBSEN

CHILD WONDER

Translated from the Norwegian by
Don Bartlett and Don Shaw

Complete and Unabridged

ULVERSCROFT
Leicester

First published in Great Britain in 2011 by
MacLehose Press
an imprint of Quercus
London

First Large Print Edition
published 2017
by arrangement with
Quercus
London

The moral right of the author has been asserted

Copyright © 2009 by Cappelen Damm AS
English translation copyright © 2011
by Don Bartlett & Don Shaw
All rights reserved

This book is a work of fiction. Names, characters,
businesses, organisations, places and events are either
the product of the author's imagination or are used
fictitiously. Any resemblance to actual persons, living
or dead, events or locales is entirely coincidental.

A catalogue record for this book is available
from the British Library.

ISBN 978–1–4448–3191–7

Published by
F. A. Thorpe (Publishing)
Anstey, Leicestershire

Set by Words & Graphics Ltd.
Anstey, Leicestershire
Printed and bound in Great Britain by
T. J. International Ltd., Padstow, Cornwall

This book is printed on acid-free paper

Northamptonshire
Libraries

E

Foreword

My heroes are kids. Brave, struggling kids. Growing up in a working-class area outside Oslo in the early sixties — a time of confusion, excitement and unrefined and rather rough social experimentation. Before oil. Before anybody had any money at all. When a social-democratic welfare state was no more than a vague and desperate idea, so unlike the nouveau-riche society it produced within just a few decades. This was a change so abrupt, radical and unheard of in Norway's history that all that is left of it is an ambiguous nostalgia and real stories on that eternal subject: how to lose one's innocence without losing one's soul. This novel is dedicated to those kids who made it. And to those who didn't. I love them all.

ROY JACOBSEN

1

It all started when Mother and I had some decorating to do. That is, I painted the lowest part of the wall, as I was rather lacking in height — it was a struggle — while she stood on a kitchen chair and concentrated on the bit below the ceiling. At that rate it would actually take several months to finish one wall. But one evening fru Syversen came round, eyed our handiwork, her arms folded across her ample bosom, and said:

'Why don't you try wallpaper, Gerd?'

'Wallpaper?'

'Yes, come with me.'

We followed fru Syversen, who lived across the corridor from us, I had never been in her flat before, even though we had been living opposite each other for several years, and Anne-Berit lived there, a girl of my age in the class parallel to mine, as well as her two little sisters, six-year-old twins whose names frequently came up whenever Mother had a bone to pick with me.

'Look at Reidun and Mona,' came the refrain. Or she invoked Anne-Berit, who, according to fru Syversen, considered being indoors, where her bed and food were, more fun than being out in the street, where life was forged with its immense array of boards and building blocks and roof tiles strewn around between blocks of flats, and down beyond, the grass-covered fields with tree stumps and logs and uncluttered brooks and thick scrub and hidden clay paths, where you could light fires from roofing felt and lumps of tar and scraps of wood, and build two-storey huts, over which famous battles were fought, by the great and the invincible, edifices which could be razed to the ground from one moment to the next and would have to be rebuilt the day-after, never by those who had torn them down. Those who build and those who destroy are never one and the same. I mention this because I was a builder, even though I was small, and I shed many a tear at finding our castles in ruins; there was talk of reprisals and bloodcurdling vengeance, but the vandals had nothing to lose save their good humour and broad smirks, already there were traces here of a division, between those who have something to lose and those who have never had and never will have plans to acquire a bean. And this world had nothing to offer Anne-Berit and her sisters, they neither built nor destroyed, they sat around the kitchen table eating supper, all day long as far as I could see, this time with herr Syversen, presiding from the head of the table in a string vest with braces hanging down over impressive bulldozer thighs that bulged over the edge of his fragile chair.

On the sitting-room walls of the Syversen family flat we saw for the first time the large-flower pattern wallpaper that would in the course of the Sixties turn Norwegian working-class homes into minor tropical jungles, with slender book shelves made of teak and supported by smart brass fittings between the lianas, and a striped corner sofa in brown, beige and white, illuminated by tiny invisible lamps mounted beneath the shelving like glittering stars. I could see the cool, faraway look in my mother's eyes, an initial girlish enthusiasm that might last for three to four seconds, I knew, before giving way to her natural timidity, which in turn would end in the expression of a realistic mind-set: 'No, that's not something we can afford. We can't do that.' Or: 'That's no good for us.' And so on. And there was quite a lot of 'That's not for us' at that time for Mother and me, because she worked only part-time at the shoe shop in the Oslo district of Vaterland so that she would be at home and ready whenever I ambled in from school, and therefore she could not see herself having the means to send the lad on holiday, which she said every time spring was in the offing, as if indeed I wanted to be sent anywhere, I wanted to be at home with my mother, even in the summer; there were many others on the estate who stayed at home during the summer, although it was common for people to pretend they didn't, or at least to say they had no wish to go on holiday.

'Isn't it rather costly?' she asked, a word she only uses when we are with others; on our own we say 'dear', and we mean it.

'Not at all,' said fru Syversen, who was wont to read Swedish women's magazines — in contrast to Mother who read only Norwegian ones — and produced a pile of Swedish magazines off a shelf in the tropical rain forest and flicked open to an article from Malmø, summoning herr Syversen from the kitchen as she did so and instructing him to show Gerd the receipts.

I watched the big man, who chuckled Right you are, and was willingness itself, and as he lumbered over to the bookcase and pulled out a drawer hardly big enough to hold much more than a picture postcard, the strange aroma of hard-working adult man assailed my nostrils and I thought, as I always did whenever this large human being came too close to me, on the stairs and in the hobby room, that perhaps being without a father was not such a bad thing after all, even though herr Syversen was good-natured and harmless enough, and always had a pleasant remark to make about some topic that did not interest me. In other words, it was his wife who was responsible for these three well-brought-up girls, who were still sitting in the kitchen and silently chomping away while casting surreptitious glances at us.

What was remarkable was that Mother was unable to dismiss these receipts with her usual set phrases; in fact, the wallpaper was indeed not very 'costly', and it had not been bought in Sweden either, but in a hardware shop, Agda Manufaktur og Myklebust, at the Årvoll Senter, next to the bank, where we did our food shopping if for some reason we did not go to Lien in Traverveien or Omar Hansen in Refstad allé and from whom, until last year, Mother had also rented a freezer until it became too dear or until we discovered we did not know what to do with it; after all, these were the years of the Berlin Wall and President Kennedy, most of all though I suppose it was the era of Yuri Gagarin, the Russian who had astounded the whole world by returning alive from certain death. It was, moreover, also the time a Mark II Jaguar cost 49,300 Norwegian kroner, a snippet of information I mention here not simply as a curiosity, but also because I saw this price, and the car, at a car exhibition at Bjerke Trotting Stadium and have never been able to forget it, perhaps encouraged by the fact that I knew we had made a down payment to the Housing Co-op of 3,200 kroner and that meant the Jaguar was worth the same as sixteen flats, a whole block, in other words. And any system that equates a car with the homes of seventy-six alive and kicking human beings of all ages, such as those living in No. 3, that's the kind of knowledge that hits you like a goods train when you are young, and it never leaves you. Think of all the smells, every family has its own smell, distinct from all others, and all the faces and voices, the estate's discordant choir, look at their bodies, clothes and movements as they sit there with their shirtsleeves rolled up, eating dinner and arguing or laughing or crying or keeping their mouths shut and chewing thirty-two times on each side. What can a Jaguar have to compare with all this? A revolver in the glove compartment? At the very least. I have thought a lot about the car, probably much too much, it was bottle-green.

'But then there's the price of the paste on top of that, you know,' fru Syversen continued, as if it had occurred to her that things were going too smoothly.

'No, there isn't,' herr Syversen interrupted. His Christian name, it now transpired, was Frank.

'What did you say, Frank?' fru Syversen said in a sharp tone, taking the receipts off him and subjecting them to critical scrutiny through a pair of jet-black hexagonal glasses, which had not been easy to find among the multitude of light-blue porcelain figures and oval pewter ashtrays on shelf after shelf, shelves which, in my opinion, should have been filled with books, didn't they have any books in this family? But Frank just shrugged, smiled at Mother, placed a leaden hand on my cropped head and said:

'Well, Finn, so you're the boss at home, are you?'

A remark I presumed was prompted by the green paint on my face, on my fingers and in my hair, and I must have looked as if I were doing a man's work to keep our two lives afloat.

'Yes, he's so good . . . ' and at that point Mother's voice broke, 'I could never have managed without him.'

Which is a sentence I quite like, because it did not take a lot to knock Mother off her perch at that time, even though we lived in a house of reinforced concrete with swallows' nests in the loft and neighbours who sat on their balconies leisurely drinking coffee, or stood with their heads under car bonnets for hours on end; I could read and write better than most, and her wages arrived on time, every fortnight, well, even though nothing at all ever happened here, it was as though we were forever surrounded by perils which we had been lucky enough to avoid so far because, to quote Mother, you cannot learn anything from things that never happen.

'You know, I'm not as strong as I used to be,' she mumbled when something or other was looming, and then she alluded — although I never asked and she never gave an explanation — to her divorce, which I suppose must have hit her like an avalanche and was only the first of a series of small incidents in a kind of enduring misery. For this may have been the era of Yuri Gagarin, but it was by no means the era of divorce, it was the era of marriage, and only a year after the divorce he also passed away, as Mother puts it, the consequence of an accident at work. My father died in a crane accident at Akers Mekaniske Verksted, a shipbuilding company. I can neither remember him nor the divorce, nor the accident, but Mother remembers for us both, even though you can never get any specific details out of her, about for example what he looked like or what he liked doing, or did not like doing in his free time, if he had any, that is, or where he came from or what they talked about in the happy years they must have had while they were waiting for me; even her photographs she keeps close to her chest; in short, this is an era we have put behind us.

In the wake of the two disasters there followed yet another, this time connected with a widow's pension; you see, my father managed to get hitched again before he fell to his death, and to have another child, a girl, whose name we did not even know, so that now there was another widow somewhere out there, receiving the money that Mother and I should have had, and squandering it on the pools and taxis and perms.

'Well, don't ask me what's happened to them,' fru Syversen said, resigned, waving the invoices for the wallpaper but not the paste. However, now at least Mother was able to round up proceedings with her simple:

'Hm, well, we'll have to see about that.' And by sending the girls a goodbye smile. They stared back at us with mouths agape and three big milky moustaches. 'Thank you for letting us have a peep. It's really nice.'

9

2

The very next day we were in the Årvoll Senter looking at wallpaper. And that is pretty sensational, for Mother is not only beset by perils, she also takes her time to think things through; the green paint we had just wasted our money on, for example, was no mindless caprice, but the result of laborious calculations that had been going on since last Christmas when we were invited to coffee and cakes by an elderly couple on the ground floor, where all the walls had been painted a different colour from our own, and it turned out they had done it themselves, the slow way, with a brush.

On another occasion she had dropped by to pick me up from a friend's, from Essi's flat where the father had moved the door to the smallest bedroom from the sitting room out into the hall, so that Essi's big sister, who was sixteen, as good as had her own entrance, from the hallway. And now it was as if all of these considerations — along with the fact that the store we were in oozed the future, new opportunities and innovation, yes, there was a sense of purity and optimism about the paint pots and the assistants' blue coats in this shop that could move a mountain — it was as if all of this fused into one momentous conclusion.

'Right,' Mother said. 'Then we'll have to take a lodger after all. There's no way round it.'

I glanced up at her in surprise, we had in fact discussed this before, and also come to a kind of agreement, as I understood it, that we would not take a lodger, no matter how hard up we were, for that meant I would have to give up the room I loved so much and move in with her.

'I can sleep in the sitting room,' she said before I could open my mouth.

Accordingly, that afternoon we not only bought wallpaper and paste, but also composed an advertisement to insert in *Arbeiderbladet*, headed LODGER WANTED. Once again we contacted the mighty bull of a man, Frank: could Frank, who had a job on the new building sites over at Groruddalen driving a bulldozer, see his way to working evenings and move the door from our smallest bedroom into the hall, so that we would be spared having the lodger disturb our private lives with his, or her, comings and goings, not to mention a total stranger

11

traipsing in and out of our newly wallpapered sitting room?

In other words, we were moving into exciting times.

It turned out that, as a joiner, Frank was nothing to write home about. He made a dreadful racket taking out the door. Not only that, he worked in a string vest, panted and sweated in bucket-loads, and from the first evening began to call Mother 'darling'.

'What d'you think, darlin', d'you wanna keep these architraves or shall I get you some new ones?'

'Depends what they cost,' Mother said.

'Won't cost you much, darlin'. I've got contacts.'

Fortunately, Mother wasn't put out by being called 'darling' all the time. And fru Syversen made sure to drop by at regular intervals to tell us she had some food ready or to inform us that the dust cart would be late today. I have to confess that I also kept an eye on proceedings, since Mother put on lipstick and removed her curlers before every session, I had hardly any time to go out into the street. Now and then fru Syversen sent over Anne-Berit, her eldest daughter, so we stood watching the solidly built Frank humping around heavy doors and sheets of plywood. Black hair covered his shoulders and back like tufts of over-wintering grass, it poked through the holes of a faded vest more reminiscent of a trawling net than an item of clothing, and in mid-toil he would groan, 'Hammer!' 'Nails!' 'Tape measure!', in a teasing way, as if we were his minions, it was a joy. But when the door was at last in position, and the other doorway was sealed, after a week or so, with new architraves and everything, and the question of payment was broached, Frank wanted nothing.

'Are you out of your mind?' Mother said.

'Though if you had the odd dram handy, darlin',' he said in a soft voice, as if now they shared some secret understanding following the successful completion of the job. Mother tripping around with an open purse and two or three blue five-kroner notes between her freshly varnished fingernails, plenty more where this comes from, Frank, all you have to do is ask — none of that made any difference, Frank was and remained a gentleman, and in the end all he took was two glasses of Curaçao.

'One for each leg.'

But now he was gone, too, and the wallpapering could begin.

Everything went swimmingly. Again Mother was on a kitchen chair under the ceiling and I was down on the floor. The wall we had spent a whole week painting was papered in one evening. Then we spent two evenings doing all the fiddly bits around the balcony door and the large sitting-room window, and one final evening on the wall adjoining my bedroom, which was now to be the lodger's. The change was there for all to see, it was explosive, it was ear-splitting. We had not gone so far as to invest in a jungle, Mother wanted something more discreet, but we stayed well within the same botanical genre anyway, with rounded borders and flowers, like golden brown scrubland in the autumn. And when two people came round the very next day to look at the room, we were in business.

No, we weren't.

There was something wrong with both of the two prospective lodgers. Then a third came, who thought there was something wrong with the room. These setbacks were a blow to Mother's confidence. Was the rent too high? Or too low? Before, she had talked about us having to move from Årvoll perhaps, to get something a bit simpler, in the area where she had lived earlier, perhaps, with her husband, in Øvre Foss, where people were still content with one room and a kitchen. But eventually a letter appeared, in spiky handwriting, from one Ingrid Olaussen, who was thirty-five years old and single, she wrote,

14

she would like to see the room this Friday, if that were convenient?

'Certainly,' Mother said.

But then she took the drastic step of being absent the day after, when I returned from school with Anne-Berit and Essi.

I had never encountered this before.

A locked door. Which was not opened when I pressed the bell, again and again. This seriously threw me off-kilter. Essi took me to his place where his mother, who was one of the few mothers on whom I could rely, aside from my own, comforted me, saying Mother was sure to be out shopping, I would see, I could do my homework there in the meantime, with Essi, who needed some help in his struggle with spelling, he wasn't much good at arithmetic, either.

'You're so clever, aren't you, Finn.'

Yes indeed, I was coping very well, it was part of the contract between Mother and me, the delicate balance in a family of two. I was given sliced bread with cervelat, which as a rule I relish, but I couldn't get a mouthful down; the strange thing is that once you have had a mother, when she goes missing, this is no trifling matter. I sat beside Essi at his broad writing desk, holding a pencil, I was orphaned and didn't write one single letter. This was so unlike her. More than an hour had passed now. (It was no more than fourteen minutes.) Only when almost two hours had passed did we hear a clatter on the road outside, which turned out to be the exhaust of a superannuated lorry trying to reverse up to the block of flats. Then I saw Mother jumping out of the driver's cab in her long, flowery shoe shop dress and running towards the entrance. On the burgundy vehicle's doors it said 'Storstein Møbler & Inventar' in gold-edged ornamental letters. A large man in a boiler suit let down the sides, another man jumped out and together they unveiled a sofa, a modern sofa bed in beige, yellow and brown stripes that Mother had gone out to buy on the flimsy basis of a letter from Ingrid Olaussen, and they hauled it off the lorry and started manoeuvring it towards the front door.

By that time I already had my school bag on my back and was galloping at full speed down to the ground floor, across the grass and up the stairs following the unwieldy piece of furniture that the two men, with curses and one cry of distress, managed to coax up to the second floor and in through the door which had been locked for an eternity, now open for the first time in my life.

Inside, Mother stood with a desperately strained expression on her face that came no

16

closer to normality on catching sight of me, because of my wretched emotional state, no doubt, and at once began to apologise, 'it had taken such a long time in the shop'. But there was no energy in her consoling words, and when she had signed a form and the new sofa was standing by the sitting-room wall where hitherto we had had nothing, but where actually it fitted very well, she had to lie down on it for a while. So did I. I lay beside her and drew in her fragrances and felt her arms around me as I instantly fell asleep: pansies, hair lacquer, shoe leather and 4711 *eau de Cologne*. I didn't wake until two hours later, under a blanket, while Mother was making supper in the kitchen, humming, as she always did.

There was no set dinner today, it was fried pork and eggs, the kind of supper that can still outdo any dinner. And over the meal she explained to me that there was something called H.P. which, in short, meant you didn't have to save *before* you bought something, you could do it afterwards, which in turn meant there was a chance we wouldn't need to wait so long to go and buy a bookcase either, not to mention one of those television sets that were invading the flats around us, so I wouldn't have to run up to Essi's every time there was something on which was not to be missed.

These were indeed heady prospects. But there was something about her that evening that still made me uneasy, something that seemed to have collapsed inside her and with it had gone her composure and peace of mind, and I — who had just been through a traumatic experience of my own — did not sleep as well that night as I usually did.

Next day I came straight back from school again, this time I found Mother at her post, ready to receive Ingrid Olaussen, and at once I got down to preparing myself, motivated by a number of reproving cautions, as though we were about to take an exam, they were quite unnecessary, it goes without saying, if there was anything I had taken on board, it was the seriousness of the matter.

'Are you alright?' I said.

'What do you mean?' she said, going over to look at herself in the mirror, returning and growling: 'You haven't got some little scheme up your sleeve, have you?'

I didn't even know what she was referring to. And within no time at all she was herself again, shooting a sympathetic glance down at me, and saying she knew this wasn't easy for me, but there was no alternative, did I realise that?

I realised that.

We were of one mind.

Ingrid Olaussen arrived half an hour late and turned out to be employed at the hair salon in Lofthusveien, she looked the part too, like a twenty-year-old, even though she must have been Mother's age. She had heaped-up, rust-red hair, with a little grey hat perched on top, adorned with a string of pearls, black droplets, so it looked as though her hair was crying. Furthermore, she smoked filter cigarettes, and it wasn't just her handwriting that was spiky, casting an eye over the room she had the nerve to say:

'Basic, right. Shouldn't you have said that in the ad?'

I didn't know what that meant, but Mother's face went through three or four familiar stages before she blurted out that it was easy for someone who didn't have a clue what it cost to put ads in the newspaper to say that.

Confronted with which statement, Ingrid Olaussen just took a long drag on her cigarette and cast around for an ashtray. But none was offered. Now Mother wanted to call off the whole business, and said that in fact we had changed our minds and needed the room ourselves.

'Sorry you've come on a wild goose chase.'

She even opened the front door for her. But then all of a sudden Ingrid Olaussen looked deeply unhappy. Her coiffed head slumped to her bosom, and her long, ungainly body began to sway.

'Goodness gracious, don't you feel well?'

Mother led her by the coat sleeve into the sitting room, sat her down on the new sofa and asked if she wanted a glass of water or a cup of coffee.

Then something even more incomprehensible happened. Ingrid Olaussen did want a cup of coffee, yes, she did, but before Mother managed to put on the kettle, she began to intertwine her long, slender fingers, as if splicing two ends of a rope, and spoke in a staccato manner, and at quite a speed, about her job, about demanding customers, as far as I was able to gather, who were always after her with all manner of criticism, not to mention the condescending owner, she also brought up a matter which made Mother totally change character and shoo me into the bedroom before I could glean any further clarification.

Through the door I heard talking, intense mumbling and what sounded like crying.

As time went on, they seemed to be on the verge of reaching agreement, there was even some hysterical laughter. And when at last

Mother opened the door, I thought they had become the best of friends. Instead it turned out that Ingrid Olaussen had departed, leaving Mother more thoughtful than ever as she prepared dinner.

'Isn't she going to live here?' I asked.

'No, she will not, I can promise you that,' she said. 'She hasn't got two øre to rub together. Her life is all over the place. And she's not even called Ingrid Olaussen, either . . . '

I wanted to ask how Mother could know all of this. Or to enquire how a total stranger might open her heart to her in this way. But a strange unease had settled over me in the course of the half hour I had spent in the bedroom, and the answers to the two questions must have been that Mother already knew her or she recognised herself in this woman. I didn't want to hear confirmation of either, I preferred to concentrate on my food, but was nevertheless left with a quite tangible feeling that there were sides to Mother of which I had little understanding, not just her sudden absence the day before, on Thursday, for which ultimately there was a reason, a sofa, but the fact that a total stranger could enter our hitherto uneventful but now over-renovated home life, break down on the new sofa, divest herself of all her secrets and then be chased away again; I was not only facing an insoluble riddle but a riddle to which I perhaps never *wanted* to find a solution.

I sat stealing furtive glances at her, my nervous, frightened of the dark but on the whole so stable and immortal mother, my bedrock on earth and my fortress in heaven, now wearing an unrecognisable face.

3

The lodger project was now put on hold for a few weeks, as though Mother was afraid to have a new mystery darken her door. But, as I mentioned before, we had committed ourselves to an agreement to save backwards, so there was no option but to put another advertisement in the *Arbeiderbladet*, at fifty øre a word. She was still testy and distracted: she put the wrong things on my slices of bread, she didn't listen when I was telling her things and she lost her place when she was reading aloud in the evenings.

'Anyway you can read better than I can now,' she said defensively when I protested. But that was not why I had learned to read, we had a heap of books, and we were going to read them all, children's books, Margit Söderholm, the Jalna series, an encyclopaedia called *Heimskringla* and Captain Marryat's *Peter Simple*, as well as one solitary book left by my father, a Finnish book entitled *The Unknown Soldier* by Väinö Linna which we had not read yet and which, according to Mother, we had no plans to read, all piled up in a box in my bedroom waiting for the bookcase which we would buy on credit, if only we could hook this damned lodger of ours. And it was on one of those occasions when she wasn't listening that it struck me I was someone else, I had changed. It wasn't a clear or a palpable feeling, but intrusive enough all the same for me to ask:

'Which of us are you talking to now: me or him over there?'

This did not go down well.

'What do you mean?' she snapped, and lectured me about my being quite incomprehensible at times, a lecture she had delivered once or twice before, perhaps it had something to do with my being a boy and her thinking life would have been easier with a daughter.

'I don't understand what you're on about,' I said, ill-humouredly, and went into my room to lie down on the bed to read in peace, a Jukan comic. But, as is the case with protest reading in general, I couldn't concentrate, I just got angrier and angrier lying there with my clothes on, wondering how long a small boy has to lie like that waiting for his mother to come to her senses and assure him that nothing has changed, irrespective of whether Yuri Gagarin has blown us all sky high. As a rule it does not take very long, not in this house at least, but this time, oddly enough, I

24

fell asleep in the middle of my rage.

It wasn't until next morning that I discovered she must have been there, as I was in my pyjamas and under the duvet. I got out of bed, dressed and went to the kitchen. We had breakfast as usual and laughed at some chicken-brain on the radio using words like 'baritone' and 'U Thant'. Nonetheless, there was an irritating distance about her that meant we couldn't quite resolve our differences, I felt, as the door across the corridor slammed and I put on my *peau de pêche* jacket and my school bag and shuffled off to school with Anne-Berit.

So had I perhaps changed after all?

Anne-Berit, at all events, had not changed. I have never known a person to avail herself to such an extent of the opportunity to be herself: pretty, self-assured and unimaginative; there was not a trace of her lumpen parents in her, she was never the one to come up with any fun things to do and never laughed until she was sure there was something to laugh at, which as a rule there wasn't. But today all this was fine, in a way, for while I was usually the one to say something, neither of us said anything, and the silence became so oppressive that she said:

'What's up with you?'

I still didn't have much to say in reply, we

just continued down the grey beaten-earth paths in Muselunden, which according to both Mother and fru Syversen were much safer than the pavement along Trondhjems-veien, even though it was here on the slope down to the road that the tramps made their homes, in small ramshackle huts which in the black, leafless wilderness of late autumn were very visible from all sides, resembling blood-spattered wreckage after a plane crash. Some scary men lived here, whom we called Yellow, Red and Black because Yellow suffered from some illness that had turned him yellow, Red was always red-faced and Black was as swarthy as a gypsy, as we say. We just had to make sure we didn't go into their huts when they called, because if you did they would chuck you in a mill and grind you into thin brown gruel and make stock cubes out of you. But none of that was relevant today, they weren't even anywhere in sight, so they didn't give me anything to talk about either, and I was in a mood to lose my temper with someone.

'Huh, you're so boring,' I said to Anne-Berit as we entered the school play-ground. To which she replied:

'Piss off.'

This is not a usual mode of utterance on her part, although it is not out of keeping with her temperament, so we parted on unfriendly terms, she on her way to the girls' class, and I to the mixed class which had been set up to determine whether it was possible for boys and girls to sit beside each other and learn something at the same time.

Being in a mixed class felt good, even though the prettiest girls were in the other one, of course it is often the case that the better you know people the more faults you find in them. But here I could rest my eyes on the blazing black hair of Tanja, who was still a bit of a mystery to me because she never said anything and answered questions in a voice whose volume even frøken Henriksen despaired of trying to turn up. But she turned round every time *I* said something and sent me little smiles, which made me feel that there was nothing else to live for; some said she was a gypsy and lived in a circus caravan outside the botanical gardens in Tøyen, and that didn't make matters any easier, for what could be more alluring than people who travel the world with a guitar, steal things and operate merry-go-rounds?

Matters had reached such a pass now that I put up my hand primarily to make Tanja turn round, a move I also tried today, on top of which I wanted to get rid of all the mess that was still churning around in my head. But instead of showing off with some witticism, I realised too late that for once I had not done my homework and burst into a terrible and incomprehensible fit of tears. Once it had started it was impossible to control, I lay hunched over my desktop like an idiot, bawling my eyes out, oddly enough under no illusions, even then, that this was going to cost me dear, and that didn't make matters easier, either.

'Goodness me, Finn, what has happened?'

'I don't know!' I howled, which was true, and an answer which, by the way, I was more than happy with, because what if I had blurted out the truth: there's something up with Mother!

Frøken Henriksen took me into the corridor and calmed me down enough for me to be able to comprehend what she was saying: she was going to send me home with a letter to make sure that everything was alright. But I objected with such vehemence — and another torrent of tears — that once again she had to wait until I had composed myself. I sat slumped against the wall staring down the deserted corridor, which conjured up the image of a hospital where all the children laugh without making a noise and the dead have already acquired wings, and frøken Henriksen, with whom by and large I had a good relationship, suddenly said:

'Have you *seen* something?'

I gave a start.

'Seen what?'

'No, no, I just wondered whether perhaps you might have . . . *seen* something.'

'Seen *what*?' I shouted again as the abyss beneath me opened wider, Mother had not only become distant and different, maybe I had also known, maybe I could have predicted it. 'I haven't *seen* a bloody thing!' I yelled.

'Take it easy now, Finn,' frøken Henriksen said, no longer quite so comforting, lethargic rather, and I sat there with some sudden memories or words in my head, we collected words, Mother and I did, and laughed at them and liked them or thought them silly or redundant, words that were so real you could touch them, like 'concrete', 'exhaust', '*piassava* broom', 'petrol', 'leather', 'shoe leather' . . . I fell into a reverie imagining myself desperate to go tobogganing, on my new sledge, and crying and pestering until Mother took me by the hand and dragged me roughly along towards the slope that ran all the way from Trondhjemsveien down to the estate; there was no longer a clear meandering river of cold glass, but a brown muddy track like a coagulated nose-bleed on a battered face.

'Do you understand now?' she shouted, making my ears ring. '*The winter's over! It's spring!*'

'Shall we go back in?' frøken Henriksen said.

I looked up at her.

'Yes,' I said, getting to my feet and trying to look as if in the last few minutes we had come to an agreement that nothing at all had happened.

★ ★ ★

But the news of my breakdown had reached the school playground, of course, and there was no mistaking Anne-Berit's smile on our way home. By now Yellow and Black had got up — Red was nowhere to be seen — and they were sitting outside their huts drinking from shiny cans and calling us over, so that Black could show us his squirrel, which caused Anne-Berit to crumple up in a strange giggle.

'Murderers!' I shouted at the top of my voice. Black got to his feet and did a Heil Hitler salute and yelled something we didn't catch because we were running for our lives towards the Youth Hostel and not drawing breath until we had passed the tennis courts, where I saw some of my friends were busy stoking a fire and I asked Anne-Berit if she wanted to join in.

She stopped, looked me in the eye and said first of all something about her mother not liking her clothes smelling of smoke, especially not of tar, and that I had enough mud on my overshoes already and some other blather, it was quite unlike her to be so talkative, so I thought she had forgotten all about my breakdown.

But late that evening I heard the doorbell ring and fru Syversen came in and engaged in a hushed conversation with Mother, who straight afterwards took up a stance in the new doorway, with her arms crossed, she eyed me as she would a stranger as I lay in bed trying to read.

'What exactly do you get up to during the day?' she said so laconically that I was unable to brush her aside. But there was not much else I could do, either, so I just lay there, gawping at Jukan until the situation began to feel like trench warfare — *had* I seen anything?

But not even now did she do what a mother should do to retrieve a lost son, instead she gave a sorrowful toss of her curls and went into the kitchen. But she left the door open, the door of the lodger's room that

Frank had installed, and the sitting-room door, so I could hear her washing up, which was my job, a chore from which I seldom managed to escape, while she did the drying and tidied away.

I flung the comic aside, got off my bed and went to the kitchen and gently pushed her away from the sink, but avoided splashing and waving the brush around for once, with the result that we ended up standing there like an old married couple with nothing left to say to each other, washing and drying milk glasses, plates and forks for Olympic gold in the longest silence that has ever reigned in this flat.

However, I had done with crying now, I could feel, so I maintained the front until I felt, would you bloody credit it, that I was going to laugh. At that moment I smacked the brush into the dirty water so that it splashed all over her face. She lurched backwards and let out a howl of fury, but caught herself and stood, sombre-faced and strange, with one hand on her hip and the other over her eyes, before plumping down on the nearest kitchen chair and saying with an air of apathy, as the soapy water ran down her hair:

'You've got a sister.'

'What?'

'A half-sister.'

Not much I could say to that. I knew about this sister, of course, who was somewhere out there enjoying the widow's pension that should have been ours. But then everything fell into place.

'The hairdresser?'

'Yes.'

Yes, the hairdresser, Ingrid Olaussen, whose name by the way was not Ingrid Olaussen, was the mother of this girl called Linda, who was six years old, and she had seen our advertisement in the newspaper because we had been stupid enough to give our names and not to use the box number, but who on earth thinks of that kind of thing?

'Box number?'

The next information lay deeper. Mother had to dry herself first. She did that in the bathroom, at some length and with great care, while I stood on the footstool, which actually I had outgrown, staring down at the washing-up brush which I used to stir the murky soapy water, leaving long, thick furrows in its wake until I felt faint and she returned, having removed the make-up which was so necessary in the shoe shop, looking as she did at the weekends, when there were only the two of us, when she was at her most attractive.

'But she isn't up to looking after her,' she said and fell silent. And again I had to stand there on my pedestal brooding and aching and manoeuvring the brush to and fro, waiting for her to continue, because still I could not bring myself to ask, and she spoke to me in such a soft voice, taking one step at a time, the way you give medicine to a baby, Ingrid Olaussen was not just a widow, she was also a drug addict, the first time I had heard that expression, by the way, she was on morphine, oh right.

'And I'm telling you this because I know you're old enough to understand,' Mother said. 'If you put your mind to it.'

But:

'Is she going to live here?!'

At last it was beginning to sink in.

'You've known all the time!' I shouted, in a sudden outburst of indignation. 'We've been doing the place up and we got a separate entrance so that they could live here!'

'No, no,' she interrupted, for the first time, in a manner which inspired some confidence and that was much needed. 'She can't take care of the girl. I've looked into it and . . . she'll be sent to an orphanage if we don't . . . '

'So she *is* going to live here?'

Mother sat without moving, but nonetheless appeared to give a nod. 'We're *not* having

34

a lodger, then?' I persisted in desperation.

'Yes, we are . . . '

'We're having a sister *and* a lodger?

'Mm.'

'But not the hairdresser?'

'She's not a hairdresser, Finn! No, she's got to go in for some treatment, I don't know . . . '

'So *she's* not living here!'

'No! I keep telling you. Listen, will you!'

★   ★   ★

Ten minutes later. Mother is sitting on the new sofa with a cup of Lipton's tea and I am in the armchair with a bottle of Solo lemonade, even though it is the middle of the week. We are getting on better than we were ten minutes ago. We are on the same wavelength. A new wavelength, for I am still a changed person, I am just a bit more used to the change, it is all tied up with Mother's new confidentiality, because she has changed too, we are two strangers speaking sensibly about how to cope with another stranger, a girl of six called Linda, the daughter of a crane driver who also happened to be my father.

I know that it cannot have been an easy decision to make, in her earlier life Mother had not been full of kind words about this widow and her daughter, but now she has clearly been imbued with an unshakeable sense of direction, solidarity some might well call it, but we are not the high-falutin kind here, we live on credit and we are inscrutable. And in the course of these two weeks Mother has not only calculated the costs, she now tells me, but she has also considered what people would say if we did *not* take the girl in. And how we would feel. As well as how she would feel being in a children's home. Besides, and I would come to appreciate this in later life, would it not be preferable to be the widow who managed to do what *had* to be done rather than the person who threw in the towel and shunned her responsibility because of something as idiotically self-inflicted as drug addiction?

This, I have to admit, smacked of a victory for Mother over the person who had gone off with her crane driver and who was perhaps the indirect cause of him falling to his death, the man whose memory still caused Mother such pain that photographs of him had to buried in a locked drawer.

With that I also have to ponder the question, which as yet remains unanswered, concerning the widow's pension.

'No, we won't see any of that,' Mother says, obviously prepared, but with a quiver of emotion in her voice. 'I wasn't intending to adopt her. And . . . '

But this is not in fact where I want to go. I want to know whether Mother, with this new venture, has at last seen the opportunity to have her wish fulfilled, to have a daughter. Then I change my mind and keep my mouth shut, probably so as not to destroy this new equilibrium of ours. I finish my Solo and go to my room to do some homework, leaving the doors open so that we can hear each other: Mother pottering about in the sitting room and the kitchen, the evening's sonatas and the shipping forecast on the radio, which means bedtime is approaching. I can chew on my pencil and look out onto the block where Essi lives, peer at the light in his window, which is off at this moment, at the lights in the windows of all my friends, Hansa, Roger, Greger and Vatten, the estate that shuts one eye after the other while I sit by the Matchbox toys lined up on my windowsill and for some reason begin to look forward to an event which a mere two weeks ago would have seemed like a catastrophe: having a sister, a little sister.

4

First of all, though, the lodger had to be sorted out, our new source of income. And that was still no trivial matter. We had three callers in as many days; Mother served coffee and cakes to a young woman who was the spitting image of Doris Day, but who exhibited two rotten teeth behind her blood-red lipstick when she forgot herself and smiled, at which point negotiations came to a halt.

We were visited by an elderly man who stank of alcohol and some indefinable pungent odour and was incapable of explaining himself, so even though he wafted more hundred kroner notes before us than I had ever seen, he too was shown the door.

Thereafter came one more man, in a hat and coat, a trifle distant, but a pleasant fellow, smelling of after-shave, the kind that Frank wore on Sundays and which I was told — by Anne-Berit — was called Aqua Velva and which could also, in an emergency, be drunk. He had clear, calm, colourless eyes that watched not only Mother but also me with a certain curiosity. He had been at sea, he said, had come ashore, and was working now in the lucrative construction industry and needed temporary digs until he found his own place.

Neither of us had heard of 'digs' or 'own place'. But there was something modern and reassuring about this man, as if he had an education, Mother declared afterwards. But in fact he seemed absolutely normal, or the way we had imagined a lodger to be, except of course that he wore a hat and coat, like a film star. What settled it, however, was the following remark, as he was standing in the new doorway peering in at my desk with all my comics and Matchbox cars, nodding slowly:

'Cosy.'

'Yes, it is, isn't it . . . ?'

'But no room for the T.V., I can see.'

'Oh, you've got a T.V., have you?' Mother said, as though it were natural to have a T.V. set when you didn't even have a place to live. 'We'll have to put it in the sitting room then,' she said with a coquettish curtsey, upon which he returned her smile with a simple:

'Yes, of course, I don't watch it much anyway.'

In a way that was it, the deal was done.

His name was Kristian and he moved in the following Saturday. By then I had moved in with Mother, who all of a sudden didn't know what to do with herself. After a bit of to-ing and fro-ing, she also ended up in temporary digs, in her own bedroom, that is, staying where she had always been, where by the way we were in the midst of preparations to receive the new member of the family, six-year-old Linda.

'This must be a bit odd for you,' she said, giving me a sympathetic look.

No, I didn't think there was anything odd about it, now I had a view of the blocks opposite, and I had plenty of friends there, too. Not only that, we were in the fortunate position of having a bunk bed which Mother had bought cheap three years ago and split into two parts. Part two was in the loft storeroom. It just needed to be brought down and assembled on top of mine, a straightforward procedure for which we didn't even need Frank's help.

But there was something else worrying Mother, and that was that the T.V. set, which had indeed been installed in the sitting room, just stood there and was never switched on, because after Kristian moved in, we didn't see a great deal of him for a while, apart from his hat and coat, which hung in their appointed place in the hallway beside Mother's two cloaks and my *peau de pêche* jacket. He hadn't asked whether the room came with access to the kitchen, which of course it didn't, it came with access to the toilet and bathroom, one bath a week. So he must have been eating out, or he kept some provisions in his room, in private, if he was ever there, that is, we never heard a peep out of him. One evening Mother decided enough was enough, went into the hallway and knocked on his door.

'Come in,' we heard. We went in. And there was Kristian sitting as quiet as a mouse in a burgundy armchair reading a newspaper I had never seen before.

'Aren't you ever going to watch that T.V.?' Mother said.

'You can watch it. I don't actually give a shit about the damn thing.'

I knew this sort of language unsettled Mother. And she told him she wasn't having any of it.

'Have you had dinner?' she asked huffily.

'I don't eat after five o'clock,' Kristian said in the same flat tone, still with his nose buried in the newspaper.

'Surely you can't mean that,' Mother said. 'Come and have some supper with us.'

Then Kristian did more or less what I do when she is in that mood: got up with a wan smile and said thank you very much.

'I don't want this to become a habit, mind you,' he added as we left the room.

'Don't worry, it won't,' Mother parried, relieved that the use of vulgar language was obviously a one-off occurrence. 'Please do take a seat.'

'If you skip the formality,' Kristian said, sitting at the end of the table where no-one had ever sat before. 'It's not right.'

'Oh?' said Mother, cutting the wholegrain bread into thinner slices than usual.

'No, we're working-class stock.'

That was quite an argument. But I was with Kristian on this. The language that Mother used whenever we met the outside world, which was so necessary in the shoe shop, didn't actually belong anywhere else but there.

'And what's this young fellow going to be then?' he asked me.

'A writer,' I said without pausing for breath, at which Mother burst into laughter.

'He doesn't even know what a writer is.'

'Well, that may be an advantage,' Kristian said.

'Oh?' Mother said again.

'Yes, it's a demanding profession,' Kristian said, and seemed almost to know what he was talking about. Mother and I exchanged glances.

'Have you read *The Unknown Soldier*?' I asked.

'Stop that now,' Mother said.

'Of course,' Kristian said. 'A fantastic book. But I suppose you don't know anything about that yet, do you?'

'No, I don't,' I conceded. But the atmosphere was now so agreeable that I could concentrate on my food while Mother smiled and said that Kristian should not be surprised if he were to bump into a little girl here soon as we were expecting an increase in the family. Crikey, said Kristian, it certainly didn't show. And they chuckled in a way that I am not going to bother to describe here, I will, however, mention that Kristian ate in the same way that he stood and walked, calmly and with dignity, waiting between each slice of bread until Mother urged him to take another, do help yourself to a bit more, etc. She could not understand what craziness it was not to eat after five o'clock, while Kristian considered there were doubtless many people in this country who would soon have to learn a little about asceticism.

'Because it's not certain that all this is going to last.'

'And what do you mean by that, if I may ask?' Mother said in a tart voice. Whereupon he pointed good-humouredly at her with his knife and smiled.

'There you go again, being formal.'

But I couldn't listen to this, anyway for ages I had been dying to get the T.V. going. We had spent the last few evenings in the sitting room, Mother with her knitting and cup of tea, me with a comic, casting restless glances at the teak colossus standing there and staring at us with its blind, green-tinged eye. The future resided in that box. The world. Large and unfathomable. Beautiful and mysterious. A slow-working mental atomic explosion, we just didn't know about it yet. But we had an inkling. And the reason it was still so utterly mute was, I gathered from Mother, that the lodger might feel that we would be acting out of turn if she were to let me press the ivory-yellow 'on' button. Or he might hear the noise from his temporary digs and be encouraged to spread into larger areas than he was entitled to in his contract, he might invade our sitting room and feel it was his prerogative, night after night, there were a lot of sides to this, it wouldn't help to bellow:

'I want to switch it on!'

We had to sit and pretend the whole caboodle was there for safe keeping. And there has never been anything less like safe keeping in our flat. Mother even read the paper to find out what programmes were on, there was 'Hit Parade' with Erik Diesen, so we might hear 'Sailor' or the waltz 'Life in the Finnish Woods', which you could otherwise only hear on a record request programme, and what about the quiz game 'Double or Quit', which I had heard Essi talk about as the eighth wonder of the world?

But now when I got up from the table and went straight into the sitting room without a second thought and pressed the button above the Tandberg badge, nothing happened. Not a sound. Not a flash of light. For thirty seconds. Then a crackling snow storm burst into my face, and I heard Kristian's voice from the kitchen:

'We'll have to sort out a licence. And it needs an aerial.'

He got to his feet, went to his room, rummaged around in a box and came out with something he called an indoor aerial, resembling the galvanised antennae of a monster beetle, which he described as junk. But after he had installed it, at least we had a few fish swimming around behind something curved and wavy lines not unlike the Syversens' wallpaper.

'I'll get a proper one, though,' Kristian said, twisting the antennae and making the waves bigger and smaller.

We sat looking at the deformed fish, Mother perched on the edge of the sofa, with closed shoe shop knees and a bent, expectant posture, as if she were waiting for the bus; Kristian was standing in the middle of the room with his legs wide apart, his arms crossed, his eyes fixed on the door to the balcony where presumably the aerial would be set up. He didn't sit down until bidden, by Mother, and then on the very edge of the chair, pensive, with his elbows resting on his knees and his chin brushing his knuckles, lending him an unsettled air, too. I was the only person who was all there. But during that evening the first foundations were laid for what I think I felt at that time was a friendship.

It turned out, you see, that Kristian was a fan of numbers, like me, lap times, dates, car registration numbers, once something was in my head, it stayed there. He knew, for example, that there were more than 60,000 T.V.s in Norway, which was almost one for every ten households; in the U.S.A. almost every single home had a colour set. He used words like 'intelligent', 'development' and 'sporadic', concepts of which Mother and I had no more than the vaguest of notions. After the fish, the screen was filled with a large Asian face, which we were to discover belonged to the man with the ridiculous-sounding name of U Thant, whom we had heard on the radio and had had a good laugh about, but Kristian knew that U Thant was reportedly both intelligent and had vision, or 'so it's said', he added. And this view of U Thant's intellectual apparatus was not only the opinion of one lodger but also the judgement of something close to a majority, a truth conveyed by the somewhat speculative 'it's said' and 'reportedly' — there was an insidious, irresistible magic to almost every sentence Kristian uttered. And even though in the following minutes, he used the words 'arsehole' (once), 'lame', 'radiator' and not least 'absenteeism', again the thought crossed our minds that he might be educated, and I could tell by Mother's face that this unsettled her more than the vulgar language; I mean, anyone and everyone can swear, the air had turned pretty blue when the door to my old room was being moved. So it must have been the combination that put her nose out of joint, that one and the same person could use words like 'arsehole' and 'sporadic', as if the man were a half-breed, a man without a home town, who everyone knows is a gypsy, which in turn implies false and unreliable;

did we have a Trojan horse stabled here in our idyll?

The evening came to an end with a brief comment from Mother:

'Yes, well, I think it's bedtime.'

She rose to her feet and pulled down the hem of her skirt. Then Kristian also jumped up, as if he had been caught *in flagrante*.

'Yes, tomorrow's another day. Goodnight.'

He went to his room, but came out again and said, 'Thank you for supper, I forgot to say that, I think,' and placed a black five-øre piece on the T.V., said I could have it, a five-øre coin from the war, told me he had collected coins himself at one time, and supposed I did, too?

Mother and I were at length able go to the bathroom to perform our nightly ablutions, which had become more extensive since the lodger's arrival, as she now had to wait till the last moment to remove her shoe shop make-up, with me sitting on the edge of the bathtub holding a toothbrush in one hand and the coin in the other.

'What do you think?' she said, looking at me in the mirror.

'Alright,' I said, referring to the T.V., although it — because of the programmes, I suppose — had not quite lived up to expectations, but this could easily be rectified, at least I had something to tell people at school the next day.

'Strange,' she said.

'What is?'

'Just hope we haven't done anything stupid here.'

'What?'

'Didn't you see his hands? He's not a builder, not in a million years.'

'What do you mean?'

'Well, you've seen Frank's . . . er . . . herr Syversen's hands.'

I had no idea what she was driving at, but looked down at my left hand, the one with the coin, nothing out of the ordinary there.

'Hope he's not a snob,' Mother said.

I didn't know what a snob was, but I didn't think it bore much relation to Kristian after she had explained.

★　★　★

In the ensuing days it appeared that the new lodger had a number of items that anyone would covet, a bayonet from the time when he had been a soldier, a microscope in a wooden box with brass fittings, a leather pouch containing twenty-eight steel balls that had been in the bearings of yellow earth-movers and could be used as marbles or just to hold in your hand — what wonderful objects to hold in your hand. In another wooden box he had a little brass spinning top with a painted green spiral pattern that made you go dizzy when you watched it. As well as that there was a chess set with steel pieces which he claimed he had made himself, like the spinning top; he was a toolmaker by trade, he told me. But he hadn't liked being a toolmaker, for reasons which he explained but of which I didn't understand a word. So he had gone to sea instead, which he had enjoyed until he was wrecked west of Ireland. Then he didn't want to sail the seas any longer, and returned to his old profession, but it had not changed in the intervening years, so, in the end, he turned his hand to the building trade.

We didn't hear any more of this job of his, which, according to Mother, was not consistent with the state of his hands, until one evening when she asked him outright, after he had paid his rent — on time — for the first month.

'I do union work for the most part,' he said with a pointed stare, and went into his room, leaving Mother and me looking at each other in bewilderment.

'Heavens,' Mother said.

With this, one mystery gave way to another.

Why could Kristian not put his cards on the table, as we had done, now that he was living here and was affable in a way that made us like him?

Now it was Mother's turn to be concerned. I had long come to terms with Kristian having been a seaman and a toolmaker, so much so that *that* became an issue too, in as much as Mother refused to let me go into his room whenever I felt like it, and that was by and large every evening. I knocked, he said 'Come in' and I went in and stood gawping until he looked up from the newspaper and nodded to the one spindle-back chair there was room for, next to the armchair in which he was seated. He carried on reading for another minute or two while I sat with my hands wedged between my knees surveying his books, the bag of ball bearings hanging from a hook on the wall and the chess board, until he had finished reading and asked if I had done my homework.

'Yes,' I said.

'I never did any homework,' he said.

That didn't cut much ice with me. I had lots of friends who didn't do their homework, and that just got them into trouble; besides, words and numbers were fun, and he must have seen that in me.

'You're a funny chap,' he said.

51

'You are, too,' I said. 'Can we look down the microscope?'

'Go on then, get it out.'

I pulled out the microscope and fitted the mirrors and the glass slides, and we studied the surface of a krone coin; it didn't look much, scratches all over the place, as deep as ravines, all the things the naked eye cannot see.

'Do you know what that is?' Kristian asked.

'No.'

'It's the history of the coin, look here, the date, 1948, it has passed through thousands of hands since then, it's been shaken about in piggy banks, cash tills, pockets and slot machines and perhaps it fell out of a taxi and pinged around Storgata one rainy night and was driven over by a bus before a little girl found it on her way to school the next morning, took it home and put it in her piggy bank. All these are *tracks*, the history of the coin, do you know what history is, lad? Well, it's wear and tear. Look here, for example, at my face, it's full of wrinkles, even though I'm only 38, and look at yours, as smooth as a baby's bum, and so the sole difference between us is wear and tear, a meagre thirty years' wear, like the difference between that coin there and a krone that was minted yesterday, such as this one.' He produced a brand new coin, with a horse where the crown had been before, and let me examine it under the microscope. True enough, it was as smooth as a windless sea. Until we changed the lens and looked even closer, then we saw that even the surface of a new coin is matt, covered with billions of tiny particles that Kristian called crystalline chips, which wear and tear were destined to remove. 'In other words a coin is not at its shiniest, at its peak as a coin, that is, when it's spat out by the stamping machine, it's more like the time when the twenty-sixth or forty-third owner fishes it out of his pocket and pays for a sausage with potato cakes and mustard at Åsbua in Bjerke — *that* is the apex of the coin's history, as it slips out of the hands of a hungry customer and lands on the counter of a well-fed sausage vendor. From thereon everything is downhill all the way, inexorably, even though it takes time. Have you ever seen any coins that have been worn right down?'

'No.'

'Nip into the sitting room and get your mother's encyclopaedia, the volume with S on the spine.'

I did as he said, and we looked up King Sverre, himself a pinnacle in the wear and tear of our country, but Sverre had not just been a warrior and king and turned the nation on its head, he had also had coins minted that were pictured in the encyclopaedia. On them you could barely make out *Suerus Magnus Rex*, which was Latin; they were as thin as leaves, so like shimmering tinsel that if you held them up to the light you would be able to see the sun through them. But here, of course, we were talking about no fewer than 800 years of wear and tear, so that was alright, for coins, mind you, Kristian pointed out in conclusion.

I looked at him, perplexed.

'And, leading on from this,' he said philosophically, 'when would you judge a human being to be at his peak?'

I had a think.

'Your age, maybe,' he said with a sly smile.

That night I took the encyclopaedia with me to bed and read the whole article about King Sverre, and although there were several words which not even Kristian used, I felt that he had been quite right.

5

Mother, however, did not like these visits of mine to his room. I should not disturb the lodger, I was told, and furthermore she didn't like me staying inside for so long after I had knocked and waited for him to say 'Come in' — sometimes he didn't say 'Come in', and then I didn't go in. The worst thing was that I came back out with all kinds of information, the average temperature in the Svalbard archipelago or the Norwegian consumption of aquavit, 3.3 million litres per year, but they had not managed to pour more than a tenth as much red wine down their throats, this was not the sort of thing to stuff into the head of a young kid.

'I am not a young kid.'

Moreover, I could tell her that what we had always called 'red sausage' was in fact known as salami and that Einar Gerhardsen, the Prime Minister, was not to be trusted even though we voted him in time after time. So an end was put to these evening visits of mine. I was not even allowed to go in and return the microscope I had been lent to study the mesh in Mother's nylon stockings. She did it for me. But when she re-emerged her cheeks were red, and she wanted to know if the lodger always hung his underwear over the curtain rod to dry.

I had no idea. But she collected herself for a new foray and ran in again to say that she did not want any underwear hanging in the window for the whole estate to see.

'Alright,' Kristian said, unmoved. 'But where should I dry it? Or wash it?'

The upshot was that he would have his own basket for dirty laundry, so that he could carry it down to the wash-house when it was her turn to wash, and throw it into the drum, after which she would hang it up for him, in the drying room. I had a feeling that this arrangement was to avoid having to touch his dirty clothes. That was Kristian's interpretation, too. And there wasn't much contact between us over the next few weeks.

That autumn the suppliers went on strike, Omar Hansen's more or less ran out of stock, and it took Mother ages to find all the things we needed on her way home from the shoe shop. One afternoon, though, we found a large box in the hallway, with margarine, bread, potatoes, fish balls, a tube of caviar, liver paste, two bottles of Solo, three bars of Freia milk chocolate and right at the bottom two copies of a cowboy comic for me.

'You shouldn't have done that,' Mother said.

'Why not?' Kristian said, who, like Frank, had connections, in the union, he said, and Mother didn't. On the contrary, it was her union that was behind the strike.

'You could at least keep it in the fridge for me, couldn't you?'

It was the same sort of arrangement as with the T.V., which Mother and I now watched every night, legally, since she had paid the licence fee in her name. Kristian was making greater and greater inroads into our lives, no matter what she did.

'How much do you want for it?' she ventured.

'What is it with you?' he said with annoyance and went into his room, closing the door after him. And the box stood there for an hour or two before Mother came to her senses and put the items in the fridge.

'There's something not quite right about this,' she said. But then added: 'Oh, well.' And she gave me one of the Solos. A Solo in the middle of the week again.

Afterwards we had one of the chocolate bars as well, and switched on the T.V. to watch 'Hit Parade' and a long documentary about a horse carting crates of beer from a brewery round the shops in town. His name was Bamse, bruiser, and he was thirty-two years old, which is a formidable age for a horse. The whole point was that Bamse's era was over now, not only for him but for the whole of his melancholy race, it was giving way to motorised transport and tarmac and, not least, speed. The programme became more and more depressing, and more and more forlorn the longer we sat there gawping, we both had tears in our eyes. Fortunately, though, it ended with Bamse and his ancient owner strolling around a meadow on a large farm and he saw his days out with the sun shining, the flowers swaying and the larks singing.

'Thank goodness,' Mother said, hurriedly switching off. We sat blinking with the glare from the T.V. in our eyes until she suddenly exclaimed:

'I'll deduct it from his rent!'

6

Then Linda arrived. She arrived by bus. Alone. Because Mother had no desire to meet the girl's mother again, that was my impression.

It was a Saturday. We ambled down to the bus stop by Aker Hospital in good time and waited for the Grorud bus, which was due at 1.26, I had been to school and had barely got home with my satchel, I hadn't told a living soul about this turn of events, about Linda, because I couldn't find the words. But in a very indirect way I had touched on the subject with a chum of mine, Roger, who had two elder brothers, I had asked him what it was like to have several siblings, an issue which he was quite unable to grasp, until he seemed to understand what I was getting at after all, and said with a smirk:

'Only child.'

Made it sound like a diagnosis, on a par with having a limp. I had of course also had a few half-articulated thoughts of my own along these lines as we were assembling the new bed — I had even slept in it one night — and especially while Mother was sitting lost in thought in the interim between the decision to take Linda and today, or when she went into the loft and came down with our enormous suitcase covered with sticky labels marked Lom and Dombås, which turned out to be full of her childhood clothes, those she had worn when she was Linda's age, six, and she went through them one by one, holding them up and thinking and mumbling and saying: 'Well, I never, and oh my God, what is this then and none of that's any good, except for this maybe?' A doll called Amalie that didn't look up to much, the stuffing poking out of a gash in her stomach — because her brothers, I was told, had performed an appendix operation on her. She had dangling legs and a loose, floppy head with dull beads for eyes.

'Isn't she cute?'

'Mm.'

She put Amalie in Linda's bed, where she had been lying now for the past week, until she was gone again, that happened this morning.

'Where's Amalie?' I wondered on waking up. But Mother didn't answer me. 'She's coming today, isn't she? Linda?'

'Course,' Mother said, as if this were sufficient reason for Amalie to be back in the loft, so there wouldn't be any misunderstandings between her and Linda, I suppose, what do I know? The sheets on the bed had been changed again, for the third time, and there was nothing between them, the bed was waiting.

Then at long last the bus came. It stopped as well. But no-one got off. Quite the opposite, a number of passengers got on, and Mother and I stood looking at each other. The pneumatic brakes hissed and the folding doors clattered and shook and threatened to close. Mother threw herself forward at the last moment and shouted 'Stop', and the conductor jumped up from his seat, came and took her by the arm and in the same movement pressed the door fully open with his knee.

'Careful now, madam.'

Mother said something or other, at any rate the bus didn't move off as she disappeared into the interior, behind the filthy windows. She was gone for ages. Then there was some shouting from inside until, at last, she reappeared, puce-faced and agitated, dragging behind her a little girl in a tight dress and white knee-stockings in the raw autumn weather and carrying a tiny, light-blue suitcase.

'Thank you, thank you,' she shouted to the conductor, who answered, 'Not at all' and 'My pleasure' and made several other comments that only made Mother's face even redder as she stood straightening her hair. I walked in a circle, staring at the new arrival, at Linda, who turned out to be small and fat and quiet with her eyes boring into the tarmac.

At length the bus set off, and Mother went down on her knees in front of our new family member and tried to make eye-contact, without much success, from what I could see. But then she completely lost her self-control, Mother did, she started hugging the gawky creature in a way that filled me with grave concern. But Linda didn't react to that, either, and Mother dried her tears and said, as she tends to do when she is ashamed of herself:

'Oh, what am I doing? Come on, let's go up to Omar Hansen's and buy some chocolate. Would you like some chocolate, Linda?'

Linda was bereft of speech. She smelled strange, her hair was unkempt, all over the place, and her fringe hung right down over her face. But she did put her hand in Mother's and clasped two of her fingers, making her knuckles go white. Then Mother lost her composure again. And I couldn't watch any more, this grasp which I knew instinctively was a grasp for life, which would change most things not just in Linda's existence but also in mine, one of the grasps that lock themselves around your heart and hold it in a vice-like grip until you die and it is still there when you are lying rotting in your grave. I snatched the small sky-blue suitcase that weighed almost nothing and swung it around my head.

'She's asking you if you want some chocolate!' I shouted. 'You deaf or something?'

Linda gave a start and Mother sent me one of those murderous looks of hers that are usually reserved for larger gatherings. I took the hint and kept a couple of paces behind them as we walked up the hill, Mother talking now in a pseudo-friendly and much too shrill voice and saying 'This is where we live, Linda,' and she pointed through the traffic fumes across Trondhjemsveien.

'On the second floor over there. The one with the green curtains. It's No. 3, the third block from the bottom, one of the first to be built . . . '

And a load more drivel to none of which Linda responded.

But after we had our chocolate, things improved a bit because Linda gobbled it down and smiled too, more confused than happy, and that made you feel a little less sorry for her, yes it did, I suppose Mother thought she had been eating the chocolate too greedily, and so there was a reason to find fault with her, or there was something one might have wished were different, which I think was good for us all because so far Linda had not uttered one word. Nor did she until we got inside the door.

'Bed,' she said.

'Alright,' replied Mother, nonplussed. 'You're sleeping there.'

At which Linda loosened the iron grip she had on Mother's fingers, scrambled up into bed, lay down and closed her eyes. Mother and I followed this game, our amazement increasing by the minute, because this was no game, Linda was sleeping like a log.

Mother said There, there, and covered her up and sat on the edge of the bed stroking her hair and cheek. A little later she left the room and crashed down at the kitchen table as if she had just returned from the War.

'I imagine she must be all in, the poor thing. Coming to stay with us. So alone . . .'

I didn't have any sympathy for this line of thought either, after all, what could be better than to be allowed to stay with us, in a bed that had been made three times already, even though no-one had slept in it? I said as much, too, showed Mother that I was already beginning to get pretty sick of this new family member of ours.

But she was not listening, she had opened the little blue suitcase and found a letter, a sort of instruction manual, it appeared, which told us in spiky handwriting what Linda liked to do — playing (!) and eating: Sunda honey and spiced cheese, and potatoes and gravy, she wasn't so fond of meat or fish or vegetables. But it also informed us that we should be 'careful not to stuff the child with too much food'. Furthermore, she had a problem with her left knee, she needed to take some medicine for it, there were pills in boxes with Linda's name on, which Mother duly found in the suitcase and held up to the light to have a closer look, two pills every night, or three. 'And give her them with a full glass of water,' the letter instructed, 'just before she goes to bed so that she won't get up in the night and raid the fridge.'

Mother lost her composure again:

'Good heavens.'

'What's up?' I said.

'So sad!' she groaned.

Once more I understood nothing, just repeated:

'What *is* up with you?'

'And she looks so much like him!'

'Like who?' I cried, feeling that I was

seriously beginning to lose my temper, not so much because of what she said, but more because of how she looked. She was referring, of course, to the crane driver, my father, Linda's father, the bloody cause of all this howling, the man who before falling to his death had managed to create so much mess that we no longer knew whether we were coming or going. And as if that wasn't enough, Kristian came home at that very minute, heard something was afoot and wanted to know what on earth was going on.

'It's got nothing to do with you!' Mother shouted, totally out of control and making no attempt to conceal her tear-stained face. 'Get out! Do you hear me! And don't show your face in here again!'

Kristian was smart enough to perceive that this was a state of emergency and retreated, unruffled. I was not so smart.

'But who do *I* look like?' I yelled. 'You've never said *I* look like anyone!'

'What has got into you?'

I was someone else and before I knew what I was doing I had grabbed her hand and sunk my teeth in the two fingers Linda had claimed for herself and bitten them as hard as I could, so that she really did have something to scream about. She slapped me good and hard, which she had never done before, and

66

we stood glowering at one another, both of us even more changed. I even felt a stiff smile spreading across my truculent face, and a cutting chill.

Then I threw up on the floor between us and walked into the hall without a word, put on my outdoor clothes and went down to the street to join the others, those who had no home, it would seem, at any rate they never were at home, the big boys, the losers, Raymond Wackarnagel and Ove Jøn and so on . . . that night we smashed the window panes in the entrances to No.s 2, 4, 6, 7 and 11 and also the little glass panel in Lien's stockroom where sago and roll-up tobacco were stored. There had never before been so many windows smashed in the Tonsen estate on a single Saturday night. And perhaps I was the only person to know why, or who at least had a motive, a strange dumb creature who lay asleep in our new bunk bed; I suppose the others did it out of habit, or because it was in their nature, it was not in mine.

There was a huge hullabaloo afterwards with an investigation involving the caretaker and the housing co-op chairman. There was, of course, no difficulty finding out who was responsible, it was the usual suspects, Ove Jøn and Raymond Wackarnagel etc, the mystery was me, the person who had never done anything wrong, who was known as a mummy's boy, and not just because I didn't have a father, but because I was a well-balanced lad, a happy lad with my feet on the ground and a quick brain, as frøken Henriksen had written on my handwriting tests, I could write and do sums, I wasn't afraid of anything, not even of Raymond Wackarnagel, I washed up almost every night, I was small of stature, but I didn't pee in my pants and was more than happy to paint a whole sitting-room wall with a brush if asked. Had I just got into bad company? Or was there an unpredictable demon lying dormant in me, too?

This gave Kristian the chance to re-enter the arena.

'Crap,' he said to the housing co-op chairman, Jørgensen, who was standing in our hall, an imposing, magisterial presence, talking to Mother about how to deal with the brat. 'There's nothing wrong with the lad.'

'How can *you* know?' came the pert reply from Mother who on this occasion had deemed it appropriate to kowtow to Jørgensen, she can do the servile bit, Mother can, if needs be, it comes from her background, the youngest of four children from Torshov, with a father who was said to drink, a lot, and a mother who, after he died, had ensconced herself in an easy chair and begun to drink, too.

'Everyone can see that, can't they,' Kristian said in his indomitable chairman's voice. 'Anyone with their wits about them.'

To be on the safe side, he laid a hand on my head and smiled, God knows why, and went to his room humming.

Mother stood with her arms crossed, fidgeting with the bandage she had wrapped around her two sore fingers, the Linda fingers, a touch less confident now about the unholy alliance she had entered into with Jørgensen, a man who determined when radiators should be bled and kick-sleds should be stacked before being put into summer storage in the bomb shelter.

'Oh well, I suppose we shouldn't make too big a thing of this,' she ventured, averting her eyes. And that was all it took to start me off crying again and blurt out that I would pay for the window at No. 11 from my savings, for that was the one *I* had smashed.

Mother looked down at me, touched, and Jørgensen knew that the negotiations were at an end, but stood his ground anyway, as if to demonstrate that it was he and not Mother who decided when he was to leave, let alone pronounce when the affair was to be regarded as settled; when he had done that, he left.

Thereafter Mother was free to start on a long diatribe about how I was to keep away from the street gang and what was I thinking of and so on. But all this was pretty ordinary stuff, quite unlike the bombshell that had hit us the day Linda arrived, last Saturday.

Now she was sitting at the kitchen table, waiting.

For supper.

In accordance with the instructions in the blue suitcase, we had already introduced the ruling that Mother would butter slices of bread on the board, and put them on two different plates and place them in front of us beside our glasses of milk. An equal number of slices on each plate, two and a half, with whatever we wanted to eat on top, whereas Mother had only one, with syrup, which reminded her of her own childhood, or perhaps mostly of what she had never had enough of, because times had been lean then, as people said. She stood by the breadboard fiddling with something in a cupboard, or in the sink, and making the occasional funny remark. And there was no more bread and butter for Linda, however long she sat there giving Mother the wordless stare, which under normal circumstances would have cracked the strongest of wills, it would, although she didn't eat anywhere near as greedily as on the first day and furthermore had realised she shouldn't grab at food on the table, such as the Sunda honey.

I knew that even if I had felt like another slice of bread on this particular evening, and it had never been an issue whether I ate two or six slices, I would not have said anything, and I received a nod of acknowledgement from Mother, since we were so united in the task of complying with the instructions in the letter. Linda could see how the land lay.

'Read,' she said.

And we read. But first of all the table was cleared and the washing up was done, if you could call it that, because Linda had enough trouble standing on the stool — which I had had to cede — and splashed her hands in the soapy water while I was even more thorough than usual, and I noticed that she didn't smell strange any more, she didn't smell of anything, like me. Her hair was also combed, shorter, and she had been given a light-blue hair slide to keep her fringe out of her large eyes so that she could no longer hide behind it. Mother asked if she knew any songs. Linda, after much hemming and hawing, finally mumbled a song title I hadn't heard before, but Mother smiled and hummed the tune, she knew a couple of verses of this particular unknown song, as she dried and cleared away, and Linda smiled coyly into the washing-up water and went pink, which we considered a good omen, for, to tell the truth, she had not smiled a lot since she arrived.

Even reading had changed quite a bit, now it had to be the Bobbsey twins again, of whom I was heartily sick, a gang of kids who had God knows how many parents and uncles and aunts, and *Mette-Marit at the Ballet School*, which Mother had read as a child and had also tried to foist on me, I couldn't stand Mette-Marit. Anyway, Linda didn't want to read very much, she just wanted to listen to the first page and a half again and again, as if she lost the thread as soon as the story got going, or perhaps because she had an especial predilection for repetition.

But lying there under the ceiling has an atmosphere of its very own, with your arms tucked behind your head, knowing you have to keep your mouth shut about your needs, knowing that this is appreciated, and Mother made sure it was, with a new look she had added to her repertoire; we had become, as I said, a team, with the task of looking after someone we hadn't quite deciphered yet, nor would we until a good three months later.

7

As I mentioned, Mother came from a pretty large family, three elder brothers and a mother who had turned grey and retired to a rocking chair. Now she spent her days indulging in games of patience, and innumerable glasses of sherry, but she always brightened up when she saw me, and asked how things were at school. It was important to do well at school. But she never listened to my answers.

'Pick a card,' she said.

I picked a card, and if it was the seven of clubs, that meant I was going to have a prosperous life, and the jack of diamonds meant more or less the same. But normally we didn't stay long, apart from on Christmas Eve, on the ground floor in an old working-class tenement in Torshov, where there was just a kitchen and one room, and in that room, which for some reason was not called a sitting room but a parlour, there was an enormous cylindrical black wood-burning stove that was always so hot it had to be shielded behind a fireguard, itself almost as hot.

When we turned up on Christmas Eve I had to join Uncle Oskar in the cellar and chop wood, which was a pleasant midway stage between the freezing cold walk from Årvoll and the pork-ribs aroma of a Christmas Eve fought out in the parlour where now there was a spruce tree wilting next to the red-hot stove. Gran still used real candles which had to be replaced all the time because the wax ran down onto the bone-dry spruce branches like snot.

Uncle Oskar was much older than the others and had been a merchant seaman in the War; he didn't have any children or a wife and was on the dole, he whiled away his time doing simple carpentry, but even so had 'coped', as Mother put it. He always arrived early on Christmas Eve and put the ribs in the oven and then chopped kindling in the cellar wood store for hours on end to help Gran, so that she would have something to get the coke going over the winter. When I turned up he showed me how to chop and pile the wood and smiled and was good-humoured and nice, but he didn't say much. And even though I looked forward to the presents, the hour down there with Uncle Oskar was without doubt the best part of the whole evening, as the others, for some reason, liked to have a go at him, especially when we

74

were sitting around the table, saying he had developed quite a stoop since they last saw him or his hair had greyed or had he still not won the pools.

My mother joined in, too, and I didn't like that, even though she was more restrained than Uncle Bjarne, who was a dreadfully serious engineer at an out-of-town paper factory, and therefore seldom seen except on this one day of the year.

The youngest of the brothers, Uncle Tor, was a waiter at Hesteskoen and Renna and Grefsensetra and . . . it kept changing. He was cheerful and lively and danced with Mother after the presents had been distributed and the drinks appeared on the table. He also danced with Uncle Bjarne's bad-tempered wife, Aunty Marit, who loosened up as the evening progressed, so much so she had almost come apart by the end, unlike her spouse, Bjarne, who was always given books for Christmas and who, as soon as he had said his piece about Uncle Oskar, liked to settle down to read on the kitchen bench where, apparently, he had also spent most of his childhood, books which he managed to finish before the evening was over and it was time to gather the herd of kids and his unsteady wife and wend his way to the taxis in Sandakerveien. The kids in question were my three cousins, all belonging to Bjarne and Marit, who conversed in dialect and were forever making sure they hadn't soiled their frocks with pork fat. The eldest, whose name was also Marit, was two years older than me and quite interesting; she liked to bamboozle me with conjuring tricks.

'Look at me, Finn,' she said, and did something with her fingers that was supposed to be magic and then, all of a sudden, in a hand that had only a split second before been empty, she was holding a Christmas heart. But this one was easy to see through.

'It's in your other hand.'

'Look now,' she ventured.

'Now it's behind your back.'

But that didn't wipe the smile off her face; she just held out one hand, slowly, as if to magic a coin from inside my ear, but instead pinched my cheek, making tears well up, and I howled with pain.

'See,' she said, turning to the others in triumph.

'Ha, ha, Finn fell for it again, hook, line and sinker.'

This expression came from Uncle Bjarne, I recognised it. He loved this sort of thing: *a spanner in the works, Mary, Mary quite contrary* (for Mother), not to mention *Knock, knock, is anyone at home?* — which he used on Uncle Oskar — idioms, rhymes and catch-phrases my mother and I considered embarrassing. She didn't like Uncle Bjarne, not him, not his wife, nor his pack of kids: I had also caught her mumbling 'twit' and 'muttonhead', or worse, when she thought no-one was listening.

But, well, there was something about Uncle Oskar, who appeared not to hear the jibes directed at him. He smiled with good humour at everything and ate slowly and to repletion after the long wood-chopping session in the cellar. He even had his work-clothes with him, which he hung in the minute bathroom before donning his blue suit for the meal. Mother was always tight-lipped and touchy when we were here, never went to the loo, because it was so dark and cramped in there, and she needed a day or two to recover, kept mumbling it was good to get it over and done with as we trudged home in the freezing cold, late at night, like last year for example, each of us carrying a rucksack of presents, past the Ragna Ringdal day centre, across the Ring Road and through Muselunden, my route to school, past the shanty huts — belonging to the men we called Yellow, Red and Black — covered with glittering snow, all looking like Joseph and Mary's stable with Trondhjems-veien's line of silent, fog-yellow Bethlehem stars in the background. Except that the idyll was broken by the sound of beasts of prey, unless it was the sound of snoring, Mother shivered and increased her pace and murmured 'Poor things' and said:

'We're doing fine, we are. Remember that, Finn.'

Though she was relieved to have got Christmas Eve in her childhood home out of the way.

★　★　★

The year we had Linda, she sent her apologies, told me she wasn't up to it, what she wrote on the Christmas cards she sent round the family I have no idea. However, we were to be on our own, the three of us. And it was one of the best Christmases I can remember, even though it got off to a shaky start. We had been to the Årvoll Senter and bought a Christmas tree which we were dragging home on Essi's fish sled when, half way down Traverveien, we discovered that Linda didn't know what presents were.

'What are presents?' she said in a very quiet voice, after Mother and I had been talking in excited tones about Christmas lists, what we might get, our sky-high expectations, Mother's relief this year at not having to think

78

about whatever it was she thought about in connection with the family down in Torshov, and about Kristian, who had not only paid his rent for December on the dot but also given her an advance for January, so she would have a bit more to play with over Christmas, as he put it.

The significance of Linda's question sank in slowly for her, it didn't sink in at all for me, even though I ought to have realised from the pallor of her face, Mother's, so all I was able to come out with was:

'Don't you know what presents are? Are you stupid or something?'

Then I heard something I had never heard before:

'Now you just shut your mouth, Finn, or I'll murder you.'

'She says *gifts*!' I screamed. 'She understands *gifts*! Don't you, Linda, you understand *gifts*, don't you.'

We stared down at Linda in expectation. But there wasn't a glimmer of comprehension. Scared by all the commotion, she had again held Mother's two fingers in an iron grip, her eyes boring into the depths of eternity, and she wanted to go back home.

★　★　★

The rest of the day was taken up with long, comforting monologues from Mother's side. About there being many ways to celebrate Christmas, Linda didn't need to rack her brains, some people gave each other presents, others didn't, there was no limit to diversity in this world, and we could in fact see that Linda was looking forward to the presents *she* would soon be getting when at length she understood what it was all about.

The Christmas hearts she was supposed to be weaving didn't go too well, either, but I showed her how to cut up an egg carton and glue two tops together and paint them in watercolours, the way I had been taught at school on the last day of term, and tied a thread to them so that they could be hung on the Christmas tree.

While we were busy doing this, Mother sent me one of her new looks, which meant that she wanted to have a private word with me, and Linda was left in the kitchen fully engaged in her egg-box activities.

In the sitting room she bent right down to my ear and asked if I thought we should send a Christmas card to Linda's mother since we had received one from her, with very spiky handwriting, and, question number two, whether we should show it to Linda because it didn't say anything nice or personal, just

Merry Christmas and a Happy New Year, printed, and she couldn't read anyway, on top of which she had never so much as mentioned her mother, not even when Mother asked, which she was trying to stop herself doing for that very reason.

I didn't need to think twice, I answered no straight off to both questions. Apart from that, it was the 22nd of December and from my experience the post was a bit on the slow side around these parts. We found that out when we put the advertisement in the paper.

At first Mother shot me a look of surprise, then of reproach, then without warning she changed and exuded the new warmth. I was even given a hug and packed off into the kitchen where Linda was poring over her third cardboard bauble, which was black with runny yellow streaks.

'You have to wait until it dries, before you paint on top,' I said. 'Look.'

I demonstrated while Linda watched. Copied what she had to do. But now that she had got going, there was no stopping her, Mother tried a bit later in the evening, we didn't have any room for more than four, maximum five, baubles on the tree, after all we were going to put a lot of other nice things on it, shop-bought baubles, tinsel, lights, hearts, flags and some clip-on birds. I had a feeling this was going to be the same process as with the reading, that whatever was done would have to be repeated *ad infinitum*, it was worrying. I think Mother was worried too, for out of the blue she said we should go out to the balcony and look at the Christmas tree, which of course was not to be moved into the sitting room until the following day, because that was the tradition in our house, she intoned in her fairy-tale voice, standing in the cold balcony doorway on the 22nd and admiring the new Christmas tree before it came indoors, as the snow fluttered down from the Arnebråtens' balcony upstairs, a scene that was redolent of Walt Disney.

Of course, this was a ploy to distract Linda. I took the hint and stayed behind in the kitchen to tidy up all our mess so that only the eight baubles Linda had made stood in a line against the wall. I had to admit that the black one with the runny yellow paint was in fact the best. When they returned and Mother said with a shiver that now it was time to enjoy a nice hot cup of cocoa, Linda had no problem focusing her attention on supper, which today included an extra slice of bread topped, in her case, with spiced cheese.

★ ★ ★

We decorated the tree on the 23rd, Mother on one stool, me on another and Linda on the floor with her baubles forming a kind of skirt around the branches, like planets in a rough and tumble solar system, and she had never even done that before, so it was another great night, which the tiniest slip of the tongue on my part could so easily have turned into a catastrophe, and Mother was in a very good mood now that Kristian was away with his family and we had the place to ourselves.

On the morning of the 24th I went into the street with Linda for a few hours. For the first time. Brother and sister. And that passed off well enough too, even though I was nervous, and Anne-Berit, the stay-at-home, made the point that Linda didn't sledge the way she should, she was always trying to come on my sledge. I let her, of course, but it meant she cramped my style, and I suppose I looked more awkward than usual. When any of the other kids spoke to her she did not answer.

'What's your name, then?'

'Her name's Linda.'

'Are you visiting?'

'No, she lives here.'

'Where, at your place?'

'Yes.'

'Are you Finn's sister?'

Neither of us answered that one.

'My mum says you're Finn's sister.'

'Mother does too.'

'Is that true, Finn?'

Silence.

'Hey, Finn won't answer. Is she your sister, Finn? Come on, out with it.'

'Where the hell's she *been* all this time?'

A boy by the name of Freddy 2 said to her face:

'Can't you talk or what?'

'No,' Linda whispered, and the whole gang laughed, Freddy 2 loudest of all, he had been given that name because there were no fewer than three Freddys in our street, of whom only Freddy 1 had any personality.

'P'raps you're just deaf?' Freddy 2 wondered.

'Yes,' Linda said.

They laughed even louder at that. But it was a good answer, which meant no more questions were asked, for the time being. We did some more sledging, to Linda's mounting pleasure, because we kept to the shortest slope, in front of the house. When we got to the bottom she grabbed my mitten with more or less the same grip she had used on Mother. We tramped to the top and tobogganed down again. But then some bright spark asked:

'You — what's your name, then?'

'Her name's Linda, I've already told you!'

'Can't she speak or what?'

'Say something, Linda!'

'D'you wanna toffee, Linda?'

'. . .'

★ ★ ★

When, after a couple of hours, frozen to the bone and aching with lumps of ice dangling from our sweaters and socks and scarves and woolly hats, we went back inside, Mother had to crack our laces to undo our boots and hugged us both, and was nice and said Linda had to have a bath now, she was as cold as ice, poor thing, and she loved having a bath, didn't she?

'Yes.'

When at last she was sitting in the bathtub and whizzing her new duckling around, a pre-Christmas present, of which there had been quite a few, clothes mostly, and Mother had laid and unlaid and relaid and unlaid the table and changed the cloth before plumping for white, she said to me:

'You seemed to be enjoying yourselves on the slope.'

'You bet.'

'I noticed you were playing with the other kids.'

'Mm.'

'You were having a good time, I s'pose . . . ?'

'. . .'

And because adults can never get it into their noodles what idiots children are, this too rose to the dizzying heights of Freddy 2-style conversation, that is, until I left her and knelt in front of the T.V. and pressed the 'on' button, aware it was time for a Jiminy Cricket cartoon. But hardly had I immersed myself in it for more than a couple of minutes when the doorbell rang.

'Can you see who it is, Finn? Think it's someone for downstairs.'

This someone was for upstairs.

It was Uncle Tor, who never visited us as a rule, even if he was working nearby, at Hesteskoen for instance, which we could see from the kitchen window, but today he had an errand, as he called it, standing there in his waiter's suit with an alcoholic smile and his blond wavy locks smothered in Brylcreem.

'Well, Finn, are you looking forward to Christmas?'

'Yes, of course . . . erm it's today, isn't it.'

'Yes, that's right.'

'Oh, it's you, is it,' Mother said behind me, fidgeting with an earring, but not without a critical look, which must have registered — as did mine — that the guest was standing there without a single present in his empty hands, this was Uncle Tor, who could give me a pair of expensive skis one Christmas and not a sausage the next because he was broke, which he readily admitted with his pearly white charm. Uncle Tor was, according to Mother, the one member of the family who would never grow up, however old he became, and with some justice too, well, in fact he had been my age for as long as I had known him. He had dropped by to pick us up, he said, the car was waiting down in the street.

'The car?'

'Yes, a taxi.'

Mother dashed over to the balcony window.

'Are you out of your mind? Have you got a taxi waiting down there with the meter running?'

'Yes, aren't you ready?' Tor said innocently, surveying the wallpaper, the sofa and the Christmas tree with evident admiration, and perhaps the T.V. in particular, which Mother switched off, and then installed herself in front of the screen with her hands on her hips and a steely glare.

'Is this something you and Bjarne thought up?'

Then things took their usual course. Uncle Tor flopped down on the sofa, sighing and fidgeting with the crease in his terylene trousers and thrust out his hands as if trying to shake his watch bracelet further down his arm.

'Yes,' he admitted, glancing at his watch.

'We've already been through all this,' Mother said reprovingly.

'Yes,' Uncle Tor said again, looking across at me, realising he ought to smile, did smile, then went back to being serious and continued to sit as if just being there was an argument in itself.

Mother said nothing, but I could see from her face that she was not only in total control of the situation, but might also even have been enjoying it. She went into her room and fetched her purse.

'You've got nothing to pay the taxi with, have you?'

'Er . . . no,' Uncle Tor said, gazing at the wallpaper again.

'Here you are. Say hello to the others and have a good time.'

Tor was on his feet.

'OK, Sis. You win, as always.'

He gave her a thumbs-up, grabbed the note and headed for the hall. But then he remembered something.

'Er . . . Could I have a word with the girl, too, while I'm here?'

'She's having a bath,' Mother said curtly, and Uncle Tor looked down at his formal get-up, ill at ease.

'Yes, well, I suppose I should have brought her a present.'

'Yes, you should.'

There followed a few more moments of embarrassment before Uncle Tor showed us one of his party pieces, a three-step shuffle on the lino, chin on chest, shadow boxing with me:

'Watch out for the jab, lad, watch out for the jab . . . '

Upon which he opened the door, said oh well and Happy Christmas, and made off down the stairs.

'Rascal,' Mother said, then strode into the kitchen, turned, came back and said, as if mustering a troop of elite soldiers: 'Come on, Finn, now you get yourself dressed and this year you'll be smarter than ever before, both you and Linda.'

We plucked Linda out of the bath water, which had become quite cold in the meantime, so much so that she was shivering and her teeth were chattering. But she laughed when Mother tickled her through the towel, these lovely, almost inaudible gurgles we had heard only once. And indeed we did look smarter than ever before, and stiffer. That wasn't such a problem for Linda who was to a large extent stationary. But I couldn't sit still while eating the meal, which even today we ate in the kitchen, no ribs this year, it was roast leg of pork with oodles of gravy.

I had to read out the names on the presents as I was the best in the family at reading. And it is strange how you get a true picture of life standing like that, with a stiff collar chafing away at you, beside a sparkling Christmas tree, reading names on presents and working out who can be relied upon in this world and who cannot. Gran, for example, doesn't get a very high score this year: Linda and I each get a card game, and Mother gets nothing. Uncle Bjarne and Aunty Marit have given us nice presents as usual, but neither has given Mother anything, while the previous year she at least got a weighty ornament which was more expensive than anything she could have afforded herself.

Only from Uncle Oskar did we all get what we wanted, Linda a jigsaw puzzle she couldn't do, a magnifying glass for me, and Mother a primus stove. But she just snorted at it, even though she had said she wanted one just like it after the old one gave up the ghost on a picnic last autumn.

Kristian, too, had bought presents for everyone. Mother got some jewellery, which silenced and irritated her, and caused her to busy herself with anything else but what we were doing. Linda got a pair of Dutch skates and I got two books, number eighteen in 'The Famous Five' series and the 1961 edition of *Hvem Hva Hvor*, an almanac, in which a bookmark had been inserted and a sentence underlined about the rapid rise of television viewing:

'It has been our experience that gifted children soon prefer reading books and magazines to spending their leisure hours in front of the screen, while there is an increasing tendency for less gifted children to spend their time watching television . . . '

'What's he mean by that?' Mother said, snatching the book and perusing it with a furrowed brow before returning it and devoting her attentions to the strange jewellery which, squinting through the magnifying glass I was given by Uncle Oskar, I could see had 585 CARAT written on it; it was a hare holding its paws in front of its eyes.

Linda was given most presents, it turned out, including from me. But that didn't matter, because most were clothes which had to be tried on and taken off and tried on again while we ate marzipan and cakes, and laughed and laughed until she fell asleep in bed amid the skates and all her clothes, and I was on the point of dropping off myself after no more than three pages of Kristian's boring book, although at least it did have a picture of Yuri Gagarin, when, sad to say, Mother came into my room with tears in her eyes, whispering something about it having been nice on our own, hadn't it?

I didn't have an answer to that; in fact, there had never been so many of us.

But, as so often before, when she wanted to tell me something in confidence, other things came out first which had nothing to do with the main point, this time it was what the family might have said about her during the evening, another thing I couldn't get worked up about.

The real problem didn't surface until a while after Christmas. There were three of us now, weren't there, she explained. But Linda would be going to school soon, and giving up the shoe shop job was out of the question, it was much more likely she would go full-time. And then the nursery up behind the church had rejected our application, there might be a place in spring, fine, but what on earth would we do until then?

Even this question wasn't addressed to me, though; Mother had already found a solution.

'How do I look?' she asked, it was the 28th of December, just after three in the afternoon.

She had put on some make-up and her shoe shop dress, now she was draping her smartest cloak across her shoulders, she asked me to look after Linda and went out starting with No. 1, then went from block to block, rang all the door-bells, said Happy Christmas and asked if there was anyone at home who might be able to take care of a little girl for five to six hours a day until spring. She got no further than No. 7, where she found the right person, a twenty-year-old by the name of Eva Marlene whom ever since we have called simply Marlene and who worked as a waitress in the evenings, at Kontraskjæret, and slept all morning in her parents' flat. And Marlene seemed fine, even though Linda ran off and hid the instant she popped her head in.

'Come and say hello to Eva Marlene, Linda. She's going to be looking after you while I'm at work.'

That didn't have much of an effect, and I can't say I blame her, the way she had been bundled from one woman to another, barely used to mother No. 2 before No. 3 was introduced. But Marlene, who at first sight could appear somewhat flighty and very nubile, judging by all the paint-work, turned out to be robust and down-to-earth, a realist, who strangely enough was employed in the same frivolous line of work as Uncle Tor, the fairy-tale industry, as Mother called it, where dreams and insanity were two sides of the same coin.

'Oh, she'll get used to me,' Marlene said in the direction of the duvet beneath which Linda was hidden, and then started looking around to get an impression of what it would be like to spend time here. 'I've got three small brothers and sisters, and I'm used to young kids.'

'I don't think we'll be able to hang onto her for long,' Mother said, in high spirits, when Marlene had gone home after downing three cups of coffee, with reference to both her nubile status and pleasing personality. 'Just hope she survives till March . . . Well, if we're very, very lucky maybe . . . '

On and on she went. For good fortune is always followed by bad, etc., etc.

So that was how the year of the Berlin Wall, the T.V. set and above all Yuri Gagarin ended, the year that had begun so like all the others, but because of something as prosaic as the combination of decoration fever and poverty had transformed Mother from being a divorced widow into a landlady and single mother of two, and me from being an only child to becoming one of two siblings in a bunk bed, not to mention what this must have meant for Linda. Though we were not so aware of that yet. If the truth be told, by and large, we don't understand much of what is going on around us; as Mother is wont to say, by God's good grace, life usually comes to us in bits and pieces.

8

The New Year began with snow. Piles and piles of it. On balconies and roofs and in fields and streets, with ski slopes and toboggan slides and children hanging on to bumpers as cars spun up Traverveien and got no further than Lien's shop before having to seek refuge in Eikelundveien. And the ethereal tranquillity that can settle over a suburb which in fact has been designed for the complete opposite, for clamour and tumult, this tranquillity that descends as the banks of snow rise and cars in Trondhjems-veien disappear from view, and where only the yellow Schøyen bus tops are visible above the white mounds, bus roofs gliding like inaudible flying carpets over the Saharan expanses; this is the countryside come to town, woods and wide open spaces, one might even say the sea, which have superimposed themselves on the urban experiment.

There was no question of us limiting ourselves to the toboggan slope outside our block now, we had to cross the street and explore Hagan, an overgrown ridge with ancient oaks, fruit trees, gooseberry bushes and a white house with only one illuminated window. The old lady we used to call Ruby sat there, she was part of eternity too, like snow and horses, and if you sneaked up there late at night, you could hear a cosmic noise emerging from the darkened house to petrify anyone who lived on an estate.

And I had to go further afield now, away from the block and the short slope, and perhaps especially from Linda, who incidentally had succeeded in taming Anne-Berit, the indoor creature, who during the first weeks of January had been out in the streets more than she had in the whole of the previous year, and had taken it upon herself to spread a protective wing over Linda, a demanding and calculating mistress, Anne-Berit was.

'No, no, no, not like that, Linda. Look at me.'

Linda did make a few brave attempts to follow orders, which were met by a shaking of the head and laughter, but also with some crumbs of sympathy, after all she was nothing less than a little doll, easy to distract, who moreover did not cry needlessly, the perfect pet for someone like Anne-Berit, who was sick and tired of her own younger sisters and took Linda to the tennis courts, which had been sprayed with water and now served as skating rinks, where Linda learned to stump around on the leather uppers of her boots or otherwise sat on the drifts eating the snow off her mittens, where she was an audience for Anne-Berit's pirouettes on the milky-blue ice as she sang Anita Lindblom's Swedish version of 'You Can Have Him' — everyone was singing 'You Can Have Him' that winter, it was on the radio and T.V., I had even heard it on the bus and at the trotting track, most of all I had heard Marlene, who was unable to so much as peel a single potato without humming 'You Can Have Him'.

And I was able to slip away.

Up to Hagan, with the big boys.

I have never been any great shakes as a sportsman, but I can be quite brave, and a person like me who doesn't give in, whatever comes his way, can easily earn the requisite dose of mocking respect; especially if on top of that he can ignore the jeers that are hurled at him.

Now there are also losers who try to get even in a way that lands them in more trouble, deeper and deeper, until the situation gets out of hand. I had a friend like that, Freddy 1, he was big and heavy and angry, nothing special at school, and nothing special in the street; he didn't have the mouth on him either, and for some reason he always wore clothes that were not quite right. That was what made him stand out, that was what gave him a personality, and the name Freddy 1, placing him before Freddy 2 and Freddy 3 who just merged into the crowd, yes, the very fact that he was big and strong but slow, a catastrophic combination of much too much and much too little in one and the same person, that was what gave him number 1 status.

When the gang grew tired of herringboning up Hagan and skiing down and herringboning up again and instead started taking the piss out of Freddy 1 about his skis, or hat, or stance, he responded with coarse insults and snowballs that never found their target. When the snowballs were returned, Freddy 1 ripped off his skis and flailed them around, to the mounting glee of the riff-raff, because he never actually hit anyone, just whirled round and spat and cried and fenced with his idiotic Bonna skis until he toppled over with a belch. Then the shouting stopped. Freddy 1 was on the ground, hurrah. The gang inched closer to see if he was dead. But Freddy 1 was not dead. He was just waiting for precisely this moment, his moment of glory.

'Are you dead, Numero Uno?'

With his last remaining energy he pounced on the boot of one of the smallest boys, knocked the poor devil over and fell on top of him and punched him in the face with his icy mittens until the victim's nose started to stream with blood or until one of the bigger boys tugged at his scarf and presented him with the tough choice of laying off or being strangled. It usually ended with the latter. Freddy 1 was no longer of this world. But in his own. In the realm of fury and snot and tears. Nothing could crack Freddy 1, he endured the punishment and never learned, this was Traverveien's toughest existence, to which statues should have been erected, in iron.

★ ★ ★

It was on one of these exhilarating evenings, as I heaved myself off the top of Hagan and raced down with the wind and snow battering all my senses, only to land with a thump on my kisser just where Hagan meets the estate, that I was observed by Kristian. Our lodger was standing there in his hat and coat and witnessed my fall, he had crossed over from the estate to see what the young ones were up to in the evening gloom.

Later that evening the topic of my skiing skills, which were by no means perfect, was brought up at the kitchen table, and the question was whether I wanted to go with Kristian on a cross-country excursion next Sunday, take the train to Movatn and ski home via Lillomarka, past legendary restaurants such as Sinober, Sørskauen and Lilloseter, as was customary for those children who had fathers.

I hesitated, not least because I was puzzled by the encouraging tones with which Mother met the invitation. When Kristian returned after the Christmas holidays she had confronted him and asked what the jewellery he had given her for Christmas was supposed to mean, an assault he had tried to ward off with roughly the same expression as when he had presented us with a box of provisions during the strike, with the same lack of success. So why this positive attitude of hers now, towards the man wishing to undertake some misguided notion of fatherly duties?

'What about Linda?' I asked.

'She's too small.'

'Is it *that* far?'

'Not at all.'

I ended up saying yes. I had said yes far too often in my childhood, it was only later that I began to say no, not that it helped much. And for some reason we had to depart at the crack of dawn. At half past seven. On skis. Kristian looked alien and strange in a white anorak and oddly antiquated knickerbockers, and he was very tight-lipped as the freezing cold day broke. In Lofthusveien it was alternate gravel and ice. So even if it was downhill all the way, I was already whacked by the time we arrived at Grefsen railway station at five to eight. The train was packed and silent, a slumbering mass of men of all ages, only men, as if in thrall to a national solemnity, an army on its way to the front. And we had to stand, so I didn't get a chance to recover. But off we set in the biting cold, and there were good trails, and it was nice and flat over the ice on Lake Movann. Thereafter, however, the nightmare began, the ascent.

'On the other hand, when we're up top it'll all be plain sailing,' panted Kristian at his lowest ebb.

The thing was we never got up top. It was just like walking up to the moon. I was merely a quivering shadow of myself when at length we swerved into the forecourt of Sinober, the first restaurant, a wondrous sight in the crystal clear winter landscape. But for some reason we were not going there. I couldn't believe my ears. We were going on. To Sørskauen. We made it, too, by the skin of our teeth, but by then I was such a wreck I had difficulty swallowing the blackcurrant toddy and waffles that Kristian treated me to, I went to sleep with food in my mouth, and when he shook me back to consciousness, I asked if we couldn't stay the night.

'Ha, ha,' he said, turning to the waitress. 'The boy's asking if we could stay the night.'

'Mm, fine thing that would be,' the woman said.

I had the misfortune to bump into one of my pals here, Roger, who was an excellent skier. But, as luck would have it, he was with his elder brothers, so we were almost equally red-faced sitting there, mute with exhaustion, beside each other on the shiny, worn wooden bench in the stuffy room reeking of wet clothes and wet men and rucksacks and bark and berries and spruce and all the Norwegian outdoor smells I have always associated with a combination of poverty and fathers. As luck would have it, Roger was dragged out before me.

But after we had had our fill of all the waffles and the toddies, we could not stay where we were, however much I begged, taking up room from a constant stream of groaning hordes crashing in through the door with loud voices and swaggering pitch-seam skiing boots, with steam and sweat and ice and snow and indefinable, thick storm-clouds of breath that they had gorged like greedy sharks for kilometre after kilometre through the frozen reality, only to release the whole foulness here in this much-too-cramped pressure-cooker of a primitive shack. The great Norwegian winter beast. The bear that never sleeps, but slashes and claws and makes an infernal racket alone and with others so as not to freeze to death, all the things I had missed because I didn't have a father.

In short, there was nothing for it but to set out and struggle on, unrelenting, an extra layer of wax, alright, then. But it wasn't grip that was the trouble, or the glide, it was my physical state. I was now so stiff and frozen after the merciless baking from the wood-burner that I was regurgitating waffles and blackcurrant toddy the whole way down to Lilloseter. Kristian had to dispense sympathy and scorn to keep me upright, for kilometre after kilometre. But by the time we arrived in Lilloseter, this last station on our socialist-democratic *via dolorosa*, it became apparent that we weren't stopping here, either, I had definitely regained my body heat, and got shot of the food.

On top of that, Kristian had come a cropper a couple of times on the slopes down to Lake Breisjøen. I fell too, but his nose-dive was a more thorough-going affair, more time-consuming, one might say, it must have been something to do with age, and philosophy. Kristian was not the type to fall, he was more likely to determine himself when he would take a tumble, and here natural forces had got the better of him. But when at long last we hung trembling on our poles at the top of Årvollåsen squinting down towards the rifle club and Østreheim, at least his smirk was gone. Not just that. He had a brand new expression on that modern face of his. I think it must have been bitterness, even though he managed to force a grin, and said there was something he wanted to talk to me about, did I think my mother would mind him having guests in his room?

An unusual question, to me, and it wasn't until there had been a bit of hemming and hawing that I realised a lady was involved. Did I think she would be allowed to stay a few days?

I answered that I doubted it.

'I thought as much,' he said, focusing his gaze on the hollow in which Oslo lay. 'What is it that she wants?' he mumbled.

A son cannot answer that kind of question, it wasn't even certain that he was referring to Mother, but then he said:

'And what's up with the girl, is she . . . retarded?'

I heard the drum rolls begin in earnest, and saw rainbows wreathe my field of vision. I gasped for breath, tightened my grip on the sticks and set off, managing to stay on my feet the whole way past the rifle club and down Østreheimsveien, but of course he caught me up again, and knocked me flying into the snow.

'For Christ's sake, Finn, you don't understand a thing!'

The lodger had turned into a monster. I could do nothing but close my eyes and be strong.

* * *

'Back already,' Mother said as we stumbled into the flat at last.

But I didn't have much to say about the skiing trip, I was hot and uncommunicative and at the end of my tether, had to have help with my boots, and cleared off to my room in a kind of unarticulated, almost a physical attempt not to say anything. Perhaps I was even trying to believe that I had not heard the dreadful word. But there was Linda in the lower bunk, on her stomach, drawing a horse, a creature only Mother and I were able to identify, and if you can't draw a horse in this life, you are doomed, you will sink like a lead weight, and this was an indecipherable horse repeated on sheet after sheet throughout the drawing pad I had given her for Christmas, for she loved horses, and they looked like ants and elephants and God knows what. She smiled and said:

'Cold?'

And I yelled:

'Can't you bloody draw properly!'

But before her lower lip could quiver into a sob, Mother was there, screaming: 'What on earth has got into you, Finn?!' And the dreadful word had not been forgotten.

'He called her retarded!' I bawled, and at that moment I saw a flustered Kristian behind Mother's deathly pale face.

'What?' she said, her voice almost inaudible. And there was silence.

'The boy's raving,' Kristian shouted, crimson-faced skier and idiot. 'Don't listen to him.'

But Mother has this ability to freeze her surroundings. And since Linda was the sole normal person among us, she just turned over the page and carried on fiddling with her crayons while Kristian and I stood to attention listening with fear and trembling to Mother's softly spoken words.

'You called her *what?*'

Kristian raised his arms to a great height, then dropped them again and tried to do an Uncle Tor, whispered into the bargain, out of consideration for Linda, I assume:

'But you must be able to see the child needs help. She can't speak, can she?'

'You called her *what*?'

That was him done for. Kristian stroked his forehead with one hand and did something I myself have never been able to quite bring myself to do, he apologised and looked as though he meant it.

'Sorry. It was inexpiable. But . . . no, there is no excuse, I know.'

He turned on his heel like the guilty man he was, in every cell of his body, and went to his room, while Mother was left standing like a steel spring, speechless and alien, until I took her hand, shook and pulled it.

'Inexpiable?' I heard from afar.

I didn't know what it meant. But then she was back. 'That man is finished here!'

I nodded, with enthusiasm. 'And Linda can draw whatever horses she likes, Finn, I can tell you that!'

'Yes, fine, but . . . '

'But what?'

'I'll have to teach her . . . something.'

By now Mother was at the end of her tether, too. She flopped down on the bed beside Linda and placed her hands in her lap and nodded slowly, mumbling, mhm mhm, before looking at me again, as if seeing me for the first time, or the state I was in, my puce cheeks and a body that was utterly drained.

'How was the skiing?' she asked.

'I'm hungry,' I said.

'Have a little lie-down,' she said. 'And I'll see to dinner.'

I had a lie-down. But not a little one. I didn't wake up until dawn the following day.

9

I was shaking with cold and experiencing terrible breathing difficulties, I also had unbearable pains in my chest. What was left of my arms and legs seemed to be encased in lead. I was unable to get up and had to shout in whispers until Mother awoke in the early morning darkness.

'I'm cold.'

'You've got your duvet,' she mumbled drowsily.

'I . . . can't get up.'

'What do you want to get up for? It's not . . .'

'I need a pee.'

'Go on, then.'

'I *can't*. I've told you.'

Then Mother was beside me.

'What do you mean? Get up now!'

'It's not working,' I said, pointing to where I reckoned my heart was. What next, Mother wondered, as I recoiled with a fully fledged howl the moment she laid her hand on me, you see, we are never ill in our family; illness is treated with the utmost scepticism, it is something Mother has brought with her from her own home where everyone had a 'lie-down' at times, in fact even Uncle Bjarne himself had a tendency to throw in the towel on the odd occasion and 'go on a cure', which Uncle Oskar told us about in a letter, news which made Mother snort, but which was never discussed at Christmas family gatherings. It would have been quite natural to ask 'Well, Bjarne, how's it going with the cure?'

Not a word.

Mother sent me a stern look.

'It's not your heart, my lad, it's your lungs.'

After muttering 'damned lodger' and 'damned cross-country skiing', and repeating that the man was finished here, she gave me a thermometer that I first had to put under my arm and then in my mouth. But it showed only 37 degrees, and I was still sore.

'I can't breathe,' I said. Mother told me to wait while she got dressed and crossed the road to the telephone booth by Omar Hansen's and called the doctor. Before he arrived, I was moved down to Linda's bunk while Linda lay on her stomach on Mother's bed watching me being examined.

His name was Dr Løge, he made me sit up, however much it hurt, and banged a knuckle and some cold, hard fingertips against my chest bone and my back, listened with his stethoscope and peered at me from under his

white eyebrows before removing the stethoscope and looking quizzically at Mother.

'Seems as if he may have cracked two or
three ribs. Has he had a fall?'

'Ribs?'

'Yes, or they're broken. We'll be able to see
on an X-ray.'

'Did you fall yesterday, Finn?'

Yes, of course I did, I fell all the time.

'But I didn't hurt myself.'

'You're not trying to tell me you broke two
ribs doing cross-country skiing, are you!'

Dr Løge looked at me with renewed
interest, he must have been in his mid fifties
and wore bifocals and peered over the top
rim.

'It was a long trip then, was it?' he asked
with a smile.

'Yes, quite long.'

'It's the most stupid thing I've ever heard,'
Mother persisted. 'Did he hit you?'

'Who?'

'Kristian, of course. Come on, spit it out!'

'Naah . . . '

'What are you two talking about?' Dr Løge
broke in.

'Nothing,' Mother said, crossing her arms
tightly and biting her lips, before her gaze fell
on Linda, whereupon she rested her face on
one hand, as if she had had as much as she

could take, and it struck me that now something incomprehensible was going to happen again, and intolerable, I began to hope she would break down, so that we would get the whole thing over and done with, but she just stood there, and Dr Løge sat and sat there with his bushy eyebrows and the clear look of wonderment through his matt glasses which magnified the pores in his skin into deep craters, when with a sudden effort of will Mother said:

'Well, I'd better be getting off. We have to . . .'

'But the boy has to be X-rayed.'

'Marlene will take care of that,' Mother said without emotion. 'I have to go to work. Up you get, Linda, and put some clothes on. Are you hungry, Finn?'

'Wouldn't mind a slice of bread with goat's cheese . . .'

Dr Løge looked from one to the next and sensed that this was more an audience than a doctor's visit, and that his time was up.

'What do I owe you for the . . . visit?' Mother asked.

He stuffed the stethoscope in his bag, grabbed his coat and sat with it over his lap, watching Linda play with Amalie on the bed while Mother went into the kitchen. He smiled and stroked Linda's cheek and asked what her name was, to which she made no response, just held out Amalie who had now had her operation wound sewn up, her floppy leg reattached and her face equipped with shiny new button-eyes.

I was given a slice of bread and a glass of milk as the doorbell rang and in walked Marlene, with apple-red cheeks and a layer of glistening snow on her lacquered hair, which she never hid under a hat. Marlene had become Mother's confidante in a very short time and was now being briefed in whispers about the situation, I suppose, I heard another sharp exclamation in the hall, like the dry pop of a silencer, as it were, and 'I can't take any more!' from Mother, 'so if you wouldn't mind?'

Not long afterwards she called to the doctor, who still hadn't put on his coat.

'You didn't answer my question, doctor.'

'Don't worry about it,' he said calmly, getting up and proffering a pen and a small pad with white pages and a blue-black carbon sheets which fluttered as he left the bedroom, like dry leaves, it is autumn even though it is winter, I thought, chewing away but I couldn't swallow any of the food and I knew I wouldn't manage the milk either, me who loves milk. As the front door banged to behind Mother, and I saw that the alarm clock on her bedside table already showed ten, I knew that Marlene must have been late today, or that Mother had overslept, and that I was going to be sick.

However, Marlene came into the bedroom and was gentle, still shrouded in the winter cold and she sat on the edge of my bed and asked me how I was, stroked my hair and joked and took a bite of my bread and said what I already knew, that we would have to go and get the X-ray done, a trip to town, that would be O.K., wouldn't it, eh, with Linda?

Yes, it would.

I got up. She dressed us both and we went down at a time of the day when the estate looked like a bed sheet covering an enormous hospital, in which all the children lie lifeless and laugh through soundless open mouths. I could hardly walk and barely breathe, I was dizzy, nauseous and shaking with a chill that I must have brought back with me from the forests.

But Marlene helped me, and I was given a seat on the bus like an elderly person, she made sure of that, even though sitting hurt much more than standing, and it was a long way, a journey I had in fact made many times before, when I was going to visit Mother in the shoe shop, but which was quite different now and we went through a district I had never seen. Nevertheless, we got off at the familiar Gasserk which was such a monstrous presence with its long, black intestines on the outside and it roared and burned and hissed and it was like a World War.

Across the road and into the casualty department.

I concentrated as hard as I could and looked at Marlene who did not lower her gaze for anybody, she who had been to grammar school, and was forthright and plain-spoken and gave my name and Dr Løge's, and yes, thank you, we'll wait, take a seat over there, will you? Then she went back out and queued up in front of the little kiosk, she waved to us through the window and bought two lollipops, one green and one orange, which Linda and I took turns to suck because we both liked the orange one best, we timed each other using Marlene's solid gold wrist watch, which she said was just gaudy junk, ha ha.

'But I was given it by a prince!'

She had even brought a book with her, which she read from in a whisper, to Linda, whenever Linda stopped her in the middle of the story she repeated the passage again and again. And I could feel that now I wasn't tensing my muscles so much any more, and was gradually able to sit back in a sprawl. But

I gave a start when someone called my name and I had to grimace when I was helped up and led into a silent, white room to be sat down on a large, hard iron chair and laid on a bench and stood inside a yellow and white cabinet where I held my breath and let it out, surrounded by only smiling people, who thereafter wrapped me up with rough, brutal hands in a large white bandage that held me erect and prevented me from breathing in more deeply than I needed to, whereupon I was bundled out again, as stiff as a poker and given a hug by Marlene, who became embroiled in yet another frank conversation with the receptionist, bent down to us, made secretive, mischievous faces, as though she had just managed to pull the wool over someone's eyes, and whispered as she pushed us out into the winter cold that now we were going to take a bloody taxi, which *she* had arranged for us!

A taxi home.

With Linda and me on the rear seat. Marlene and the driver sat at the front smoking filter cigarettes and talking as if they had known each other all their lives, the way Marlene talked to everyone and the way everyone talked to her. Marlene was born to mend all the wayward and the weird in life with her words, her beauty and her red-lipped smile. She talked the driver into taking us right up to the entrance, the lad's not well, you see. And it created something of a stir because, as it happened, school was over, and the black Volga we rolled up in was almost on a par with an ambulance. Anne-Berit asked Linda what was going on, although I didn't hear whether she got an answer. But I made a few more faces and was very stiff, as Marlene signed a slip of paper and said bye-bye to the driver before steering us through the crowd of kids in through the door and up the stairs.

★ ★ ★

Mother was already home from work, and in quite a different frame of mind from when she had left us, gentle and full of energy, with food on the table, rissoles and creamed cabbage, and she wanted to know exactly what we had done during the course of the day and most of all how I was.

Well, not so bad, I ate as I had never eaten before. But then I had to have another lie-down, this time in Linda's bed, on the lower bunk.

'Linda can sleep with me,' Mother said, pinching her cheek. Linda had been on my bunk once and there had been a hell of a

118

to-do, caused by fear of heights, Mother reckoned.

I stayed there for a full week.

That might have been a bit over the top, seven days in bed on account of a few ribs, but I read the whole time, books and comics, and Linda entertained me by sitting still in Mother's bed and looking in my direction, in case I needed anything, volume four of the encyclopaedia, for example, a glass of water with fizzy drink powder, and I paid her with small scraps of paper with numbers on, I called them bank notes, which she collected in a little shoe box and I forced her to add them up, to keep a kind of balance sheet, to no avail, but she did at least want to keep them in piles, sorted by size.

I also had some visitors, first Anne-Berit, who was disappointed to find that my bandage was not a plaster cast. Then Freddy 1, who had been sent by his mother with two Fox chocolate bars and hung around the beds, ill at ease, not knowing where to sit, until I made room for him on my bed. We ate the chocolate and played Snakes and Ladders, Ludo and a card game called Pig. While Linda watched.

'Is she not going to play?' asked Freddy 1.

'Nope.'

'Why not?'

'She doesn't like games.'

'Doesn't *like*?' Freddy 1 wondered with an intrigued grin, and glanced over at her through his long fringe, Freddy 1 had always had longer hair than everyone else, apart from when he had his hair cut, then he had shorter hair than everyone else, and always looked as if he groomed his hair with a hand grenade. 'Can't you play Pig?'

Linda didn't answer. She was making heaps with the money.

'I can teach you,' Freddy 1 said.

'No,' I said loudly, and he looked upset. 'O.K., have a go then.'

Freddy 1 explained, but Linda looked away.

'See if you can chuck 'em,' he suggested. 'Like this!' And he started throwing cards around the room. Linda thought that was fun, she even laughed, with laughter that sounded like a wish had come true, I don't know whether it was hers or mine.

But Freddy 1 didn't want to take off his coat for some reason, and when at length he left, because he was beginning to boil, I presume, Mother said:

'What's wrong with him?'

'What do you mean?'

'He's twice the size of you.'

★ ★ ★

120

On Saturday afternoon there was a din coming from the sitting room, and when I went to investigate, I found Kristian and Mother involved in a heated exchange which stopped as soon as they caught sight of me.

'I just wanted to give you this, Finn,' Kristian said meekly, holding up his chess board. 'As a farewell gift.'

'You've no business giving him anything at all,' Mother said.

I beat a hasty retreat, even though I would very much have liked that chess set. But as I was leaving for school on Monday morning I saw that his hat and coat were still hanging in the hallway, and in the afternoon I asked Mother how that could be, but all I got by way of a reply was some mumbling about the lodger having been given a period of grace until he found himself something else.

I would have liked to ask more questions, or say 'Eh?', at least. But this was not the easy matter it used to be. It was past ten o'clock, I still remembered in a vague, hazy kind of way the morning I woke up with three broken ribs, and Mother was going to work even though she was supposed to finish at one that day. Perhaps it was not so strange, or perhaps that was exactly what it was. Furthermore, she was back at home when we returned from casualty, and that was perhaps not so strange either, at any rate it wasn't worth making any enquiries or delving further, that was just the way things were, the distance between us that had grown with Linda's arrival, which I thought we had succeeded in bridging, had instead increased.

★   ★   ★

I was out a lot during the weeks that followed, came home from school, threw my bag in the hall and went out again, even pretended I didn't hear when Marlene called me, did I want a bite to eat? This isn't the sort of thing you choose to do. These are decisions that make themselves, and you can allow yourself to be guided by them because something new is happening — such as the coming of spring; for Linda it is a skipping rope and paradise, she has never seen any of this and has to learn everything from scratch. But she is still slower than the usual beginner, and not many weeks pass before my interest in the poor mite is on the wane. And I have to avert my eyes. Well, actually, I don't, I have a kind of observation post up on Hagan which gives me an uninterrupted view of the estate, and from there I can see Linda sitting on the steps, alone, outside our entrance. And then I have an observation post on the slope facing

Trondhjemsveien, and from there I can see her, too, alone, and even though I don't show it and I allow myself to be swallowed up by the various sudden wave-like movements that surge through a motley group of kids and carry them on to ever new adventures, I see her all the time, and that irritates me, because it seems to me that she is sitting exactly where she is sitting with the sole intention of making me look at her. I go down and ask.

'Why are you sitting here?'

She doesn't understand the question, smiles, and she is happy to see me and gets up and doesn't even take my hand, but stands there shuffling her feet, waiting for *me* to take her hand and get up to some fun, which I often do when no-one is watching.

'Don't sit like that,' I say.

'?'

'With your head down, I mean. Sit up.'

I show her how, and she sits up straight, I nod, but it is not to my complete satisfaction, because something somewhere inside me tells me the reason she is sitting here alone is not just due to the fact that all the others are idiots, but that there is something about her, I can't work out what though.

I take her with me to a coin-tossing game, push her into the crowd of spectators with an invisible hand, or I show her a knife-throwing game, one which also requires a crowd of spectators, or else she can make dams with the slush in the street, which as a rule only involves the participants themselves. But none of this is much to Linda's taste, it seems, even though she is fond of repetition.

She also has the chance to witness another of Freddy 1's breakdowns, this time over his new bike, which is not new but old and black and bought by his father off scrap dealer Adolf Jahr in Storo for fifteen kroner, and is about as much use as a wooden leg. His performance is so dramatic that Linda takes my hand and tries to drag me away, I almost have to tear myself free, wondering how the others do it, how they get away from clingy younger siblings. But I see no way out, this skill is invisible, I can't even see anyone clinging, as if everyone, great and small, knows how to deal with siblings and friends. And Mother?

Over dinner she says:

'Well, how was it today, then?'

'Great,' says Linda with a smile, and then Mother doesn't ask who she played with, or what she played with, instead she looks relieved that nothing bad has happened.

★ ★ ★

Marlene starts sending Linda on shopping errands, up to Lien's, which is usually my job, so that we have potatoes and bread for when Mother returns from work. But also that little journey crosses my field of vision. From Hagan I see Linda go into the shop and she does not re-emerge for ages, and then she is empty-handed, so I have to go down and ask what has happened, only to have the note written in Marlene's handwriting shoved in front of my nose. I take Linda into the shop again and explain to her that the idea is not that she should hide behind the shelves but nail herself to the floor in front of the counter and she shouldn't budge an inch, neither for women, nor children, until fru Lien catches sight of her, and then she should pass over the note, snappy, like this.

Two days later she comes out empty-handed again.

'What's up this time?' I ask, irritated and out of breath after having to break off what I was doing yet again. Once more I am shown Marlene's list, and realise at length that there might have been a problem deciphering her handwriting, was that one or two loaves?

'You've got to *speak*,' I say. 'Come here.'

We go back, I demonstrate my skills to Linda and catch myself shouting, all too late, however.

'One *loaf!* Wholegrain!'

'Goodness me, Finn,' fru Lien says, rolling her eyes. I blush in the crowd, take the loaf and drag Linda out.

'Now you just carry this and go home — *alone*,' I say sternly, still crimson to the roots of my hair. But she doesn't want to, she stands hugging the bread with both arms, as if afraid it will make a getaway.

'Come on now. I'll watch you until you have passed No. 8.'

After much hithering and thithering she goes, backwards almost, down Traverveien, but not around the corner, not at all, she stops right on the borderline between her world and mine, and starts mooching around and looking up at me, until there is nothing else I can do but go after her yet again and walk home with her, where I say to Marlene, who is listening to the radio and humming and singing while pairing off an ocean of small, almost identical socks:

'Can't you bloody write properly!'

'What are you talking about?'

'This!'

I show her the note and explain, but Marlene is not the type to be knocked out of her stride by any old scribble, not even her own.

'Why don't you ask fru Lien to learn to

read?' she says. 'Smart-arse.'

I close my eyes and visualise a deserted plain with a tiny apple tree. Then I open them again and tell Linda who is still clutching the by now almost flattened wholegrain loaf:

'Tomorrow I'm going to take the note off you, then you'll have to *say* what you want, got that?!'

★   ★   ★

Above all, this was the spring when old one-eyed Ruby disappeared from the house in Hagan and the last light was extinguished in her window. And so we children could tear down the rest of the fence and climb the trees and burn the heaps of wood and launch the final destructive attack on the house itself, smash the windows and break down the doors and burst in and steal all the things that were not there, for the house was as empty as the sky and razed to the ground by two bulldozers in a single hour.

A new day-care centre was going to be built here, and a shopping centre with a hairdresser's and an Irma supermarket and a photography shop and a fishmonger's and shoe shops, because the satellite town is devouring everything, even inwards to its own core. Blocks of flats have appeared now at the bottom of the estate, cars, children, roads and noise are springing up, there is only one way this is going, to hell, according to our lodger, Kristian, who is not moving after all, it transpires, he is content to exchange his winter coat for his spring coat and walk up and down the new short cut, which he has been doing for close on six months now, are his temporary digs going to become permanent?

And one more thing: was it nine o'clock or eleven o'clock the day that Mother couldn't face taking me to casualty?

The last item of old Ruby's furniture to be carried out of her house was a venerable old piano. Inside there was a concealed treasure. Sound. We had heard this sound for many years as we sneaked up in the autumn murk through the towering oak trees with our torches and encircled the one eye that shone, and were stopped in our tracks — by sound. No-one had a piano in Traverveien. But there was one here, in this ancient house in our midst. It was now being carried out by four strong men in white overalls, all the same age, the same height, the same hair colour and the same thick, black-rimmed glasses and all with short grey beards, which not only made them look like soldiers in the same army but also quadruplets from the same family — they were carrying out this shiny, black wonder in a perfect, silent synchronised dance as we stood watching from our unnaturally static positions and for the first time I knew what we had heard all these years, thirty, forty children, fifty, sixty . . . of all ages. In the end there were 183 suburban children who had heard music for all those years and had not known where it came from, until it went silent. Now we stood there paying our last respects, to a coffin being borne to the grave.

'There weren't *so* many of you present, were there?' Mother said.

'Yes, there were,' I said. 'I counted them and I remember.'

'Don't give me that again, Finn, please.'

'Ask Linda, then.'

'*Don't*, I said! *Don't!*'

She covered her eyes with one hand, which she had done the morning I woke up with three broken ribs, and which at long last I realised meant it was me she couldn't take any longer, she couldn't take listening to what I had to say, it was *me* she couldn't take, not being hard up, not a sudden death, not a lost love, not a pestering lodger nor a Linda who was so quietly wrapped up in her own eternity. No, it was *me*. And I realised that on the evening I was talking about the 183 children who had stood in the involuntary line bidding a dejected farewell to a piano, she was incapable of listening because this was not a sign of childhood but of nascent decadence.

'Well, was it a grand piano or an upright?' she asked, crossly.

'Makes no difference,' I said, and left, for good.

10

Then a letter arrived. With a crossed-out addressee and our name written in spiky handwriting, in pencil. It was from the health clinic in Sagene where I myself used to go for check-ups before the school nurse came onto the scene. Now it was Linda's turn. And Mother had the bright idea of taking me along, to have a rib-check, as she jokingly called it; she had never succeeded in coming to terms with this injury of mine, you don't break three ribs doing cross-country skiing, do you. Besides she knew the staff in Sagene, and trusted them more than Dr Løge who had been called only because his practice was in the vicinity.

This was indeed to become an hour of truth. Which started with Nurse Amundsen declaring that Linda seemed somewhat unco-ordinated, distant, sluggish . . .

'Sluggish?' Mother said with a new facial expression.

Fru Amundsen nodded pensively. 'But what about this problem with her knee?' Mother enquired.

'Knee?' said fru Amundsen, she was big

and old and dressed in white like fru Lund in the school canteen, had brought four children into the world, lived through two wars and seen most things. But she couldn't see any sign of the trouble with Linda's knee that had been mentioned in the letter in the blue suitcase.

'Yes, you know, she takes medicine for it,' Mother persisted.

'Medicine?'

For a moment Mother didn't know whether to nod or shake her head, and ended up doing neither.

Fru Amundsen leaned over Linda, who was seated on a long, crinkly piece of paper over what resembled an operating table, took off Linda's shoes and rolled down her tights and felt the left knee with her large hands.

'Does that hurt?'

Linda cautiously shook her head. 'And now?'

More head-shaking. Fru Amundsen grabbed her under the arms, lifted her down and asked her to walk towards the wall where the eye chart was hanging, turn around and come back and then walk to the padded door and turn again. She asked what her name was, but Linda did not answer until her enquiring look had received a nod of approval from Mother.

'Linda, yes, that's a lovely name. How old are you?'

Again Linda needed a nod from Mother.

'Six.'

'So you'll be starting school in the autumn?'

Linda nodded.

'She can already spell,' I said.

'Can you? Well, there's a clever girl.'

'G,' said Linda.

Fru Amundsen nodded appreciation, lifted her back onto the table and shifted her gaze to Mother.

'And what is the medicine you've been giving her?'

Mother told her. 'Does she sleep well?' fru Amundsen asked.

Mother nodded. 'A lot?' fru Amundsen asked. And Mother had to nod again, and mumble under her breath:

'Yes, actually she does.'

Fru Amundsen flashed a serious smile and said wait here and went out, while Mother started to roll up Linda's tights and put on her shoes.

'I can do it myself,' Linda said as she tied a bow in laces.

'Yes, I know, my love, but now I'm going to do it.'

Mother pulled the laces so that they were

an equal length, like bows on a Christmas present. Then she suddenly found herself giving Linda a hug, where she was sitting, on the crinkly paper, a hug of the kind that extends right across the entire Atlantic Ocean, and I knew now that the mystery surrounding my three ribs was not going to be solved.

I stepped onto the scales and moved the weights to and fro, and then stood under the angle iron on the wall to measure my height, Mother didn't stop me, she just stood with her nose buried in Linda's hair, giving her hug after hug, as if someone were planning to run off with her, so I went ahead and opened the white, safe-like cupboard on spindly legs and peered in at all the bottles lined up on glass shelves like small, tubby dwarfs, picked out one of them and shook it and began to unscrew the top before Mother intervened, but only with a flick of the hand, a weary, resigned gesture.

Then I screwed the lid back on, closed the cupboard door, took the pointer hanging beside the window, gently pushed Mother aside and pointed to the letters on the chart for the blind, one after the other down the pyramid, and made Linda say them, we carried on doing this until fru Amundsen returned, this time with a young man we hadn't seen before, but who seemed friendly and shook hands with all three of us and asked Linda to walk across the floor and back, as fru Amundsen had done, whereafter he led Mother into another office.

'The children can wait here,' he said over his shoulder as they left.

We waited.

Fru Amundsen gave us an old Donald Duck comic which I read aloud. Then she took us into the waiting room because other people had to come in. Then she came back for us and said we could sit on a small, black leather sofa, which in reality was just a very wide armchair, while she sat behind her desk catching up on her medical records for the day, because now it was beginning to get seriously late.

Mother was only half with us, so to speak, when she returned. She had little make-up left on, her eyes were red-rimmed and dry, and the grip she had on Linda, after having signed three forms with a nib that was needle-sharp, was as firm as the one Linda had applied the day she alighted from the bus.

Nothing was said until we were outside on the pavement listening to the roar of the rush hour traffic, and we realised how quiet and desolate it had been inside the naphthalene-ridden institution.

'Right,' Mother said to herself, with force. 'Right.'

She glanced up and down the busy road, as if to plot a route, while Linda and I looked up at her, tense, what was going on here?

O.K., now we were going to a butcher's Mother knew, to buy some pork and sliced meats, then we were going to a bakery, which she also knew, from her childhood, I gathered from the way she was speaking, much too loud and familiar with the lady behind the counter, who gave us a cake each. After that we took a trolley bus and changed to the Tonsenhagen bus in Carl Berners plass where we also had time to buy two bags of peanuts from the machine outside the Progress factory. When at length we arrived home it was to be pork with gravy, since in our family food is the way we like to settle crises or signal that dangers are over.

But this time events came in reverse order.

This was the evening that there was to be no medicine for Linda, it went down the lavvy, two full bottles, while the prescriptions were locked safe and sound in the drawer with the photographs of the crane driver and Mother, her happily-married life. As proof, she said, after Linda had gone to sleep. She also said that we might have some tough days ahead of us. Plus:

'There is nothing worse than stupidity, Finn. And your mother has been stupid. Stupid, deaf and blind. And do you know what makes folk stupid?'

'Er . . . no.'

'Fear. That's why you must never be afraid, my boy. And you must go to school for as long as you can. Will you promise me that?'

Yeah, yeah, I'd never had any plans to do otherwise, and I didn't see Mother as some shrinking violet either, although she was frightened of the dark and could never really feel at ease even before Linda came into our lives despite the fact that we were doing fine. And what was going to happen now?

'I don't know,' Mother said. 'We'll have to take things as they come.'

That was what we did, and it started in the middle of the night when Linda stood beside my bunk wanting to play. Then she wanted to go to the lavvy, after that she wanted something to eat. But she couldn't sit still and instead ran out to the sitting room to fetch something, only to forget what it was she was looking for, she said oops and went back to the kitchen, where something else occurred to her and she ran back and scurried around the meagre space that is available in a three-room flat minus one for a lodger. Then she began to shake and knocked over a chair, then she sent a glass flying and began to fling her legs and arms about. Mother held her tight, locking her in a vice-like grip, put her to bed and restrained her while I ran into the sitting room and sat on the floor behind the television with my hands over my ears, unsure whether I was dead or alive, with the screams and a tingling in my skin, with the smell of Bakelite and teak oil searing my nostrils, and I read the Chinese symbols that were supposed to make the electricity work, but which could not drown the noise, until the enormous sitting-room window turned grey and filled with light, like drawing paper, and I heard Mother shout that I had better get myself off to school.

Which I did, without any breakfast.

There were only four lessons today, though, and when I returned nothing had changed, Mother was in bed with Linda, who was wriggling and squirming, and her face was blue and white. The whole flat smelled of vomit, of Linda, who never cried but who was beside herself now, like a circular saw cutting through rock. But I knew Marlene had dropped in, for there was food on the table, and when I had eaten and still didn't know whether I would live or go up in smoke, Mother shouted through the door I couldn't bring myself to open — out of fear that I

would see something I would never forget
— that I could watch T.V. and sleep in the
sitting room.

But the night was to be no more peaceful.

At six the following morning Kristian came
in wondering what the hell was going on and
found himself being chased back into his
room.

'And you stay there!' shrieked Mother, who
obviously had the strength of a horse and was
carrying Linda round the flat and comforting
her with strange words I had never heard
before, incantations that did not work and
therefore had to be repeated *ad infinitum*.

But then at long last she fell asleep, and
Mother sent me off to school, this time with a
packed lunch and an absent-minded hug, and
admonitions not to say anything, not even to
Essi, be strong, she said, as though the
terrible things that were going on inside
Linda were only the half of what would assail
us if anyone on the outside caught wind of it.

As I was leaving, along came Marlene, who
was not stupid and never had been, and spent
the whole day with Mother, who didn't go to
work that day, either.

That evening Linda slept for more than
two hours before the hullabaloo started
afresh, just as I was about to go to bed. But
by then Mother had also managed to get

some sleep. And again I was lying in the sitting room with cotton wool in my ears and a tingling sensation in my body as the battle raged on in the bedroom. I didn't wake until Marlene was sitting in the armchair beside the sofa asking me how I was.

'How are you doing, Finn?'

'It's ten o'clock,' I said, sitting up with a start because I thought something was wrong.

But there wasn't. I was soaked in saliva and sweat. Everything was calm, still and light. In the middle of the floor stood the doctor we had spoken to at the check-up in Sagene, in his coat, without a hat, and he uttered some reproachful but friendly words to Mother, who had put on some makeup and looked ready for work. She couldn't be expected to do everything on her own, he said, whatever that was supposed to mean. And she answered:

'That child is not going to any home!'

'No, I appreciate that, but . . . '

'*She's never going to leave this house. Never ever!*'

The doctor said no again and hung his coat beside Kristian's, as if he lived here as well, and carefully took Mother by the arm, led her into the kitchen, sat her down on a chair and started to examine her arms and hands which had acquired some bluish-red crescent shapes

I guessed were bite marks.

Linda was also sitting at the kitchen table, having breakfast and drinking cocoa, she was smacking a tea spoon on the cocoa skin and smiled sheepishly as I padded in. Mother burst into laughter in a way that reminded me of death, and I felt Marlene's hand on my head, steering me towards the table and I seemed to be pressed down in front of a plate with four slices of bread, typical Marlene slices, buttered and cut to the sounds of 'You Can Have Him', I grabbed one and took a cautious nibble.

'Linda's been ill,' Linda said.

'So have I,' I said and shivered and chewed as the visitor beside me stopped doing what he was doing and everyone's eyes focused on me. Mother had to get up and go to the bathroom to wash her face and apply make-up for a second time, and came out again blinking at the doctor and the light and asked if she was fit to go to work, 'looking like this?'

'And you're asking *me*?' he smiled.

'Who else should I ask?' she said.

'Yes, well, if you absolutely must. I'll give you a lift.'

'She's not going to work,' Marlene decided, and Mother crumpled, half turning, but in doing so made a stupid movement with her head in my direction, believing I wouldn't notice, and the doctor seemed to catch sight of me in among the others and bent over the table and the plate and my food and asked, with that broad mouth of his, if I had done my homework yesterday, and I had, good, he said, then he wanted to know how many pupils there were in my class . . .

'Mixed class? Ah, I see. Any nice girls in it?'

'Tanja,' Linda said, and the doctor smiled while I was trying to recall if I had in fact done my homework yesterday. I had, yes I had, I remembered the hymn verse and the piece we had to retell from our reading book, about Halvor who comes home and is very upset; I knew it off by heart, which was not the purpose of the exercise as we were supposed to use our imagination and write it in our own words. I had done that, so, anyway, I wasted no time in telling them about what happened in Heia to the sick horse that couldn't stand up after a fall in the forest, and how the vet thought it needed some water, then it perked up, the nag did. And strangely enough, for once, everyone was following and laughing and seemed to be very interested, Mother too, I just had to finish the story and drink my milk and get up and go to school. But it was getting on for eleven o'clock.

'You can stay at home today, Finn.'

'Tell me again,' Linda said.

11

It is quiet and warm and summer and holiday time in the streets of Årvoll, and I have to teach Linda to climb trees, I feel. She is no longer afraid of heights, has become thinner and is a tiny bit taller, I don't want to exaggerate, it is easy to exaggerate when there is progress; in our house we take things one step at a time, we are prepared for the worst and we are caught on the hop if things just go moderately well, for example a whole evening in front of the television without Linda having any relapses, as Mother calls the last vestiges of her old life.

But she has grown stronger. When we practise on the clothes drying frame in front of our block, she can not only hang by her arms for eight seconds, she can also swing along the bars, two, three grabs, or perhaps four, before she falls into my arms. Linda trusts me, I always catch her, I like to be trusted.

'That tickles,' she says.

When I stand on the iron bench and help her up onto the frame, she can also sit astride the gap between the frames reserved for

Blocks 1 and 2 and cling onto the clothes lines with enough pluck to hang on for four to five minutes. The days are ours. And Freddy 1's. Freddy 1 is not on holiday, either, he is big and heavy and no climber. But he can swing himself the whole way along the whole frame making it shake and sway like the rigging on a sailing ship in a storm. And while Linda is sitting over the gap he lies down on his back on the concrete flagstones with his arms behind his head and tells her to jump onto his stomach. She doesn't dare.

'Come on,' says Freddy 1. 'It won't hurt.'

Linda considers it, and I suspect that Freddy 1 is lying on that particular spot so that he can see up her yellow-flowered dress. I suggest that she lies on her stomach and slides down from the bar and lets go when she can't hold on any more. She does as I say, and after an awkward fall of a metre and a half she lands with her sandals firmly planted in the stomach of Freddy 1, who coughs and goes red in the face just as Mother comes out of the bomb shelter wearing sun glasses and carrying a deck chair and two women's magazines.

'What are you kids up to?! I mean, really, Finn!'

Freddy 1 was ready to defend me, I could see it in his face, but not a sound emerged.

Mother came running over and helped him up onto the iron bench where the washing baskets are put, glancing around anxiously to see whether Freddy 1's mother might be keeping an eye on us from her window or balcony. But Freddy 1's mother was not keeping an eye on anyone, she was asleep, and Freddy 1's father was on a building site, and his elder sisters at a summer camp. Freddy 1 didn't want to go to the camp, not on your nelly, he wanted to be at home in the streets during the time when not a single one of his tormentors was there, the time his tormentors spent in hell, which is what Freddy 1 considered a holiday to be.

We listened to Mother's warnings and helped her to assemble the deck chair. It took a while. Then we messed around with a ball and sat on the grass demonstrating our boredom until Mother was sick of us and asked whether we didn't have anything better to do.

We crossed Traverveien and went up to Hagan, out of her sight, where one of the oak trees had branches within reach for even someone of Linda's stature, where even Freddy 1 could scramble up to base two, as we called it, at the top of the trunk, where the massive branches fanned out and formed a kind of platform, a floor of solid oak with room for four, five or even six children and from which Freddy 1 had once pissed on the head of Freddy 2, who hadn't been able to climb any higher than base one.

We could see the glowing heat haze over the city centre and the new Disen blocks and Trondhjemsveien and our own estate lying there with deserted streets and the flats and the fields that were in the process of being mown and becoming lawns that had to be tended by the caretaker and Oslo City Parks and Gardens, which of course is a contradiction in itself, an estate without people, an empty shell after all those who had returned to where they had come from, to teach their children to dry hay and to fish and to row and climb trees — Essi, who had been driven by car across the mountains to Romsdalen, Vatten who was in Solør, and Roger in Northern Norway, not to mention all of those who were on Hudøy Island summer camp and had nothing to do but yearn for home in Hagan and us and the dizzying view of the world we sat enjoying, the way it is without all those who belong there, a strange time, the summer, a mystery, on a par with the winter.

But this was to be no usual summer.

In the first place, Linda was there and that put a stop to most of Freddy 1's ideas, which by and large consisted of stealing something we didn't need, from a cellar or an attic storeroom, a kilo of flour, shoe polish, peas, which at least we could use in our pea-shooters, or maybe best of all empty bottles from the Trotting Stadium which we could get the money back on and buy ice creams with. I couldn't take Linda on any of this.

Secondly, because Kristian was sitting at the kitchen table when we came in that evening, Kristian in some khaki shorts that were much too big for him and an even bigger khaki shirt, which made him look like Doctor Livingstone in *Illustrete Klassikere*. He had a surprise up his sleeve, it was to transpire, did we want to borrow his tent and go on holiday?

'You're just saying that,' said Mother as we slid onto our chairs and I wondered what had occasioned this audience, because Kristian had not been seen since the time Linda fell ill, and that was almost two months ago.

No, really, Kristian had a house tent, as he called it, on an island in Oslo fjord called Håøya, and it was there all summer, he liked to take the boat over at the weekends, he said.

'House tent?'

'Yes, a six-man tent. With an awning as well.'

I wanted to ask what an unmarried lodger

was doing with a six-man tent, but he gave me the answer unprompted. 'Well, it's nothing special. I got it cheap — it's a bit fire-damaged.'

Mother began to laugh.

'You can hardly see the marks,' Kristian protested.

But the very fact that this tent didn't seem to be worth much made it almost attainable, indeed it made it seem like an irresistible temptation.

'Aren't you going to be there yourself?'

'No. It's not being used, that's what I keep telling you. It's padlocked. Here's the key.'

He rummaged around and produced a tiny key that looked as if it would fit a jewellery box, held it up for everyone to admire and placed it on the table between our plates. And it was not fire-damaged, it was so shiny and bright all we had to do was to get weaving.

'Then Freddy 1's coming too!' I shouted.

'Stop that now, Finn. We're not going to any tent on an island . . . '

'Why not?' Kristian said. 'You can lie outside and sunbathe just as well as here.'

'Stop it now.'

'You have got quite a tan. It suits you.'

'Stop it, I said.'

'And the kids need some fresh air . . . '

'Tent,' said Linda, taking the key with

tentative hands and staring at it, before dropping it in her glass of milk.

'Linda!'

'Freddy 1 has never been on holiday!' I shouted. *'It's a crying shame!'*

'Why do you call him that actually — Freddy 1?'

'Because that's his name!'

'Give me the key, Linda.'

Linda stuck her hand in the milk, fished out the key and gave it to Mother who wiped it and her hand with the tea towel, shaking her head. But then she stopped and examined the key, the way she had examined the golden hare she had been given for Christmas and had started to wear in the shoe shop, I had noticed.

'And sleeping bags?' she asked, all at sea.

Kristian had considered that, too. There wasn't a thing Kristian had not considered. Even a collapsible, green canvas bucket which we could use to transport water from the outside tap and hang on a pine tree beside the tent, a bucket with a valve at the bottom that could be opened and closed, and if we hung it high enough we could stand underneath and take a shower, which was very pleasant if the sun had warmed the water first.

But by now Mother was thinking this was

beginning to sound too planned, as if he was trying to wheedle his way in with us, what with the T.V. and the food and the golden hare and the chess board, which in the meantime by the way I had been allowed to 'borrow' and at this moment was set up on my desk.

'Freddy 1's coming!' I repeated irrepressibly. 'I'm not going without Freddy 1!'

'Don't *you* start!' Kristian snapped, looking as though he was going to smash his fist down on the table.

'What's that supposed to mean?' Mother said, taking my side straight away.

'Ugh, what a crew,' Kristian said, rising to his feet in his huge khaki get-up and striding towards the door.

'Angry,' said Linda as his door was slammed shut.

Mother sat down, we didn't move, eyeing each other across the table, and there was the shiny key and Kristian's half-eaten piece of bread and they spoke to us in a way which prompted us to look at each other with even more gravity and Mother to wipe a few despairing strands of hair from her face and sigh:

'What has got into us? *All he wants to do is lend us a burned tent!*'

We had never heard anything so funny, we

collapsed over the table, killing ourselves with laughter, unable to stop, and we had no plans to, either, for this was perhaps the only thing which could bring us back to our senses. Mother got up and flung open the door to the lodger's room and shouted out:

'Come and finish your food and don't sit there sulking.'

Now things were beginning to take shape. Kristian came back with a semi-annoyed smile on his family-less face, but diplomatically resumed his place and went through the motions of continuing his meal while Mother poured him some more coffee and said that, of course, we appreciated his offer, it was just so sudden, what about from Tuesday onwards, for a week, what did he think about that?

'Fine, fine, no problem.'

But it would be wrong to say that I had finished having my say.

'Freddy 1's coming!' I repeated while Mother was still riding the waves with a devil-may-care wind in her sails.

'O.K., but then you and I are going up this minute to ask!'

She had her sandals on in a flash, and I was barefoot anyway, it was summer, down the stairs and across the deserted lawn at a pace that gradually decreased as Mother thought things through and asked me some probing questions about Freddy 1's mother, whom she had seen often enough, but with whom she had never exchanged a word, but there were rumours going round . . .

Mother's galleon carried us up to the third floor, where I rushed to ring the doorbell. But no-one opened. We heard a good deal of shouting inside, an argument about who would open the door, I guessed, between Freddy 1 and his mother, a battle which the mother lost.

She came to the door and was calm and pleasant and looked with raised eyebrows from one to the other as we explained our errand, and she answered, fine, that would be nice, and:

'Of course Freddy should go on holiday. He's never been anywhere in his life.'

But Freddy 1 still did not show himself. And I thought that was a bit odd, because he was inside listening to find out who it was and what we were talking about. I shouted that he was coming on holiday with us on Tuesday.

'Do you hear me?!'

To that, however, Freddy 1 replied no.

'*What* was that!' his mother shouted, turning in his direction, still without shifting herself a millimetre, she guarded this door,

152

not even *I* had crossed this threshold, Freddy 1's only friend.

'No,' he said again.

I saw Mother roll her eyes as Freddy 1's mother made the typical desperate-mother grimace that was mastered to such a level of perfection on this estate, and shrugged her round shoulders and said something to the effect that there was no making sense of this boy.

But I couldn't give in and shouted back that we were going on a boat and would be on a huge island and would go swimming and live in a tent.

Freddy 1 was unbending.

'No!' came back the response, as adamant as before. And by then Mother had had enough. She muttered a flurried goodbye to Freddy 1's mother and grabbed me by the shirtsleeves and dragged me down the stairs and on to the deserted grass that still tickled, nice and sun-warm beneath my bare feet, now she was in a real temper.

'Blinking nonsense you've got in your head, Finn!'

As though I had abused her trust in the most appalling way.

'He'll be kicking himself now!' I yelled. 'Let's go back up!'

'Are you out of your mind?!'

153

'I know him. He'll be kicking himself!'

'I'll give you kicking himself!' Mother hissed in my face and simply turned on her heel and stamped off.

This was a blow to my plans.

I ran after her, but said nothing for the rest of the evening, didn't mention Freddy 1 once, not even when we got down to packing. It was a good thing that Linda had just been given a new school bag for when she started at school; Mother went up into the loft and dug out an old rucksack which must have been through a couple of world wars, said goodness me, stuck her nose inside and held it up and ran her eyes over it with a woman's disgust and went back up into the loft and returned with the suitcase bearing Dombås on the address label.

'You can't go camping with a suitcase,' Kristian said, who was spending the evening in front of his television, he got up and went into his room to return with a canvas-coloured bundle of fabric that turned out to be a kitbag, with strings and brass rings and two shoulder straps so that it could be carried on your back. 'This is what I take.'

'Oh yes,' said Mother, looking warily at the shapeless sack.

Kristian pulled out a map of the island to show us where his tent was and ringed a water tap, a shop, two beaches and a party area — we were itching to leave. Each of us glowed like a sun. And when he put a cross by a secret jetty where you could lie on your stomach and fish for crabs I felt goose-pimples all the way down my spine like bristly fur. The only fly in the ointment was Freddy 1. And when I sat by the window before bedtime to see whether he was sitting by his window, full of regret, he was nowhere to be seen, the boy who lived on that windowsill, either to keep watch, to lower something, to heave water balloons out or simply to sit there staring. But by then I had at any rate managed to devise a plan. It wasn't a very good one, but then even good plans have a tendency to go down the pan.

12

On Tuesday morning we set off at the crack of dawn, in sunshine, dragging Kristian's kitbag down to the bus stop and onto the bus, where the conductor joked that we would have to buy a ticket for it, and we got off at Wessels plass and lugged it down to the harbour where the boat would be waiting for us. But it wasn't. We were three hours too early, it emerged, because Kristian's timetable was last year's.

There was so much to see here, though, sailing ships and ferries and yachts and swarms of people buying fish and shrimps from an armada of fishing smacks and cutters bobbing up and down in the sewage-tainted water, and whole trains that regularly ploughed their way through the crowds with lots of noise and hissing and whistling and green flags and uniformed men hanging on the outside, waving with their hats and shouting to the unwary that they had better move out of the way, the train was coming, for crying out loud.

After we had placed our kitbag with care on one of the jetties, it looked like a small sofa, Mother said that she had a little errand to run and, for God's sake, keep an eye on Linda while she was gone, make sure she didn't fall over the edge.

'*Hold* her!'

'Yes, yes, yes.'

But no sooner had we started to argue about how hard I should hold her than Mother was back.

'Look what I found,' she beamed.

There was Marlene with so much make-up on that at first we didn't recognise her, and a man we had never seen before, but who introduced himself with a smile as Jan, Marlene's boyfriend. They were both wearing burgundy uniforms, like the confectionery sellers in Ringen Cinema. They were on their way to work, up there, Jan pointed, in the direction of Akershus Fortress. Marlene grabbed Linda under the arms and lifted her and hugged her and said how big you've got, my little girl, although she could hardly have grown a millimetre in the two weeks that had passed since we last saw her.

'And Finn, too,' she said, to balance the books.

When they heard that our boat wouldn't be leaving for a good two hours they invited us up to Friluften Restaurant for a cup of coffee, there are not many customers so early in the day, and perhaps they have something else as well, who knows, Jan said with a roguish wink to me, swinging the kitbag onto his back and carrying it as it was obviously designed to be carried, it looked brilliant, and we followed them across the Town Hall square and the railway line up to the restaurant where we sat down at what Jan called the Mayor's Table — the Mayor often sat here drinking beer, smoking cigars and holding important meetings — on the outside edge so that we had a view of the whole harbour.

Mother ordered coffee and an almond cake while Linda and I had enough ice cream for our whole estate, in fountain-like glasses on such high stems that Linda had to steady hers in her lap.

Then we sat on our own while Mother went off on an errand. Jan came over and asked if sir or madam would like any more and whistled and made bowing motions left, right and centre in a way that made him look disturbingly like Uncle Tor.

But this was very different from the last time I had been to a restaurant which, as far as I could remember, was in the middle of a forest one bitterly cold January day; here white, large-patterned cloths covered all the tables, black-headed gulls hung over us in guffawing flocks, the Town Hall bells chimed and the train sang as it clattered past beneath us and the boats came and went and the harbour throbbed and the cranes swung and swayed along the wharves as far as Akers Mekaniske Verksted where our father had once worked, and died.

The only thing we could not hear was foghorns, which I would have liked, and I described them to Linda. But what use were foghorns in the sunshine? We were already so far from home, we weren't afraid, we weren't hungry, we weren't even bored.

But then once again I spotted something you spend a few days or weeks or maybe half a lifetime trying to understand, like the clock whose hands point in the wrong direction: Mother was back and standing by the entrance talking with Marlene, who was balancing a silver tray on upright fingers badly wanting to take two glasses of beer to one of the tables, Mother and Marlene in discussion about something or other, excited and emotional, but also concerned, Mother, who caught sight of us sitting where she had left us, so wonderfully exhausted from all the ice cream, and she waved and said something with her red mouth which we couldn't hear in all the buzz of conversation, whereupon she opened the bag she was carrying in her hand and held up a small bathing costume, for

Linda, I could see. Marlene turned and smiled to us in the sunshine and waved, then said a few parting words to Mother, floated off like a burgundy swan between the white tables and placed first the tray, then the glasses in front of two be-suited men at the back, and smiled and took out a little notebook from her apron pocket and laughed at something one man said, and wrote something, and said something again, and received money which she counted in her left hand before curtseying and responding to another witticism by turning her back in a wonderful sweeping movement — it was a dance, on roses, a High Mass, but what was it that I had seen?

Mother came and showed Linda the bathing costume, which was dark blue and had a large, yellow water lily at the front, she said she should put it in her satchel because we had to go now. Jan put down a tray with two prawn sandwiches on the neighbouring table, hurried over and heaved the kitbag up on his back and carried it in the way it was meant to be carried, out of the restaurant, down the stairs, over the train lines to the boat, yes, he even climbed on board with us and made sure we got a seat right at the back, at the stern, the observation post, as he called it, because it is not the ridge of hills around the fjord that should be viewed as you leave Norway's splendid capital but the town itself as it retreats into the distance.

'See you,' he said with a wink to Mother, who looked like a sleeping angel as she made herself comfortable on the worn leather-look seat and leaned against the railing, raising her face to the sun and I suppose closing her eyes behind the jet-black glasses.

The town vanished in a golden haze, with the Town Hall and the cranes at Akers Mekaniske Verksted like a last farewell salute as I sensed that something was happening inside me, in my innards. And in my mouth. It filled with liquid. It must have been the huge ice cream on its way back up. And then it came, not over the railing because I had no idea what was going on, but all over the deck, a white Amazonian flood between gym shoes and sandals and sleeping bags and fishing rods and passengers who jumped up shouting all manner of things. I stayed down on my knees in a kind of praying posture, astonished at all the lumpy cheese-like matter there had been room for inside me, red and yellow bits of fruit so whole and untouched they looked as if they could be re-used. Mother helped me to my feet and said my poor love and a number of other embarrassing things and tried to wipe me down with toilet paper while a sturdily built male figure in a black helmsman's jacket and clattering wooden clogs shouldered his way through the crowd with a broad grin and a slithering hose and started flushing down the deck, after first shouting so that everyone could hear:

'Right, so today we've got another sickly landlubber, have we, on a mirror-calm sea.'

* * *

The unimaginable dizziness did not wear off until we came ashore a good hour later and I could lie on my back on the quay and stare up at the sky with my eyes closed and lie still until everything was calm inside and around me.

We were on the island of Håøya.

A green paradise in the middle of Oslo fjord. With narrow paths for walking and not many houses and three beaches and some flat grassland that wound inwards to a forest packed with birdsong and rocks and slopes and thickets and scrub and insects and deep ravines, this was the kingdom of the dragon, we just didn't know yet whether it was good or evil.

It appeared that an order of its own reigned out here, predominantly manifested in one person who came to talk to us as soon as we

162

arrived on the quay, no doubt because we were the sole passengers to need a rest after arrival while the others launched themselves into a kind of race to the centre of the island, all vying for the best camp sites, we were soon to learn.

He was the age and size of a grandfather I suppose everyone must have dreamed about at one time, a bit on the short side, and dressed in what looked like a tailor-made costume for this particular island and this particular season, very long shorts, well, a sort of cross between bathing trunks and a uniform, which gave him the appearance of an outdoor type and a policeman, plus a small skipper's cap with a white plastic anchor, pulled well down over an iron-grey mane, an equally grey beard and small bright eyes that were both intense and friendly, but also evasive, especially when he clapped them on Mother who was now sporting a bikini top and had put her sun glasses on top of her hair, turning them into a tiara of black diamonds.

After she had given him a few faltering details and told him we had left our map behind, he sighed and mumbled:

'Ah yes, Kristian, that Kristian.' And his sun-tanned face displayed a whole musical score of differing expressions. We were quite unnerved, but fortunately he saw that and informed us in a low voice that you couldn't just come and expect to have a tent pitched here for ever, there were such things as moving days, so that people didn't grow roots and occupy the same spot for weeks on end. By which he meant that you could not stay in the same position for more than two nights. After that you had to pull up your tent pegs and move somewhere else. Furthermore, you were not allowed to consume alcohol, and there was something about food and a shop that I didn't catch.

'You can call me Hans,' he muttered by way of conciliatory closure to all these rules of which we understood neither the wording nor the purpose.

'Why?' I asked, and felt my leg being kicked by Mother, who continued to stare at the little skipper with an element of pleading in her eyes, we weren't the kind to stand around unaware that we were in someone else's power.

'Well, er, that's my name,' he said, disconcerted, and steered his gaze from Mother's bikini top down to Linda who had simply decided this was none of her business.

Mother:

'So there is no tent here then?'

'Well, there is, yes,' Hans said in his

inscrutable wisdom, at which point Linda woke up, looked at him with a serious expression and drawled:

'We've had an ice cream.'

'Er . . . is that right? Well, it must have been good, I imagine.'

'Yes.'

Silence. Linda:

'We're on holiday.'

'Yes, right. Mm . . . '

That was all it took. Hans grabbed our kitbag and said come along with me, and also carried it as it was meant to be carried, led us across the field where the holidaying masses were in full swing erecting their tents, then turned down a narrow path and guided us through dense hazel thickets up a slope between a few crags until a small, flat grassy clearing appeared in the otherwise hilly terrain, a high-lying oasis with a view over the sea and a few other islands, unless it was the mainland, whereupon he stopped and listened, as if for a tent, only to discover it, so to speak, our six-man tent; for there it was, next to the forest in the northern corner of paradise. It was as blue as the sea and the sky and the day, there was a large awning too, which was orange, two semis, one whole house.

Mother asked if this was the one, and Hans

said yes, this was Kristian's tent. There followed a vague, to put it mildly, account of — I presume — what it actually was that entitled Kristian to have his tent sited here, a permanent fixture, as it were, contrary to all the regulations, plus a request that if anyone should stumble upon us and ask when we were going to move, we should say we didn't know we had to, take down the tent and pitch it over there, six to eight metres closer to the forest, but at an angle to it, so that there would be no more room for another tent for sure. If, however, no-one asked, which was more probable because this place was a secret, then we didn't have to dismantle the tent at all, a statement that left us with a somewhat disquieting sensation with which we were already all too familiar, the feeling that we had to live under cover and on someone else's terms.

Mother said thank you and that's nice, and 'I would never have thought it'.

'And there's no sign of any fire damage, is there?'

'No, I think it was only one pole and a bit behind here,' Hans said, nodding towards a brown stain which we would never have spotted.

But now I had the key, and I unlocked the little padlock and crawled into the awning, where the temperature was two hundred and nineteen degrees centigrade and there was a terrible stench, from a pair of gym shoes, it turned out, which Hans coaxed out with a stick and hurled down the slope. However, it was possible to open the tent at the front and the canvas at the back, so that a gentle, liberating summer breeze could sweep through the boiling greenhouse. Inside, there were sleeping bags and lilos, a sun lounger and four rickety camping chairs, an equally rickety table as well as the famous canvas bag we were supposed to use to fetch water and hang on the tree, over there.

'And you can make a fire here,' Hans said, motioning towards a circle of stones surrounded by another circle made of old tree stumps to sit on.

'Yippee!' I yelled.

'Oh no,' said Mother.

'I want to have a fire, too,' Linda said.

While Hans smiled as though he were already an associate member of the family, or had gathered at any rate that here were people he could really impress, three novices to be initiated into the joys of camping.

'You'll find some dry wood in the forest,' he told me and instructed me to take the canvas bag, showed me the way to the closest freshwater tap, as well as how to hang the bag on the tree. Then something was also said about the mysterious food, that there was only one shop here, and apparently it opened for just a few hours on certain days, which hours was a bit unclear, so you would be wise to get stocked up with food from a boat that called in now and then from Drøbak, that too at rather irregular times, or go there yourself and shop, which perhaps was the easiest, yes, I reckon it is, he concluded.

So, the long and short of this seemed to be that people shouldn't take anything for granted out here and make themselves so comfortable that they stayed.

'Yes, well, that's the way it is,' Hans said with a contented smile.

But by then Mother had begun to mooch around instead of getting to grips with the unpacking, a sign, I deduced, that now we could not take any more goodwill from Hans without running up the same enormous debt we already owed to Kristian. He sensed that.

'Well, let me know if there is anything. I'm in Vika.'

Mother thanked him again, shook his hand, and Hans left.

We were alone in a paradise we had not lifted a finger to deserve, but it would be wrong to say we didn't know how to appreciate it. We were in raptures, especially me, as usual. But there was no doubt that a load had also been taken off Mother's mind in the last hour, the endless journey, by bus and boat, and Linda had already gone to sleep three times, in different sleeping bags, and got up again before the primus stove had been lit and the pork and the sausages had been thrown in the pan. Summers are often given a name or several, and at first this one was called the summer Linda learned to swim.

13

Now, this was no simple matter, of course, teaching Linda how to swim. You see — after stopping the medicine — she had not only begun to sleep less and eat less, she had also shown tendencies to go her own way. Mother had brought this subject up with me on a number of occasions.

'Don't you think Linda's been pretty headstrong recently?'

In particular, there had been a huge fuss about a month ago when there had been some disagreement over the working practices of the tooth fairy; the rate for molars and front teeth had, it transpired, soared since my time, upon which I had taken the liberty to remark, only to be put down brutally by Mother. But Linda had insisted on giving me the krone coins she found in her tumbler in the morning, which led to the rate taking a sudden dive to an all-time low, which Linda refused to accept and so on and so forth, we had been talking about these teeth for weeks.

Now, Linda was a great fan of water and put on her bathing costume with my old swimming belt before breakfast and was out all day until she was dragged ashore by force. But she would not do what we told her, stay in the shallow part, she waded out so far her feet were off the bottom and she bobbed around like a fishing float, up and down with her tightly pinched lips, treading water, or whatever it was she was doing, which meant that Mother and I had to paddle around like buoys and try to manoeuvre her in the right direction, in other words shorewards, while shouting — to no effect — that she should waggle her arms. She used them to cling to the belt and nothing else, which was quite unnecessary since Mother had tied it so tight it left a chess-board pattern all over her upper body.

It was one of the old style swimming belts, lined with reindeer fur, I think, which absorbed water and slowly but surely shifted from being a floating device to a lead weight, and at regular intervals had to be slapped against a rock or trodden on so that some of the water drained out, and was often hung up in the sun as well. However, it never dried out completely, it was wet the whole summer long, and cold, making Linda shudder every time she put it on, with the result that she preferred to keep it on all the time, which Mother would not allow.

'You'll get ill, you will.'

Furthermore, she was badly sunburned, on the shoulders and face, which was about all there was above water, and she had to be covered in Nivea and forced into a white blouse, even when she was swimming. At the same time Mother again did what she always regretted afterwards, but still could not stop herself doing, she enquired about what Linda had done in previous summers, questions which were enough to make Linda stand up and walk away, regardless of what we were doing, as though she had been summoned by a higher power, so that Mother or I, or both of us, had to run after her and walk beside her and say whatever came into our heads, until she came to a halt and looked at us with the expression that said she had heard something she liked and at that moment she forgot everything the thoughtless question had caused to swirl up inside her.

Linda had a way of fixing us with her gaze that made me wonder what actually went on inside her. In fact, looking at Linda was like pressing your eye deeper and deeper into the lens of Kristian's microscope in the hope that you might catch a glimpse of something recognisable, or comprehensible.

★ ★ ★

Luckily, this summer could also be called the summer with Boris, whom I met on the second day we were on the beach. He was my age, my size, with a quiff like mine, came from an estate much like ours, and was interested in comics and books and coins and trees and ball bearings and words and outer space, he didn't even have a father, yes, we were as good as identical.

But he had an 'uncle' who was there with his mother and some elder brothers and 'cousins', so Boris was the odd one out, that was why his 'uncle' introduced us to each other.

'Hey you, can't you play with 'im 'ere?' I heard beside me from out of the blue while I was on all fours digging in the sand for what is only to be found in heaven. And there stood a large, bald man in black, and far too tight, bathing trunks which did not appear to be accommodating anything beneath a naked, nut-brown belly, and with a cigarette dangling from the corner of his mouth. At his side stood Boris, sinewy and small and brown, as though he had lived here all his life, clad in over-sized bathing trunks, and his eyes bored down into my hole of dreams which was slowly filling up with black water. I don't think I gave him much of a response. The 'uncle' took the hint and said:

'Do you know how to catch crabs?'

'Er . . . ,' I said.

'Boris'll show you. Won't you, Boris?'

With that he turned his back on us and waddled off in beach shoes that flipped on and off and seemed to stick to the soles of his big feet while he flicked ash into the water and trained his eyes on a pink point somewhere in eternity in the cloudless sky.

Boris didn't move and looked around, and I suppose I did too, until he looked practically straight at me and said 'Come on' and started to walk over the sand to a big rock in the water.

I waded apprehensively after him, two or three metres behind, feeling my mother's eyes fixed on my back, out to the rock, I hadn't been there before, and stood with barnacles chafing against my feet; I admired Boris who strode straight through a big pile of seaweed without suffering any ill effects and bent down into the sea until it covered the roots of his hair and he brought up a cluster of mussels which he threw at my feet.

'How are we going to open them?' I asked, pretending to know what this was all about.

'We'll smash 'em,' Boris said. 'With this.'

He had his own stone for the purpose, and under the stone there was a line and a plastic bag. Boris' line and Boris' plastic bag.

'The gunge sticks to one of the shells,' he said. 'That's what the crabs are after.'

We were fishing for crabs. We crouched down with the sun beating down on our backs and chucked a mussel in and pulled up a reddish-green crab and put it in the plastic bag which we filled with sea water. Boris showed me how to catch the buggers and bring them up, not too fast, not too slowly, you have to be patient, and perhaps more than anything else he showed me there was nothing to be frightened of, not even with crabs, if you know what you are doing, all the time I had Mother's eyes on me, Mother who was lying in Kristian's deck chair on the beach and squabbling with Linda about whether a quarter of an hour had passed or not between her last swim and the next swim, which for the sake of family peace ought to have started twenty minutes ago.

'Can you swim?' Boris asked.

'Yes,' I said.

'Come on,' he said again and waded out, launched himself into the water and I followed suit. Across the bay, towards the promontory on the other side, a stretch of water I would never have dared to tackle alone. Nor would Mother. She stood beside the deck chair with one hand shielding her eyes, a monument to all mothers who have stood in the same way on beach after beach for summer after summer throughout history watching those they love above all else fade into oblivion — I swam and swam, a distance immeasurable in metres or happiness. Next to Boris. My new friend who, I could ascertain now with even greater pleasure, did not swim any better than I, we were about the same, we pitched along nicely next to each other and I suppose we were just two small, identical heads growing smaller and smaller, like peas, and in the end pinheads, before disappearing from sight on the horizon of death and eternity.

After crossing the bay we clambered out and sat on a smooth rock in a foreign country and looked back, at the sculpture to all mothers who was still standing there, so tiny, transmitting her warmth and warnings and visions of horror and all the things a mother should beam through space. I felt my smile extending across my face and stood up and waved to her and said:

'Look now.'

'What at?' Boris asked.

'She's not waving back,' I said.

'Eh?' said Boris.

'She's angry,' I said, sitting down.

Boris pondered, looking at me with a new smile because he felt the same as I had felt as we were crossing the equator, namely, that here something had happened, not to lay it on too thick, that would last and outlive us both. But we were in the mood to lay things on thick that day, that summer, we laid it on thicker than ever before. So when Boris said 'Come on' for a third time, what else could I do but follow, out of everyone's sight into the scrub, Boris' world, into the immense wilderness of gnarled trees and bushes, a slumbering pyrotechnic display of ravines and bird song that pounded your ears, and sun and shade and heat and cold, along a path only Boris knew, until I got to know it as well, for this was indeed the realm of the dragon, and the eagle owl, with a fine talcum-white dust sticking to our wet feet, making them look like bones, a powder that was found only on this path, up to a mountain overhang where all of a sudden everything became brighter and another bay revealed itself fifty metres beneath us, with a single orange tent.

Boris said we should lie down and wriggle towards the cliff edge. Down below I spotted a person on an airbed beside the tent, a woman lying and sunbathing topless, with enormous copper-brown tits, and she wasn't wearing any shorts, either, I realised a bit later.

'She's there every day,' Boris whispered.

I stared. There was no-one else to be seen. Just this overwhelming creature lying there as still as a corpse or fast asleep, looking like nothing I had ever seen before and striking chords within me I had no inkling existed.

'My brothers call her F.T.B., full to bursting,' Boris said.

'She's old,' it struck me.

'At least fifty, yes,' Boris said knowledgeably. 'But you can't see so well from here. Shall we go closer?'

'No-oo . . . '

We lay on our stomachs studying F.T.B. It was impossible to take your eyes off her. It made no difference that she was old or a long way down or stone dead, she grew and grew the more we gawped, tanned and attractive, a stranded whale in the electric sunshine.

'My brothers say she knows we watch her,' Boris whispered.

'What?'

'Yes, and she likes it.'

'Eh?'

'Wait till she goes for a swim, then you'll see.'

We lay waiting for F.T.B. to go for a swim. She took her time. Not that it mattered much. But at last she woke up and grabbed her wrist-watch beside the airbed and checked it, then brushed some invisible particles of dust off her stomach and sat up and was even bigger, looked around and brushed something off her shoulders and thighs, pollen I supposed, or insects, after which she at last got to her feet and stood with her hands on her hips like a lazy afterthought and sent her gaze on one languid, not-expectant circuit after another around the steaming summer landscape.

Then she took the first step down towards the sea, waggling unsteadily over shells and barnacles and sharp stones, her arms out to the side like stabilising wings and her back to us, onto the furthest rock, where she paused again, took another look around, across the sea and the land and the trees and the ridge, stroked her shoulders again, bent down to test the water, and now we had her in side view.

'She looks everywhere,' Boris whispered in a very low voice. 'Except here.'

'Eh?'

'Look at her — she never looks *this* way!'

I still didn't understand. And now Boris began to be impatient, said she was here every summer, and it wasn't just he and his brothers who knew.

'Look.'

I cast my eyes around and registered that the spot we were lying on was flattened, like under a tent.

'Adults come here, too,' Boris said solemnly. 'Men.'

'Who?'

'Well . . . the warden anyway.'

'Hans?!'

'Mm. But I don't think my uncle knows about it.'

'Why not?'

'I don't know . . . '

I had the impression Boris regretted bringing up his 'uncle'.

But now F.T.B. allowed herself to be swallowed up by the water, and that was another eye-opener, for, like whale spotters from a crow's nest, we could see *down* into the sea, *through* a huge, green magnifying glass which made her bright and sharp like a broad-winged bird, swimming out at an inert, geological tempo, stroke by stroke, breast. And indeed as she turned soundlessly onto her back and fixed her gaze onto us, at that moment, I was struck by the familiar feeling that either *she* was blind or *we* were invisible. A twin-domed cathedral of rubber floated before us below. Still with this blind gaze directed at us. And something happens to you when someone spots you — you see yourself from the outside, your individual strangeness, that which is only you and moves in only you, but which nonetheless you have not known, such that it is never you yourself who is revealed but someone else, an imitation, a criminal, before however you have to admit you have had this within you the whole time, you just didn't know about it, until it was too late, but by then you have also become someone else.

'We have to go and let the crabs out,' Boris whispered, breathless, and wriggled silently backwards onto the patch of flattened grass. 'I always let the crabs go.'

14

But this summer could also be called the summer with Freddy 1 even though nothing went according to plan, for which I was also prepared, I thought. For two days after Boris had shown me F.T.B., he came up to our tent and took stock, nodding in acknowledgement, then went to my mother and introduced himself as if he were a man of twenty-eight.

'I'm Boris,' he said, looking her in the eye.

Mother, taken aback, gave a flustered smile and I decided I would have to try that one myself some time, to achieve a similar effect.

Mother had spent the last two days telling me off — for crossing the equator — and comforting Linda, who had discovered she had been swimming in salt water and wanted to go home. In addition, I had been rapped over the knuckles for not picking up her new signals; the thing was, Hans was still dropping by, up at the camp site and down on the beach, with some new rule or golden nugget of advice, and he took his time about it, and Mother considered it my duty to stay close to her although she felt no need to explain to me why, it was my duty to *understand*.

'Do you see?'

'Er . . . mm, yes . . . '

'So why did you leave me then?'

Now she was looking down at Boris as if he were the type of son she would have liked to have had.

'I've been told to tell you the shop's opening in half an hour,' Boris said, 'and that you can buy smoked sausages and bread and something to put on top, I don't know its name . . . liver sausage, at least that's what it was last time.'

'Oh?' said Mother, instantly on the alert again. 'Who told you?'

'No-one. I told myself.'

She stood eyeing him, impressed, then turned to me with a rather different expression.

'In that case I think you should have this, Finn,' she said, taking out her purse and giving me a shiny tenner. 'Go down and see what you can find. And not ice cream!'

'They don't have any ice cream.'

'Is that right?'

'Yes, they don't have much of anything, and I'm not sure children are allowed to shop there.'

'So you're saying I should come along?'

'It's probably best, yes.'

Mother got Linda out of the tent, where she had barricaded herself in, waiting for the holiday and the salt water to pass, and we walked Indian file down the narrow serpentine path to the camp site, Mother seizing the opportunity to ask Boris how he knew where we were staying. He didn't reply, but reacted in a way which indicated that there wasn't much on this island about which Boris was not informed.

When we arrived at the quay we sat down and dangled our feet in the water while Mother went on to the mysterious shop, which in fact was no more than a grey house situated on the slope where the cart track met the path from the quay. We chucked pebbles into the sea, and Linda again moaned about salt in the water.

'Yes, and a good thing too,' Boris said airily.

She sent him a quizzical look. 'Yes, you float better like that,' he said, studying her.

Linda's mouth seemed to be saying 'Eh?' 'Yes, you can't drown in salt water,' he explained.

Linda glanced from Boris up to me. I nodded. And Boris sat watching her attentively, as though on the verge of making a discovery, an expression I had seen on several faces over the last six months and had never liked, this was a hurdle we would have to cross.

'Can't you swim?' he asked.

'Course I can,' she answered.

'What's the problem then?'

'Eh?'

'Well, you don't have to drink it, do you?'

Linda looked back at me with that invisible shadow of a smile which could make concrete hover.

'Can she swim or can't she?' Boris said to establish some definitive clarity on the matter. I nodded and Linda said:

'Mm.'

'Alright,' said Boris with indifference, and threw some gravel into the water, squinting across the sea and down into the quay, and scratching his nose and a long-healed graze on his left knee for no reason, so I knew for certain that we were over the hurdle, and that he too was wondering what we should get up to next, just as I do when I have reached the tipping point between having such a great time I am almost exploding and beginning to get bored.

Then Mother returned, shaken to the core of her soul, I could see from her aggressive gait, with a grey bag she was trying with little success to conceal under a blouse she had brought along from our camp site, which, by the way, we had nicknamed Daisy after a fairy-tale cow, that was Linda's idea.

'What a place,' she said, sitting down.

'Yes, they're not really allowed to sell anything here,' Boris said.

'And then we're supposed to hide the food. Well, I mean to say!' Mother said, opening the bag, which contained two kilos of smoked sausages, a bunch of carrots, two loaves and half a kilo of margarine which had already gone soft in the sunshine. Since both Linda and I love smoked meat, she abandoned all her principles and gave us a sausage each, after first taking the skin off one with her long nails.

'How about you, Boris, have you had breakfast yet?'

'Er, no,' Boris said. 'My uncle doesn't have breakfast.'

'Goodness. Would you like one?'

Boris took a sausage, too, and ate it with the skin on, like me, the sound of crisp skin cracking between front teeth, and mouths filling with the cold smoked taste which is both hard and soft and beats even roast pork hands down. Mother had one too, with the skin peeled, like Linda. When we were finished we took another one. And we had a good laugh about that, us sitting there, not giving two hoots about Parliament and the

Government, and ate as many illegal sausages as we wanted.

Then we leaned back on our elbows and dangled our feet, the smell of seaweed and forest and pollen and Nivea teasing our nostrils, the quiet buzz of insects, and we said nothing, which is very unusual for us, we normally prattle non-stop, it struck me in all the silence, then Mother mumbled with closed eyes that we could sit here for ever, and we smiled, but the boat will be here soon, she went on, it's Saturday.

'Saturday?' I awoke.

'Yes,' she said with a strange sigh, which I knew meant a change of rhythm, and she drew up one knee and leaned over to share a secret with us, Boris too, staring down at her nails as she made small trails in the soft, grey woodwork, telltale letters. 'There's something I have to say.'

Briefly, what had to be said was that Marlene and Jan were coming over on this boat, you remember Jan, don't you, from last Tuesday?

We nodded.

Mother would be catching the same boat to town and staying there for a few days, to run a few errands, which is our standard term for activities which are either boring or secret or embarrassing or necessary or all of the above.

187

But when Linda's jaw fell, and Mother nudged it back into place, and beamed: 'You'd like to be with Marlene, wouldn't you?' I knew that this was in fact not only what was going to happen, it had also been well planned, it was the continuation of a story that started on the Town Hall quay, or at the restaurant, maybe before that too, Mother had of course concocted a plan with the one person in whose hands she could leave us, Marlene.

It also struck me that without Boris and the island and all the other things that had happened of late, which I scarcely understood, only that they were growing in significance inside me, I might well also have started to blubber.

Now, I didn't even ask what the errands were that she had to run, nor did I raise any kind of objection, and she scrutinised my face with curiosity. But I just stared northwards, over the bay, where sure enough the boat hove into view, like a floating black-and-white Liquorice Allsort, appearing at the right time in the right place, as in a film, where everything turns up on cue and all you have to do is open your mouth — and receive. Now we could also hear the sound of the engine, iron and pistons and banging, the muffled echo from the ridge and the forest behind us which merged with the lapping of the sea and the insects and the silence that reigned for once in the family, a family which fortunately on this occasion had been enlarged by one, Boris.

He got to his feet and ran barefoot up the quay and expertly caught the mooring rope the boatman threw to him. And Hans, who had also made an appearance, nodded assent to Boris, it went without saying, Boris who knew these things like the back of his hand, who helped Hans afterwards with the rickety gangplank and stood to attention like a naked doorman, showing the stream of new, clothed summer visitors the way to paradise, novices and veterans alike, we could recognise them now by their style, the former in a state of bewilderment, identical to our own when we arrived a mere four days ago, and those who were in the know, the fight for territory, off at top speed towards the island's splendours.

Jan also turned out to be one of the veterans. He came ashore with more luggage than an American emigrant and exchanged a few old-hand pleasantries with Hans before coming over to us, with Marlene, who was wearing slightly less make-up today and who once again lifted up Linda and hugged her and remembered me just in time while Boris repeated his party piece of the morning and said 'I'm Boris', which I decided was perhaps not such a brilliant number after all.

I stood back a bit, to be frank, while Mother went up to the tent to fetch her bag. I admired the huge food hamper that Jan had brought, as well as a large plastic-covered creamy-white box whose apparent purpose was to keep our food cool; there was dry ice in it which Jan had got from an ice cream company, he said, and showed us a block of ice with smoke coming off it, which he claimed would last for many days before melting, if it stayed in the box, mind you, but by then he would have had a fresh batch sent over by boat, because he had contacts in Diplom-Is.

'This is in fact a genuine ice box,' he said with a proprietary air, placing a small, tanned hand on the wavy lid.

Yes, indeed. And it had to be transported to the tent by cart, which we borrowed from Hans who had begun to address Mother in formal terms and who said, as she passed, he hoped he would see her again soon, fru Jacobsen. Mother was more concerned with hugging Linda goodbye, and so on. Besides, I was standing there brewing up a storm. She could see that.

'You know I love you, Finn,' she said. 'Whether I get a hug or not.'

I suppose this was meant to be a kind of olive branch to someone who had seriously begun to consider what was appropriate and what was not, but instead it was said in such an embarrassingly shrill voice across the quay and the crowded ship's deck that there was no hug, no nothing. So she repeated how much she loved me, just in case some deaf ninny had not caught it the first time round, and went on board and waved from next to the stern in her flowery dress, which should have made me smell a rat this morning; on the island she wore a bikini top and a bathing costume, a dress was town-wear, a uniform, to be worn in shoe shops and on tarmac streets, which she put on only when Linda and I would not be with her, as the boat chugged northwards again.

★   ★   ★

Now it was me standing and staring after someone disappearing over the horizon. Of course I could have jumped in and swum after her, I would have bloody caught up with the crappy boat as well, I imagine, I did at least consider the idea, but rejected it and followed the others up to Daisy and just as tears were about to flow from my stupid mug I felt that they weren't going to come after all.

191

The tears remained inside me. It wasn't so bad. Or that was how bad it was. All this was so new, it had come in stages or like small landslides over the last six months, as if to sort of hammer it home that the distance between Mother and me was growing and growing, as if guided by an invisible hand hard at work to create a final farewell.

Then the tears did well up. But no good ever comes of crying; if there is anyone who should have known that, it was me, for ever-watchful Marlene heard it, of course, and turned and crouched down and said:

'There, there, it'll be alright.'

This was the very worst thing she could have said, in the worst possible tone:

'What will be alright?' I shrieked. '*What will be alright?*'

I was like a casualty in a cheap soap opera, staring imploringly into the summery face of placid Marlene the Wise, and I thought I saw the all-too-clear signs that she was wondering how much I knew, or how little, and how much I could take, then she decided on the best course of action, still beset by doubts, I later concluded, she straightened up and said roughly:

'Pull yourself together now, Finn. Your mother needs a few days on her own. And it's about time too. Come on.'

She took three steps along the path through the rustling hazelnut coppice and turned and held out her hand and repeated in a manner that brooked neither disagreement nor discussion that I should come and show her the camp site, without further ado.

Yes, if there is anyone you can rely on in this world, it is Marlene. Marlene is a rock, like Mother used to be, not a fickle dove in a storm whose composure can crumble any day of the week, Marlene is as solid as the ground you walk on, round the clock. She never lets you down, she is always even-tempered and she doesn't know the meaning of fear, she is the type of mother we should have had. Look how she dealt with Boris, for example. He was already up at our camp site sounding off about his local knowledge to Jan, but Marlene knew how to cope with him.

'Run along and play with someone else now, Boris,' she said with the same intractable smile. 'I have to have a little chat with Finn. I've got a letter for you,' she called in my direction.

Yes, and Boris made himself scarce without any fuss, and I was free to show them how the primus worked, the one we had been given by Uncle Oskar for Christmas, pump here, open the valve, meths, light up and so on, a letter did you say?

I had forgotten it, my plan. The letter was from Freddy 1, the first letter I had received in my life, if we exclude the one that accompanied Linda, but I assume that had been intended for Mother anyway, and even though the one from Freddy 1 could not exactly be classified as a normal letter, with an envelope, stamp, addressee and all that, it was at least a folded sheet of paper with a ragged margin left by the spiral and two lines of quite elegant, dark blue capital letters: 'I'M NOT GOING ON HOLIDAY. I'LL LOOK AFTER THE BALL BEARINGS.'

So Marlene knew about my plan, which basically had been to get Kristian to call on Freddy 1 and give him the leather pouch with the ball bearings in exchange for him agreeing to catch the boat and come out and sleep under the awning with me, where I had been alone while Mother and Linda occupied the main part of the tent.

★ ★ ★

If Marlene had imagined that this rejection by Freddy 1 might take my mind off Mother's departure, she was quite right. However, I realised something else as well, I realised that neither Kristian nor Marlene had put much effort into persuading Freddy

1, on the contrary, they had accepted his refusal as a reasonable end to the matter, after consultation with Mother, maybe, which in turn meant that Kristian must have betrayed our secret, that was the kind of person Freddy 1 was, he inspired people to exclude him, and that made me furious. At the same time I knew that I would not have seen through this game if I had received his letter yesterday, when everything was normal, there's something odd about his eyes, Mother had said once, with an unmistakable wince.

I hated that.

So I decided to keep my distance, also from Marlene, and Jan. But now there he was, in a short-sleeved, blue and white striped jumper, showing us how dry ice was so cold it could burn, look at this, a chunk was dropped into the bucket of water, and it didn't melt, it made the water boil because it brought together extreme opposites, a mystery it was impossible not to be fascinated by. I ran to fetch Boris, who didn't know about dry ice either, and we experimented with it until Marlene said that if we didn't stop there was a good chance we would be drinking warm milk for the rest of the week.

When Boris and I left Daisy, later, I at once began to tell him about Freddy 1, because I could not fail Freddy 1 the way Mother had failed me, and I talked about what he liked and didn't like, what he could do and what he couldn't do, I let words tumble out, one after the other, and I continued when we were down on the beach to swim and catch crabs, lying on the bare rock-face staring up at the sky I talked about Freddy 1, for there were very few people on this earth who could measure up to Freddy 1.

Boris too had a Freddy 1, he talked about him while we kicked a football around or lay watching F.T.B., and especially when we did dangerous things, for example when on one occasion we were on our way down from the crag above F.T.B. and bumped into Hans, the warden, who loomed up on the path and stared daggers at us, which is where I discovered that Boris did not exhibit the slightest sign of fear, he cold-bloodedly returned the glare, until I realised that it wasn't *us* who had been caught red-handed but Hans, a grown man, who is a lot more blameworthy in anyone's book than a child.

Yes, it wasn't only us who were going through this experience, there were also the friends we could never let down. Such as when we swam across the bay to sit on the big rock to avoid being with Linda and Marlene who, day after day, lay on the spot Mother had colonised, Linda who could swim like a submarine now, without a swimming belt, in the shallow water, surfacing only to breathe, and that was not often, and then stood laughing with closed eyes and the tip of her tongue carefully licking the corner of her mouth to taste the terrible salt water; as the days went by she became browner and browner, browner than me, on the parts of the body not covered by a bathing costume. She also became more agile and climbed after us in places where less than a week ago we could have been certain we would have been left in peace, she ran over beaches and fields without looking too ungainly, soon with such calloused soles that she could also walk on forest paths and piles of barnacles without displaying the stupid barefoot-walk that is so prevalent on Norwegian beaches. Traveller children have soles like wood. They don't bat an eyelid. Travellers, gypsies and Indians. With grimy faces, bleached, bristly salt-water hair, grazes on their elbows and knees and scratched insect bites. While our eyes just became bluer and bluer as the summer wore on, the most everlasting of all summers.

15

More dry ice arrived. Food arrived, in varying quantities at surprising times. A blacked-out boat arrived at night with alcohol, which Hans knew about but did nothing to hinder. All of a sudden, mackerel was being sold from a fishing boat at the quay. It was party time for the young with fires and potato races and 'You Can Have Him' and a kiosk that had opened to sell Solo and sausages and lollipops. There was football and climbing, up steep rock-faces. And there was dancing for the adults, with 'You Can Have Him' yet again, some sang along and some came to blows and Jan and Marlene lived out their love with disgusting, deep, French kisses. Meanwhile we sat in the darkness watching everything, Boris and Linda and I, it was our island, so much so that when we stared into the pulsating cabinet of horrors that was the dance floor for grown-ups, we were able to count at least three pairs of men's legs with talcum-white dust up their calves.

And then of course F.T.B. also came on the scene, it just took us a while to recognise her, unfamiliar in clothes and in these alien surroundings, in a white cotton dress, and with arms and legs so tanned that they merged into the summer darkness and transformed her figure into an enormous snow-flake as she swung from one man's arms into another's, it wasn't even revolting, it was how it should be, we were at one with this summer, we no longer had an age, only bodies and lungs and blood that pumped vim and vigour into the tiniest nooks and crannies of existence.

* * *

And all this time we were living in our peaceful oasis. While the rest of the tented island resembled an estate in constant departure mode, forced as the tenants were to up sticks every third day to rush off to a spot they had eyed with envy, in the hope that the tent there would be taken down, or at least that there had not been time for a queue to form in front of it, for a day or two they could occupy the prized site before having to dread the next move just one day later. It was obvious that since you had camped for two days on a much-coveted spot you would have to spend the next two slumming it, in order once again to seize the right to a place in the sun. These were merciless market forces

199

which I followed with interest and privileged sympathy, through the doughty example of Boris' family, the exotic 'uncle' and the nice, talkative mother whom the 'uncle' kept smearing with sun cream because she was so strangely pink and delicate and on top of that so sensitive to draughts, poor thing, plus three brothers and three 'cousins', all doomed to a restless nomadic existence that ensured that only one solitary day out of three would be reasonably peaceful.

'But at least that's something,' said the 'uncle' in a philosophical vein, presumably to mollify the six youngsters whose job it was to pitch and un-pitch the tent, under his imperious direction. 'Uncle' gave every command with a cigarette dangling from his lower lip and ash rolling down his sweaty and ever browner belly and the tiny trunks that didn't appear to house anything at all.

'Yep, one day in three, in fact that's a whole week over the three weeks we're here.'

If the system had worked, that is. And everyone knows it didn't. Some people are more conscientious than others. With the result that even that one week often went up in smoke for those who needed it most, it was like the Trotting Stadium in fact, where those who least need the money always win, or as Freddy 1 says: 'Crime pays.'

But we weren't involved in any of this.

For once. We sat outside watching everything, from above. We moved our tent once, about half a metre, the water bag hung from the same tree throughout the summer, the fire burned within the same circle of stones — by the way, that, too, was illegal.

But since we were estate people this did not give us any sense of superiority, it was more like shame. However, the shame was never such that we felt any need to dismantle the tent and wander down to participate in the peripatetic Nazi regime on the flats. It was and remained a fitting shame, it was for internal use, in the sense that we followed Hans' advice and did not specify where we lived, if anyone asked.

'Over there,' we said, or simply 'I don't know'. Mother had her own take on this, she was new to the island, she said, didn't even have a tent, ha ha . . .

But now she had gone and wasn't coming back.

A few errands? A few days?

Linda mentioned her three times. When Mother wasn't there to see her swimming with her head above the water for the first time, a sight which would even have brought tears to the eyes of Our Lord. Otherwise, she was happy with Marlene who dressed her in a summer frock and then took it off, only to put on another one, like a present that could be wrapped and unwrapped, and given and received, again and again. After a while she made two friends, of the same robust calibre as Anne-Berit across the corridor at home, older, annoying girls, who looked at her as if she were an interesting pet, a reaction which, by the way, Linda was beginning to resent, something was happening in her too, or it had already happened, such a gradual process that it was impossible to discern until it was too late and it could never be undone. Then one day Boris too was gone. Without warning.

★ ★ ★

I got up early as usual and washed under the bucket and cleaned my teeth and gave breakfast a miss, there wouldn't have been any until Jan had woken up anyway, Jan liked a 'lie-in' after all the evening visits he made to the other tents occupied by dubious characters whom Marlene greeted with very measured hellos when they spoke to her on the beach in the light of day.

I went down to the camp site and on to the bay where I knew 'uncle' had made his latest territorial conquest.

But there was just a light, sickly green

patch of flattened grass. I proceeded to the site at Dragevika, didn't find any Boris there either, and walked round the whole island in the course of the next hour without success, before returning to Daisy where Marlene and Linda had got up and were sitting on a blanket having breakfast.

'Where's Mother?' I asked.

'At home . . . ' Marlene said evasively.

'It's almost three weeks since she left,' I continued, a hundred per cent sure of my facts as I had seen a calendar on the quay when I was trying to work out which boat Boris could have left on.

'It may take a little while longer as . . . '

'*What* will take a little longer?'

Marlene sent me a serious look as I stood there thinking I had a right to an answer as I had not mentioned Mother one single time since she left. Somehow, not mentioning her was a way of clutching onto some faith in her, I realised now, because I didn't receive an answer and it was as if she had gone for good.

* * *

That day it began to rain. Not for the first time. But now the heavens were opening. We sat in the tent listening to the hammering on the canvas, playing cards, and we were browner than ever before in the primus fume-saturated gloom. We played Crazy Eights, the one card game Linda knew, and we let her win until I was sick of it, because it was no longer necessary, and she had begun to take it for granted, all the things she couldn't do, as if it did her any good, so I got up and went into the awning and put on my trunks and went down through the rain and felt the dust sticking to my feet, splashed and loped through the puddles across the sad camp sites, there wasn't a person to be seen, down to our immortal beach, not a living soul, and nothing else either, just rain.

I waded out into the surprisingly warm water and started to swim, and I swam and swam, and this time I didn't even turn towards the headland where before we had crawled ashore to have a look at F.T.B., but kept straight on, I was leaving, on my way from the island, from everything.

But I was not alone.

Marlene was swimming next to me, without making a sound. Marlene had got out of bed and come after me and caught me up with her superior crawl. Then she changed to breast stroke and we swam like Boris and I had, side by side. She said:

'Great, isn't it?' without looking at me.

I saw no particular reason to look at her,

either. I swam. 'You're a smart lad,' Marlene said. 'You knew the whole time, didn't you?'

I hadn't known anything at all, but this nonsense made me see the light to the extent that I knew all I could do now was carry on doing what I was doing, swimming.

Marlene turned onto her back without losing any speed and said into the rain that was still beating down on us — the surface resembled a grey porcupine, and from the forest on both sides we heard a torrent of water crashing down on billions and billions of leaves, like an avalanche of sand and gravel and stones careering down from the sky over the forests and the sea — and Marlene said:

'Your mother is in hospital having treatment. It's nothing serious. She just didn't want you children to worry . . . '

My silence was not to be broken. I was on my back now as well, and opened my mouth for the raindrops that had grown colder while the water I was in was becoming warmer and warmer. 'But perhaps that wasn't such a good move?' Marlene continued, and with that everything went even quieter in the storm. But here at least it was possible to cry without anyone noticing. In a different tone of voice, Marlene said:

'I know I should have told you before.'

Two strokes. Three.

'Told me what?' I said.

'About your mother,' she said.

'Oh, that,' I said, feeling an unfamiliar toughness beginning to take shape. It was about time. The determination that this should never be allowed to repeat itself, the hatred and the bitterness at not being able to decide whether to thrust a knife in her or start to weep so that she could console me like a second Linda, for I was no child any more and yet I was, and I wanted to be neither, but someone else, again.

16

This is what it is like being on holiday. It makes you begin to see that you could have been someone else, had you only lived somewhere else, been surrounded by different people and houses from those that stand on either side of Traverveien like two intrepid mountain ranges containing mothers and sons and treachery and friendship. It is a deep revolutionary insight. You could say it was a warning sign, both the onset of a collapse and a new beginning.

We got up in the sun that always shines after the rain has done its job and discovered that for the first time we could see over to the mainland, through fresh, clear air. I showed Freddy 1 the kingdom of the eagle owl, the bird that can see into the future and therefore has no reason to live, yet it does. I showed him the dragon and F.T.B. and the football pitch and taught him to dribble with a ball, and we were always in the same team, The Gang F.C. I had become a Boris, initiating an invisible friend into all and sundry and not telling that stupid little sister a thing, Linda, who didn't talk about Mother at all now and was incapable of experiencing the loss and the fury that I felt. I was nursing a secret, it was expanding and contracting inside me, like a pulse, great days, I suppose I have to admit that, we had become veterans who caught mooring ropes and positioned the gangplank and laughed at the helpless new arrivals, and I came to the realisation that if you are in any doubt as to whether you are any good, you just have to ask yourself if you are able to keep a secret that is bursting inside you, *someone else's secret.*

Then summer was over.

The boat was leaving. Our boat. We had seen hundreds of departures and this had made us think. Travelling home from an island like this is like carrying a grand piano from a condemned house, the past is irrevocable, childhood is over and all hope is gone — I arrived a month ago an innocent, naïve and happy child. With a mother. I am travelling back home as a cynical orphan, hanging over the railings, and staring down into the frothing wake from the chugging hulk of rust overcrowded with ignorant, sun-sated holidaymakers along the Nesodden peninsula.

We drag the kitbag and satchels and ice box up through the city centre and into the tropical heat of the bus and get off at

Refstad with the kitbag and satchels and a box, which no longer contains dry ice and smoked sausages, and pause for a second or two in the diesel-laden air, and stare down Trondhjemsveien to the blocks of flats in Traverveien, and recognise ourselves again.

We not only recognise ourselves, we even nod in somewhat aggrieved acknowledgement of the fact that the buildings are still standing, strangely silent. It is always silence that puts the world in another light than its own. The silence of snow in winter. The silence of the industrial holiday. And now a silence which is not ours, because we are not in it, but standing outside ready to enter with kitbag and satchels and summer-tanned arms and legs and backs. We step into our town and do not recognise it because it is evident it has been ours even without us. We smile, a little nervous and shy, and we can hardly wait any longer, we have to run. And shout. There are echoes between the blocks and in the entrance hall. We want to hear the echoes. A *vox populi* from the mountains.

Is there *no-one* here to welcome us?

No, there is not. Estate stay-at-homes don't stand on balconies and in doorways to receive estate holidaymakers. Estate people know better, even if they have never been to heaven. *This* is heaven. *This* is what counts. So don't come all that abstract stuff about absence with me!

But at least there is a letter. On the kitchen table. And everything around this single letter is so unlived-in that Jan has to open the veranda door and the kitchen window so that the late summer can sweep through the stifling atmosphere, the way we aired a tent a month ago. But it doesn't help. For the person who should have been here is not. Nor is the lodger. Just this accursed letter that Marlene opens with slow, concerned movements, which she manages to hide as usual, though not from me, I know better now, and she unfolds a sheet of paper and reads it before dropping a casual remark in our direction:

'O.K., she'll be here in a couple of days.'

Then I do what summer has taught me. The absence and the paradise. I say:

'Let me see.'

'See what?'

'The letter,' I say coldly, demanding tangible proof that she is not lying. Marlene cannot give it to me.

'It's addressed to me,' she says evasively.

'Let me see,' I repeat.

'It's private,' she says.

'Alright,' I say and go into my room so as not to witness Linda again having to be spoon-fed the news that Mother is still not here, Linda who has been looking forward to seeing her ever since Marlene broached the subject, when we started packing at nine o'clock this morning and Linda didn't want to go home and leave the salt water and the tent and the wonderful island, but she was coaxed into leaving with 'There'll be another summer next year' and, best of all, 'Now we're going home to Mamma!' Which she proceeded to talk about non-stop during the long trek on the boat and the bus and across the road and through the estate and up all the stairs, only to come here and find a bloody letter! Which Marlene opens and reads in all her radiant idiocy. I can't look at it. I can't listen to it. I go into my room and can't be bothered to unpack. I sling my school bag onto the bed and open the window and sit on the sill and wrap my arms around my knees and scan the nearest mountain top waiting for Freddy 1 to appear in his window and recognise me. Freddy 1 does not. Freddy 1 stays true to form. And that is *something*, to quote Boris' 'uncle'.

17

We have all sorts on this estate. We have a blind boxer and a taxi-driver whose eyesight is not a lot better. We have two ancient sisters with a greying Alsatian which barks every time it hears the word newspaper. We have people who pick 123 litres of lingonberries every autumn and are nonetheless able to eat them all. We have a motley crew of energetic little scallywags who climb drainpipes and trees and build huts and smash windows. We have people who collect bottle tops and matchboxes and beer mats, but who never touch a pack of cards because it is godless. There are people here who stammer and lisp, there are tone-deaf men who whistle in the stairwells, we have a lady with a cleft palate and a family man who buys a new Moskvitch every spring to keep faith with the Sixties. There are people here who set off New Year rockets inside their flats and kick in doors and crack their heads on tarmac. We even have some right-wing voters. We are a whole world. A planet orbiting so gently and brutally through the Sixties, the decade that would change a hat and a coat into a blistering guitar solo, the decade when men became boys and housewives women, the decade that transformed the town from being something old and worn with its memory intact to something modern with galloping Alzheimer's, the decade of inbuilt obsolescence, the Norwegian cultural revolution's social rock-cruncher, when even the system of coordinates went to pot — you could send a pig in at the beginning of the Sixties and out would come a matchbox at the other end. An over-rated, duplicitous and misunderstood decade, *my* decade.

★　★　★

Then Mother returns home, four days after us, four days that we have spent in the flat with Marlene. The errant mother, a faraway look in her eyes, pale and dressed in new, unfamiliar garb, who smells different and has shorter hair as she hugs us and sobs and tells us how she never stopped thinking about us and missed us, and doles out her affection in equal portions between Linda and me, which of course Linda won't stand for, she wants to have Mother all to herself and clings to her, and that is fine by me, because it gives us something to laugh about, perhaps, Mother who has had stomach trouble, she says, but now she is well again, Mother who reappears from the great unknown, claiming she has had an iffy stomach and is forced to hear an equally errant son's first sentence:

'I don't believe a word of that.'

'What did you say?'

It is amazing how adults can serve you up the most threadbare of lies and then take offence when they are caught out.

'You've been with Kristian,' I say, without quite knowing where the words come from.

'*What* did you say!' she says, echoing her own stupidity. But Marlene grasps the seriousness of the situation.

'Show him your hand.'

'What?'

'Just do it.'

Mother holds up her right hand with an expression of bewilderment and shows me a floppy plastic bracelet, which looks like a roll of tape, with her name on it, I can see, once I have collected myself, and some numbers, but then she snatches back her hand — as if afraid I would find out more.

'That doesn't mean a thing,' I say, turning to leave.

'You're not going anywhere, Finn,' she shouts after me. 'I'm serious!'

That is what she thinks. Finn does go.

Little Finn. The mummy's boy. He walks down the stairs, still barefoot, it's the 17th of August. Everyone is back from holiday ready to start school on the Wednesday, Wednesday the 18th. The street is full of children, bikes, noise, laughter, love and war, you just have to throw yourself into it.

Freddy 1 is as white as snow and even a little taller than when we left him. But he has some ball bearings in his hand which he shows off and is admired for and now he tries to sell them to Raymond Wackarnagel. But Wackarnagel knows they aren't Freddy 1's ball bearings but mine and orders him to give them back — I have always had a soft spot for Raymond Wackarnagel, the good bad guy in the decade that invented him.

'They weren't for keeps,' I say grumpily to Freddy 1 who is put on the spot, and he is nowhere near as good at lying as Mother. 'You can't sell them. They're *mine*.'

'I was going to buy them back of course.'

'When?'

'Don't know.'

Freddy 1 has a think.

'How much will you give me if I give you them back?'

'They're bloody mine!'

'Yes, but I've *got* 'em!' he says in a raised voice, and I can see he has a point, standing there with his right hand clutching his pocket. And now Wackarnagel has turned his back on us to address more pressing concerns.

'Ten kroner,' I suggest and I see Freddy 1's jaw drop, his overheated brain must have been reckoning on between thirty and forty øre; he always thinks small, does Freddy 1, even when he is at his greediest.

'Eh?'

'Yes, they're worth over a hundred kroner,' I say.

'Don't talk crap.'

'They are,' I say, giving him a Boris look, a no-bullshit look, as calm as the sights on a gun, and Freddy 1 falls for it, that is the reason Freddy 1 has been put on this earth, to have the wool pulled over his eyes, he hauls out the leather pouch, heavy as lead, worth its weight in gold, which has made him go weak at the knees and he holds it in his hand and is about to open it when I see my chance and grab it.

Of course I do.

I snaffle *my* pouch. But without moving from the spot. I don't run away with my own valuables, even if Freddy 1 is twice my size. And he has no choice but to pounce on me. But it is not Freddy 1's day today. It never is. It is not always mine, either. But today it is. I smack the pouch into his hooter, he falls to his knees, and he holds his face, blood trickling through his grass-stained fingers.

Around us everything has gone quiet. And it is time for a quick getaway. But I am still rooted to the spot. With the pouch dangling from my right hand. And in all probability Freddy 1 is lying there checking to see if he is going to die again. He won't this time, either. He straightens up and looks at me and doesn't recognise me. He has been knocked down by a different person. Now this scene has attracted about as many spectators as can be gathered in Traverveien on this 17th of August, and that is the whole street, thronging round this mismatched pair of mismatched friends who have declared war on each other.

I feel the shakes starting somewhere beneath the soles of my feet and spreading upwards through my stomach and shoulders until a familiar voice breaks the silence:

'Take it easy now, Finn!'

Wackarnagel wants to settle this matter; it is not a fight, only a misunderstanding.

However, my nerves jangling, I stand looking down on Freddy 1 wondering in all seriousness whether to finish him off with the ball bearings. It is an all-embracing thought. It permeates my bones and my blood. All I can see is Freddy 1 and all his wretched awfulness having his skull smashed by this unlikely weapon given to me by Kristian, for which in fact I had had no other plans than to hold them in my hand, to feel how good they felt, these ball bearings that I used to bribe Freddy 1 to come on holiday with us, that bloody holiday, they have become an extension of my arm, a club and a murder weapon, and Freddy 1 sees what is going through my wrecked brain, his eyes like floating prayers in a storm.

'*Finn!*'

Wackarnagel says my name the way it has to be said. And as I lower my hand and look around and pretend I am not out of my mind, I discover the pouch and close my fist around it, as if the whole scene were merely about getting Freddy 1 to return something to me he had borrowed.

I walk barefoot across the grass into the entrance to our block and up the stairs, feeling the cold stone steps under the soles of my feet, into the flat where my mother is in the kitchen with a tea towel and a coffee cup, and I say:

'Sorry.'

Carry on into my room where Linda is in bed flicking through a picture book I gave her so that she could learn the alphabet before starting school.

I lie down beside her and ask her questions, what is that letter — an h — and that letter, and that one. She answers, as she always does, and we think of animals beginning with such and such a letter, if possible different ones from those the book suggests, we want a dragon and an eagle owl and a pig and salt water and *piassava*, because Linda loves words too, long and short. I have to stick my nose into her hair to check that she has had a bath this evening. Linda has relied on me all summer long, and I haven't told her the truth, not about anything. I say:

'That's an aitch. Some people might say it's a haitch, but that's a lie. It's an aitch. Can you say it?'

Linda says aitch. I take out the pack of cards Gran gave me for Christmas and say that now she is going to learn to play whist, it is more difficult than Crazy Eights, but it is a proper game, and Linda does not want to play. Nevertheless I spread out the cards over the duvet cover and start explaining.

'You've got to play!'

She looks down and to the side and tries to wriggle out of it. But I will not give in. And she learns. It is the last day before school begins, the last day of a holiday that has changed everything. It comes to an end with me teaching Linda something she doesn't want to learn, I have no choice, nor has Linda, while Mother pops in now and then, and stands watching us and pops out again without a word, and comes back and stares because she doesn't understand a thing about what we are doing.

18

The first school day starts with a ring at the door while we are sitting in deep silence having breakfast. Mother goes to open it, comes back and whispers, all in a flap:

'It's that friend of yours.'

That is how she refers to Freddy 1. I am taken aback, but go into the hall anyway and see Freddy 1 with a swollen nose and two fearful shiners, but also an eager smile, Freddy 1 who says we are going to school together.

I let him in, he sees the breakfast table, Linda and Mother, heaves off his satchel, sits down in the place usually occupied by our lodger and scans the table and says:

'I'll have one with brown goat's cheese.'

Dumbfounded, Mother smiles.

'Right, help yourself.' She passes him a knife while wincing in my direction, which is meant to signify 'What sort of manners are these?' But of course she *has* to ask: 'What on earth happened to your face?'

'Nothing,' says Freddy 1, fumbling with the margarine as I lower my eyes, overwhelmed by more shame than I can deal with and a muddled fury that blazes up again. Fortunately, though, Mother takes the knife off him and butters a slice of bread that Freddy 1 wastes no time squeezing into his gob before explaining the reason for his presence, and so we can barely understand what he says. But it is about the ball bearings again. The fact of the matter is, I gave him two of them, he claims, he can prove it, look.

He produces the letter I wrote before we went on holiday, where it is actually stated that I promised him these two ball bearings.

But that was on condition that he joined us on the island!

While Linda and Mother try to follow, we toss this back and forth until it occurs to me that this might be where I have a chance to be myself again, so I give in and go to my room and take two ball bearings from the pouch and give them to him, two ball bearings which Freddy 1 stares at with a singular gleam in his bloodshot eyes, and then stuffs in his pocket and says he wants a glass of milk.

'There you are,' Mother says, banging the glass down hard on the table. '*And what do you say, then?*'

'Thank you,' Freddy 1 and Linda say in involuntary unison. And we laugh and watch Freddy 1 drink up his milk in the same time it would take to pour on the floor.

Then we go to school.

*   *   *

Mother has started working full-time at the shoe shop, but she has taken today off to accompany Linda to school, later the idea is Linda will go with us when her lessons are at the same time or with the twins across the corridor.

As usual, though, I haven't been paying enough attention. I have been blind, full of Mother's lies and a summer that was still churning around inside me, so I keep Linda at arm's length, and at least a week passes before one day I run in through the school gates after all the others and discover that she is on her way to the E-entrance, to the special education class, with satchel and an expectant smile. I stop her:

'You're not going in there, are you?'

'Yes,' she says.

I sense the rush of anger and the goose-pimples and realise that she has been going in here every day, to every lesson, for over a week, without my noticing because I have been avoiding her, for fear of having to look after her, or to numb the shame that wells up in me every time anyone sees her for the first time and has a suspicion that there might be something more to her than just being small and helpless.

I grab her brutally by the arm and drag her into the playground in a desperate hope that all this may be due to a misunderstanding, that perhaps she should be going to the C-entrance where the other first years are housed. But there is no misunderstanding. Behind us herr Samuelsen, a teacher, comes out to the gateway in his grey smock because he is one pupil short, and shouts:

'Come on now, Linda, the bell's gone.'

'No!' I shout over my shoulder, pulling her away.

'I beg your pardon?!' Samuelsen says, beside us in a couple of rapid strides, more surprised than annoyed, as far as I can judge, he is not one of the monsters, more the high-pitched clerical type, with opaque spectacles and a voice as soft as velvet. But I have lost the little common sense I had remaining.

'She's not going in with those idiots!' I scream, and Linda starts crying and Samuelsen's complexion changes colour and he sticks out a huge, hairy bear's paw and sinks the claws in my neck and says without mercy in a voice that is neither soft nor clerical:

'I'll show you what idiots are, you little

bugger — come here!'

And drags me like a rag doll across the playground while shouting over his shoulder that Linda should join the others and take out her exercise book, get on with her work, page eighteen, draw . . .

I recognise the smell of adult man in my nostrils, cigarette smoke, water buffalo and boiled vegetables, and try to break free, in vain. By the time we reach the headmaster's office I am so battered and bruised that I hardly hear what he says. On the other hand, there is no mistaking the headmaster's voice.

'Sit down there!'

This was Finstad, he went under the name of Flintstone and was a chain-smoking, rock-solid representative of the old school, grey suit, grey skin, dead straight side parting, armed with two elegant Parker pens in his left-hand breast pocket, one blue to write letters, one red to sign executions.

As soon as Samuelsen had left the room he asked whether I had the slightest idea how it must feel for poor wretches to be called idiots, stubbing out a half-smoked cigarette in a way that told me there was no point telling him about the merciless tribal laws of the playground which stated that a pupil who goes to the special class not only changes behaviour and appearance but also clothes and parents and language and becomes a catastrophe of a child no-one will play or be associated with, not even if related, indeed even the strongest-minded are willing to disown their own brother in cases such as this, not to mention sister, bloody hell, there were biblical proportions to this.

It was, however, these very family ties that were to give this rollicking a new twist.

'Is she your *sister?*' Finstad asked in amazement, leaning back in a kind of waiting mode and lighting another cigarette.

'Yes!' I screamed. 'And she knows her alphabet! *Every bloody letter!*'

'Don't swear!'

'She *can read!*' I insisted with saliva running down my chin and neck. And he must have concluded that he was dealing with a hysterical creature here who required more than the usual display of power, for he stubbed out the new cigarette as well and stood up and settled on the edge of the desk and wrapped his hands round his kneecaps and calmly asked what my name was and which class I was in, questions which I only just had time to answer before another outburst overcame me:

'She's not going to that class!'

'Stop this right now!'

'*She is not going to that class. And I will*

never stop! Never!'

I remained seated as I spelled this out, and now he switched into another gear, that of the objective philatelist:

'So you say she can read, right, hm, interesting . . . '

I was breathless, but nodded energetically as he walked over to a huge filing cabinet and produced a folder containing two sheets of paper and pored over them, then replaced them in the folder and the drawer, which he shut with a bang. He sat down and at first gazed deep in meditation out of the window, then lit another cigarette:

'In fact your mother requested this in person.'

'What!'

He nodded, with conviction furthermore, two or three times. But I simply had not heard him.

'She *can* read, I'm telling you!' I stated for the last time. And the cigarette break was extended even further before he said:

'If what you say is correct, she will be transferred to another class.'

Then I saw something I had never seen before. Flintstone smiled.

'I can see from our records that your mother has a job,' he said.

'But she's at home when *I'm* at home,' I

lied, knowing full well that it was problem children who had working mothers.

'In a shop . . . ?'

'Mm.'

'Have they got a telephone there?'

'Yes. Two.'

I dictated the numbers, and he wrote them down and acted impressed that a man of my cast could contrive to remember two six-digit numbers in the correct order.

'Have you ever rung them?'

'No.'

'But you know the numbers off by heart?'

'Yes.'

'How come?'

I noticed that he was beginning to zero in on me, what the hell was all this rubbish about telephone numbers supposed to mean, as if the old buffer didn't know that all kids walk around with some neurotic code in their heads ready to be activated whenever disaster strikes. He said:

'That's unusual.'

'Eh?'

He smiled again, got up and went back to the filing cabinet to pluck out two new documents, and it was no simple matter deciphering them either, I suppose they must have been about me, the trail I had left after frøken Henriksen's charitable reports, he read

228

them and replaced them and seemed to have even more food for thought.

'What was that about my mother?' I managed to mumble.

'It's got nothing to do with her,' he answered absent-mindedly, writing some figures on a blank sheet with the blue pen, whereupon he raised the sheet, told me to look at it, put it back down and asked if I could remember any of the figures.

I remembered all of them. He chuckled with satisfaction while I wondered whether Linda's case would be decided on the basis of my ability to remember a string of numbers, perhaps I should have rattled off how many litres of aquavit the Norwegian population consumes per annum, or what a new Hillman costs at Økern Cars & Buses, all the things Kristian and I had talked about, or, the height of Sweden's tallest mountain. It is called Kebnekaise, you only have to consult a reference book.

I could feel I was beginning to become, if not irritated, then at least even more confused, and it was at that moment that I realised he had tricked me, he had tricked the anger out of me.

'You should start to play chess,' he said.

'I already do.'

'Oh? On an organised basis?'

'Eh?'

'In a club?'

'No.'

'There's a good club in Veitvet, did you know that?'

I didn't answer. But with that the conversation was at an end. The headmaster lit another cigarette. 'Go to your lessons now, Finn, and I'll review the matter.'

I got up and noticed the sweat on my body had dried, although the scars from Samuelsen's claws were still making themselves felt. I hitched my satchel onto my back, but still couldn't make myself leave.

'Naturally, I can't promise anything,' he concluded, rolling the cigarette in front of his narrow lips as if relishing the thought of shoving it crosswise in his cakehole as soon as I was out of the door.

I bowed my head and left, through the ante-room where the receptionist fru Nilsen sat in her tight, dark secretary-skirt and oval glasses, she was chain-smoking too, and into the empty corridors and the classroom without knocking and I sat down and took out my books ignoring the massed gimlet eyes on me, or even frøken Henriksen's piqued questions about where I had been.

'With the headmaster,' I limited myself to saying, which caused Tanja to turn and smile,

Tanja who had been absent from school in March, but was back again now because her father's circus wagon had had a puncture, according to Freddy 1, and here at long last there was something else to think about.

'They demolished the homes of Yellow, Red and Black this morning,' I said out aloud.

'What?'

Frøken Henriksen was not used to me speaking out of turn or in riddles, I was her pet, to be honest, but on my way to school I had seen three grown men standing in a line and crying like babies at having their ramshackle sheds razed to the ground, and that sight was far preferable to the thought of Linda.

'They demolished the homes of the men living in Muselund Park,' I said. 'With bulldozers. The police were there, too.'

'Oh yes?'

'And I stood and watched. I did.'

I looked down, as if in an act of devotion. Frøken Henriksen was clearly in two minds as to how deep to let herself be drawn into the case of Yellow, Red and Black, so I said they had been arrested for living in their illegal shacks because Oslo Parks and Gardens was going to sow grass there, not only in Muselunden, but also on the slope up to Trondhjemsveien where the wonderful

231

wilderness was doomed. And since a couple of the others also felt spurred on to air their opinions on the matter, without putting up their hands, frøken Henriksen launched into a discussion of social outcasts, the needy, as she called them. Freddy 1 said:

'You mean the tramps, don't you?'

'No, Fred, I don't, I'm talking about people who may not have received the love they deserve, and who for some reason or . . . '

'Uuugghh,' Freddy 1 exclaimed with a broad grin and cast around for an audience. He was rewarded, by the usual gang, but not by me, not today, I stared straight ahead and saw frøken Henriksen take a few quick steps towards him.

'They were merchant seamen in the war,' I chipped in.

'What's that?' Freddy 1 said artlessly.

Frøken Henriksen stopped, gathered herself and returned to the dais.

'Yes, Finn, can you explain to us what a merchant seaman is?'

'No. But it's something to do with the war. My uncle was one of them . . . he chops . . . wood.'

'*Wood?*'

'Yes, he chops wood in the cellar.'

Frøken Henriksen started to tell us about the pitiful fate of Norwegian merchant seamen during the war, not to universal applause, to tell the truth we were all heartily sick of the doleful documentaries that rolled over our T.V. screens night after night like funeral processions in a gloomy minor key. But now I could rest my eyes on Tanja's hair and listen to frøken Henriksen's voice; she has a wonderful speaking voice, one of very few bearable adult voices. Mother also speaks well, but now and then she can be a bit shrill. Marlene speaks with composure and the same tone, come what may. Jan's voice is too thin. Kristian talks like the radio, and Freddy 1's mother has a voice that no human being can be in the vicinity of for more than a minute without losing the will to live.

That was what I was thinking while I sat admiring Tanja's long hair, which was like a river of shiny ink, I leaned forward over my desk to smell her fragrance, a mixture of flowers and petrol, no-one smells like Tanja, no-one has a more beautiful voice, just a pity she seldom uses it; yes, it is so rare that you sit there the whole time thinking 'Come on, girl, talk, I'm dying to hear you!' And I haven't even mentioned Linda's voice, because it is her I can't bear to think about, while frøken Henriksen's congenial tones have now come to Leif Andreas Larsen and the Shetland Busmen and she slips seamlessly into the Cold War, which is why we must all have a bomb shelter in the cellar with big iron doors that can't be opened by children under twelve, this is the nuclear age, at which point she returns to Yellow, Red and Black, and I can see that Freddy 1 is aching to interject that Black likes to show his squirrel to young girls. But even Freddy 1 has a hold on himself today, even Freddy 1 is touched by the fate of Yellow, Red and Black.

As the bell rings I get up at the same time as Tanja and happen to nudge her with my elbow, an electric shock goes through me and I apologise, you see, I had a friend this summer who taught me how it can pay to put on a show of manners, and for some reason at this moment I also think of F.T.B., the sign of dangers to come — why is it we humans simply don't break down?

'Where have you been?' I ask, and to my surprise my voice carries.

'What?' she says, without a word of explanation. We have been sitting within the same square metre for a good three years, minus the months she has been off travelling, and this is the first time I have spoken to her, so it is no wonder we are a bit rusty, but I manage to repeat the question.

'Rumania,' she replies.

I have never heard anything more alluring.

'Bucharest,' I say quick as a flash and follow it up with a few more nuggets of wisdom about Rumania as we leave. 'Isn't that behind the Iron Curtain?'

'The Iron Curtain?' Tanja mumbles vaguely, knitting her brows. And since I am unable to enlarge on this, I continue to pine for Rumania.

'Are you from there?'

'No, I'm from here.'

'What were you doing there?'

'Family,' she says.

'So *they're* from *there?*'

'Mm.'

I wondered whether I should surpass myself and say that I was also from here, but by now we had reached the playground, and although it was impossible to go on talking in the full view of everyone else it was no easy matter to bring the conversation to a close. As if by an irony of fate, Freddy 1 came over and asked straight out what we were talking about, so Tanja was able to lower her eyes to the tarmac and retreat charily towards the gang of girls, by whom she no doubt dreamed that one day she would be accepted.

Freddy 1, who had recently enjoyed a certain amount of success with both the ball bearings and his black eyes, which in the meantime had first turned yellow and then gone back to normal, had also hovered in peril of landing in the special class and maybe for that reason had one or two things to say about the business, at least he felt a strong need to declare that the whole thing was unfair.

'Uhuh?' I said, biding my time.

'Well, you don't *start* in the special class.'

'No-oo?'

'No, *first*, you go to a normal class, right. When the teacher sees you're too stupid, *then* you go to the special class.'

There was no getting away from what I had heard from Flintstone a short while ago, that Mother, the very iron in the fire, had not only sanctioned a heartless decision on the school's part, she had even requested it.

* * *

On my way home I walked with Linda and a new girlfriend of hers called Jenny, who was big and quiet and oddly erect, with all her buttons meticulously fastened, and who carried her satchel in a manner which made her look as if she were in the army.

'Where are the twins?' I whispered.

Linda pretended she hadn't heard and instead enquired why I was accompanying her home. I had to think on my feet now, and

I was not fond of this new alliance even though Jenny could be mistaken for a female version of Freddy 1. Nor did I understand what they were talking about because when they did open their mouths they mumbled, and smiled quietly into middle distance, as though they were members of an association of mutes. And as we passed the gleaming blood blister of clay that replaced what had once been the homes of Yellow, Red and Black, I took my leave of them with the feeling that I had done something right, but it had gone seriously awry, not even running helped, but I did run, thinking about Tanja, who had drawn much too close, and a sister, who for all I knew, was being certified as abnormal, once and for all.

19

No sooner had I entered the doorway than I was met by a storm of rare proportions. For a start, Mother had received a call in the shoe shop, which was not permitted, and secondly I had called Linda and her classmates idiots. She had never heard the like, how could *I*, of all people, and so on and so forth . . .

But I was on my mettle.

'*You* had her put there,' I said coldly, looking at her with a feeling I had never known before, but which nonetheless was part of me. However, instead of defending herself she caved in in a manner which was to have less and less effect on me.

'But, Finn, you can *see* what she's like!'

I certainly could not see what Linda was like, and I said so. 'Haven't you got eyes in your head?' she persevered.

I repeated:

'*You* had her put there.'

'But don't you understand? Otherwise . . . otherwise . . . '

'Otherwise what?'

'Otherwise she would have had to go to a different school.'

I needed a few seconds to digest the import of her words.

'Lippern?' I whispered in disbelief, a school for the mentally handicapped on the other side of Torshovdalen, in children's parlance a combination of cowshed, prison and laboratory, the most stigmatising place on earth.

Mother covered her face with her hands again and was a wretch you just felt like putting out of her misery, she was an adult for Christ's sake, and what is the point of anything if you haven't got the stomach for a fight!

'I can't take any more,' she howled. 'I can't take any more.'

Nor could I. I walked out.

*   *   *

The same evening Linda was playing with one of Marlene's little sisters, and mother and son had the arena to themselves, almost; the T.V. had broken down and an acquaintance of Kristian's had popped by in white overalls, equipped with a tool-box weighing a ton and containing lots of tubes and fuses in small detachable trays. It could of course have been entertaining to watch him unscrewing the back of the T.V. and start examining the contents of the silicosis-infected lungs and the heart and blood vessels. I said this as well, those things, they're the intestines, aren't they? But he just looked at me with an earnest expression.

'No, this is a technical appliance. There is nothing human in it.'

'But there's a shock in it, isn't there?'

'What do you mean?'

'It can give you a shock, can't it?'

'When it's plugged in, it can. It's called electricity.'

'Oh yes.'

'Don't you know what electricity is?'

'No-oo . . . '

'Electricity, you must have heard about it.'

'No-oo . . . '

'*Finn!*' I heard Mother shout from the kitchen, at her shrillest, and I called back, at my most obnoxious, two roles which, once we had adopted them, we did not find so easy to throw off. But the great thing about roles is that at least you do not waste time wondering what to do. I asked whether the man thought I should plug in the T.V. so that he would get a real thunderbolt and perhaps drop down dead, then Mother appeared and dragged me into the kitchen and asked me what the devil I thought I was playing at.

'Perhaps I should start in the special class,' I said. Her expression threatened another slap, but I retreated smartly, and then something quite different struck me.

'I want to see the photographs.'

'Which photographs?'

'Of my father.'

'What are you talking about?'

I went back to the sitting room and asked the man if I could borrow a screwdriver.

'There you go.'

'Haven't you got a bigger one?'

He gave me a bigger screwdriver and I went back through Mother's minefield and into the bedroom and inserted the screwdriver in the crack above the locked dressing table drawer and sat down on her bed — two metres between me and the mighty crowbar which so far had not done any damage, but was there, a deed waiting to be done, which took Mother's breath away as she ran in after me.

'You say she looks like him,' I said.

'What?'

'You say Linda looks like my . . . our father. I want to see if it's true.'

She seemed to be on the point of acquiescing when I felt the next sentence taking shape. 'Are you her mother?'

'What on earth do you mean?'

'Are *you* her mother?'

'Finn, please!'

Tears poured down my cheeks, I could barely see.

'You say she not only looks like *him*,' I said. 'But she's like *you* too.'

She stood for a while, then sat down and started stroking my hair, clumsily tousling and ruffling it, but for once I didn't mind, and so we sat looking at the huge screwdriver, the well-worn wooden handle smeared with grease and black oil, fearing that this might pass, this apparent reconciliation.

'It's difficult to explain, Finn,' she said. 'But I don't mean *like* in that way, a family resemblance.'

'How then?'

'Perhaps that we've had the same *experiences*, in our childhoods . . . '

'Bad experiences?'

She pondered and said:

'Yes.'

I probably gave the impression I understood what she was talking about, even though I didn't want to hear any more. She brushed a few strands of hair from my face, leaned forward and lifted her jewellery box from the bedside table drawer, opened it and gave me a sheet of paper which was in fact a stamped document proving I was who I was, Finn, born in Aker Hospital at half past eight in the morning on the right day of the right year, the crane driver's son and hers, yes, even the name Finn, for they had already decided to call me that when I was planned, it had been my grandfather's name — if I turned out to be a boy, that is.

'This is the most valuable thing I possess,' she said gently.

'Uhuh,' I said, looking down at the document, there was also a signature, a doctor's.

'That's why I keep it in this box. Do you understand?'

I nodded. She held up the envelope and showed me it was empty.

'And there is no other birth certificate here, see?'

I nodded again, a few kilos lighter for each spoonful she fed me. 'There's just this one,' she continued.

'Mhm, mhm, mhm,' I said, mostly to myself.

She put the certificate back into the envelope, fished out a little key, went to the dressing table and removed the screwdriver.

'You can have a look at *one*,' she said, and inserted the key into the lock. 'Our wedding photograph.'

'It doesn't matter,' I said, getting up. I had discovered that although she might have been worse than useless over the special class business, she was still my mother and if this confrontation had not been about precisely *this* when it started, it had certainly become so, the most important of all questions had been answered with a yes. For lack of anything better to do I grabbed the screwdriver, took it back and apologised once more.

'Well,' she said behind me. 'Now at least you know where the key is.'

20

A couple of days later Kristian was sitting with us over supper. I had spent the afternoon trying to pen a letter to Tanja, a letter which in addition to including such names as Rumania, Moldova, Albania and so forth was to encompass the whole immeasurable beauty of my life, coupled with the equally gigantic headache of making it all cohere.

But for once I could not find the words.

Standing between slices of bread and a glass of milk there was a bottle of red wine with two stem glasses which Mother kept in the sideboard and as a rule appeared only when they needed to be dusted. Linda was in a good mood, she compiled a list of four things to make sandwiches with and asked us to vote on them while Kristian was talking about the earthquake in Persia that had cost thousands of lives, he explained what the Richter Scale was and pointed out how lucky we were to live in Norway and not in a divide between two tectonic plates. Meanwhile Mother was drinking red wine, now and then dabbing her lips with a napkin, and she said to me with a trace of a smile on her face:

'Fancy you standing up to the headmaster and saying that.'

'Yes, I have to say that boy *has* got something,' Kristian chuckled, seizing the opportunity, but he was put in his place at once by Mother's glare, the glare which says, here she is, having to listen to something from a lodger's mouth which might be construed as criticism.

'What else could I have done?' she cried with cheeks ablaze.

'It's not the children there's anything wrong with,' Kristian muttered. 'It's the fact that they insist on putting them into . . . '

Mother had to come to his aid.

'Pigeon-holes?'

'Er . . . yes, that's it.'

He forced a smile, looked around for a way out and caught sight of Linda. 'How's it going, Linda?' he said in a booming voice. 'Are you enjoying school?'

'Yes,' said Linda, running into the room for her exercise book and a pencil and she began to write what were supposed to be letters, Mother had to put a hand over her eyes and restrain herself.

'Why do you always speak to her in such a loud voice?' I asked Kristian.

'Do I?'

'Yes.'

'I hadn't noticed.'

'What are you getting at, Finn?'

Mother had removed her hand from her eyes and fixed them on me, with her threatening expression. I laid my head to the table top, turned to face the kitchen unit and whispered softly:

'Linda?'

'Yes,' Linda said, engrossed in her scribbles on the other side of the table.

There appeared to be something on Mother's mind, while Kristian again looked as though he had missed an opportunity, then for some unaccountable reason he flew into a temper. But straightaway Mother placed a hand over his — and in a flash I saw it, not only what Linda was doing to us, showing us who we were, unveiling us, but also the inane face of a man who had lost control of himself, and I wondered for one dazed second whether I should finally tell her what had happened to my ribs, that the lodger had skied after me on that freezing cold winter day an eternity ago and tried to knock some sense into me, as he called it, so that I wouldn't tell Mother that he had called Linda retarded, this fateful secret that I had been carrying around for all these months, without knowing why, it just would not come out, and her calming hand which covered his, the intimate calming hand, it had been there before.

I got up, went into the sitting room, switched on the T.V. and was watching a children's programme without taking in the measurements of a bird box for a starling, without hearing what was said about the boys' marching band at a school in Valdres, as various instruments glided by, French horn, clarinet, trumpet . . . when another row erupted in the kitchen, and Kristian jumped to his feet and headed for his room, only to be stopped in his tracks by Mother's shrill tone once again.

'We were going to celebrate today, weren't we?'

They were going to celebrate the fact that Mother had been promoted, she was going to work in the garments and hats department as well, it was not a promotion as such, but most likely it meant a bit extra in the pay packet.

There was just this letter of mine I had to write to Tanja.

So far I had written two essays about the holidays, one about Linda and me on the island and one for Freddy 1, about his stay on the same island. We had been on holiday together, each in our own tent. Freddy 1's was green and a little less spectacular, for once he hadn't made a fool of himself, and I had made him write it in ink for just half of the money he offered me. We both benefited from this.

So what was it about this letter to Tanja that was hard to write?

Was Tanja expecting a letter from me in the first place? It is not easy to say, enigma that I am. I had a quiff, I was a bit shorter than she was and had not said a word to her until just recently. And of course there is something unique about a letter; every time anything serious happens, a letter follows; only matters so important that they cannot be uttered aloud are in a letter; the purpose of letters is to tidy up, in all kinds of ways, they function as written evidence, legal formulations, letters are for ever — and at last the blockage was gone.

I switched off the T.V. and went to my room and wrote a four-page letter to Tanja, even shed a tiny tear, the type of crying Mother calls good, for want of anything to be happy about, I suppose, and slipped it into an envelope on which I wrote her name, Tanja, it was almost as overwhelming as Rumania. Then I sat musing on whether to draw a stamp on it as well, but concluded it was childish and instead settled down to read *The Unknown Soldier*. In the meantime another bottle of red wine had appeared on the kitchen table.

I didn't often go to bed before Linda, but now it had happened twice in less than a week. I read through the first seven pages again. Like Linda. But I had written an important letter and had felt the feverish unease flow out through my fingers and the pen nib onto the paper, as neat handwriting, images from inside me that were suddenly there, so tangible, on a piece of paper and could be *read* — and the secret that Mother had stirred into life by touching the lodger's hand went dormant — but why, actually? Kristian's dirty laundry had become an integral part of ours, string vests, socks and large trade union trousers hanging side by side with my shirts and Linda's tights in the cellar drying room, the wardrobe of a nuclear family of four, there had also been some snide remarks in the street.

'What are your mother and that lodger of yours up to?'

He sat at the kitchen table almost every evening, he stood on the stairs chatting with Frank as if they were neighbours, he had even taken part in local community work, building the new sandpit down by the bus turnaround, in addition to his ever-increasing number of comments about Linda and me, as if it was any of his business, served up with those stock expressions you could read on the mugs of all the other *fathers*. So why didn't I tell her about my ribs?

Because I didn't trust her, however much she looked after this document in her jewellery box that proved I was who I was, it didn't prove anything at all. But then I did have Tanja . . .

21

Now, I never handed over this letter. Although I carried it around in my satchel for some time. And the mere knowledge that it was in this bag which I slung on my back every morning, which I lined up with the other satchels in front of the entrance to the school playground, laying satchels, as the school calls it, this school bag that I swung around my head and fought with and hurled across the ice and kept my pencil case and books in — it was like walking around with a huge power inside me, a latent ability, a hand grenade waiting to explode. The thought that at any moment I could take out this letter which had succeeded in reconciling me with my inner unrest and slap it down on Tanja's desk was so immense that it overshadowed all the defeats I experienced when my courage failed me at potential hand-over moments because I discovered something about her, about Tanja, which made me feel that perhaps she, like Mother, had not deserved such a long letter; after all, this was the type of letter you write just once in a lifetime, the one time you really mean it; all subsequent letters pale by comparison with this one, are reduced to copies and fakes because they are based on the experience of the first letter, the first and the only one. You don't sweet-talk in the letter of your life. You tell the truth.

★ ★ ★

At the end of September the miracle came about at long last, also in the form of a letter. It was a Wednesday, it was like a summer day that had got the seasons muddled. I ran home at extra high speed planning to do a quick turnaround in the hallway and join a street cart race when Mother suddenly turned up, two hours before her normal time and in the same furious state she had been after receiving the telephone call from the headmaster. With a letter in her hand.

'Is this your doing as well?' she barked.

I had the letter shoved under my nose like a revolver muzzle and understood nothing from the typed lines except that Linda would be transferred next week to the class for which she had been originally registered, for a trial period, it stated, along with 'after due consideration' and 'in consultation with the special class teacher and the school nurse' . . . Greetings, Flintstone.

'No,' I said, which was the truth.

253

However, I suppose I must have looked as if I needed time to think, as I always do when Mother corners me, there are a lot of aspects you have to consider. She took this as a confession though and strode out of the door to pay a visit to Eriksen in the adjacent block, he had a telephone, and, shaking with indignation, she rang the headmaster on his home number.

On her return she was more weary than furious and at once started to tidy a cupboard, which is what she does when she wants to be left in peace or is at a loss to know what to do with her hands, clearing up all the things that accrue in the course of a lifetime whose sole *raison d'être* is that it is comforting to know that they are there.

What, however, surprised me was not the telling-off I had been given, but that it should be so terrible that Linda was finally allowed to start in a proper class. So I asked. And straightaway she was on the edge of the abyss.

'*Because I can't take any more disappointments!*' she screamed into the idiotic cupboard. '*Can't you get that into your head?!*'

'Disappointments . . . ?'

I must have been hearing things.

'Well, imagine she doesn't make the grade! I won't be able to bear it!'

Had I been quicker on my feet, or eighteen years older, it would have been reasonable to ask if Linda had been allocated to the special class so that she, *Mother*, would not be exposed to potential disappointment. Instead I committed the deadly sin of asking whether there had really been so many disappointments in her life; you see, I didn't go around every day remembering my father and the divorce and the widow's pension and the *horrible* stuff she had experienced in her childhood. She stood in front of me and asked me point-blank if I was pulling her leg, or what.

I had to go back into my room and read my letter to Tanja in the hope that it would have its usual effect on me. But scarcely a couple of minutes had passed before she came in and sat down on Linda's bed and said:

'Sorry, of course it's not your fault that they're moving her . . . '

'No, it isn't,' I said.

'Just hope she'll make it.'

'Course she'll make it.'

But her eyes became even more sorrowful, now she had found Amalie sleeping under Linda's duvet, grabbed her and sat with her in her lap, the rag doll with two disjointed childhoods behind her.

'She is *so* like me, Finn.'

'Mhm . . . '

'It's all there.'

'You didn't go to a special class, did you?' I essayed.

'No, I didn't. It's not that . . . '

'Well, what *is* it then?' I cried, in order to have it out once and for all what it was that was tormenting her brain, and maybe mine too, and preventing us from being the people we were, and she said something about Linda lacking concentration and coordination and a number of other Latin-sounding words that did not mean much to me and which she gave up trying to explain.

'You'll understand one day,' she concluded and caught sight of the letter I was making a half-hearted attempt to conceal. 'Have you been sent a letter, too?'

'Nope, it's one I've written.'

'Who to?'

'Tanja.'

'Who's Tanja?'

'Erm,' I prevaricated until she remembered the scene I made in the spring, about this self-same Tanja, who I reckoned at that time ought to have been allowed to live with us since there were so many of us here already, so that she wouldn't have to set out on the long trek to the country I now knew to be Rumania.

'The one you wanted to stay here?' she laughed, patting the duvet to signal I should sit down. Then she began to tell me I couldn't go through life feeling sorry for all and sundry, she reminded me I was always dragging cats and dogs home I wanted to adopt, you'll mess up your life, Finn, if you think that you're here to save others, like that Freddy, for example . . .

I objected, saying how else could you spend your time, while realising once again how deeply I had missed being able to sit here, without any screaming and shouting, hearing her say that now we would have to concentrate on Linda, Mother and I. I answered, almost triumphantly, that we didn't need to worry about Linda because she could read already.

'No, she can't, Finn.'

'Oh, yes, she can, and she's only in the first class. None of the others can read any-way . . . '

'But no-one has practised as hard as we have, every day for almost a whole year. We have . . . '

'True,' I persisted without raising my voice. Again Mother looked as if she was going to have a relapse and scream, but then seemed to be mulling things over instead, as though maybe I had a point, and she asked how it could be that Linda never managed to read the simplest of words when she and Mother were relaxing together over a book. I said:

'She can't be bothered, I suppose.'

'Now you're pulling my leg.'

'No, I am not,' I said. 'She *can* read, even words she's never seen before.'

'If only that were so,' Mother sighed.

'Where is she?' I asked.

'At the twins'.'

I stood up, crossed the corridor, rang the Syversens' bell and brought Linda back to the bedroom where Mother was still sitting with Amalie in her lap. She gave a tired smile and stroked Linda's hair and asked how she was today, and Linda answered, as always, that everything was fine.

I told her to take a seat beside Mother, gave her my letter to Tanja and asked her to read it.

'I can't,' she said with her teasing smile, to make *me* read. But it didn't work, not this time. Puzzled, she looked up at Mother. For once, though, no help was forthcoming, Mother was already preparing to hide her eyes behind a trembling hand or two because this was now not only a university entrance exam, which no-one in this family had been anywhere near taking, but a doctoral *viva* in basic survival skills.

'I'm little,' she said.

'Are you heck,' I said.

'Do I *have* to?'

'Yes,' I repeated, this was a matter of life and death, and Mother had to exert her iron will not to shout: 'Come on, pack it in, Finn, let's go and eat and leave her alone,' etc.

Linda looked glumly down at the paper, took a deep breath and read:

'To the Tanja who packs up all her things every year and travels to Rumania and Sardinia . . . ' And when she also succeeded in more or less stumbling her way through the impossible 'Czechoslovakia', Mother hoisted full sail and began to behave in a manner that I would prefer not to have to describe.

'It's *my* fault! It's *my* fault!'

Linda's eyes grew wide in horror and she was assaulted with clumsy hugs and what I assume must have been outbursts of joy, although they were more like the throes of an excruciating demise. Mother jumped up holding her forehead as if she were unable to remember her own name or where she lived. And Linda was even more bemused. But I managed to snatch my letter before the more earnest sections were revealed, stuffed it in my satchel and took Linda into the kitchen to do some cooking, to make rissoles.

'With onions,' Linda said.

'With onions,' I said, taking the oval aluminium can from the fridge and giving her a large carving knife and showing her how to peel an onion, like this, like this, and started on the rissoles which were already half-cooked and needed little more than to be put in a pan with a lump of Melange margarine, I was prattling away non-stop because I had some vague notion that I should drag out the time, the longer it lasted the more composed Mother would be when at length she emerged to sort out the food, this is the kind of thing a son knows, heaven knows how, sooner or later his mother will come to her senses and take over and just laugh at the mess.

And so she did. Mother does not let you down when it really counts. Here she comes, with dried eyes, restored and calm and says oh, good for you, before grabbing the carving knife and — as I said — taking over. Mother rules the roost. In the meantime Linda and I sit facing each other drumming our knives and forks on the table and chanting bitumen and tarmac louder and louder and faster and faster until Linda explodes with laughter.

This is Freddy 1's magic formula, which he still goes around mumbling; I have a suspicion his single reason for doing this is that he imagines they are elegant words, or because he is half nuts and can't get them out of his head — he is full of weird words, red words and green words and words which are nigh on colourless, and in the end they all sound like a cry for help.

22

It would soon be Linda's birthday. And here, too, she was on new ground, a new-born baby, an innocent, so the day had to be much more than the annual routines we others go in for, and it also marked an unparalleled performance in the reading test, with invitations to all the little girls the street could muster, Mother was going to bake, Marlene would sing, Kristian would do magic tricks . . .

And what would I do?

Nothing, I knew, something was beginning to take control of me, I was beginning to stay outdoors, until late at night, I sat in a tree in Hagan or in the bomb shelter or wittered on about setting up a room in the loft, temporary digs without Kristian, and when Mother asked me one day if we should invite some of my friends too, that did it.

'On *Linda's* birthday?'

'Yes, is that so strange?'

'Er . . . yes, in fact it is.'

'What about Essi?'

'I don't play much with Essi any more.'

She didn't say much for a while, probably

out of fear I would suggest Freddy 1, but a bit later she made the suggestion herself.

'That Freddy, he could come, couldn't he?'

No sooner said than done. So when the evening arrived I hid my jacket and shoes in the bike room in the cellar; as the first guests, the twins, showed up, to a huge fuss, I managed to nip out unnoticed and down the stairs where I bumped into another guest, quite literally, Freddy 1, who was trying to hide something behind his back.

'What are you up to?' I asked.

'Er . . . don't know,' he said sheepishly.

We stood eyeing each other, a meeting we could well have done without, both of us, I knew. Then one more guest appeared, Jenny, more straight-backed than ever, and I was able to slip into the bike room and change my clothes.

I left and went up through the estate, into Eikelundveien, along Liaveien, off to the right and up into relatively unknown territory. I had been here on my bike before, with pals, but a bike is one thing, on foot you are closer to the ground and a lot less mobile, both in time and space, more present, so to speak, in foreign parts. Around me there were gardens and detached houses in undeviating straight rows, packed with private life and stoicism in warm felt slippers. Then it started raining, it developed into a storm, sleet, and after passing the market garden I found myself opposite the boiler station on my own estate, again filled with that strange feeling of what it is like to return home without a single thing having changed.

But I had got no further than halfway down the estate before I spotted the fourteen or so colourful vehicles parked alongside the boundary fence between here and Gamlehagan, surrounded by raucous loudspeakers and an exotic jangle that could only mean fairground music. I remembered hearing about this, that a fair was coming to Tonsen, with a wheel of fortune and tombola and pyramids of tin cans you could take a shy at with small bags of peas, as well as a shooting gallery.

It was above all the latter that attracted my interest — I had in fact used an air gun before, at Østreheim, and was a pretty good shot, Uncle Tor had called me a natural talent. It had stopped raining by now as well, this was only October after all, it was somewhere between seven and eight o'clock in the evening and a last surviving angled ray of sun beamed down on me; furthermore, I had seventy øre in my pocket.

But there was a queue, formed and administered by Raymond Wackarnagel and his henchmen, and a violent altercation was developing at the shooting gallery between the robust owner, a broad-shouldered hulk, who spoke Swedish in a way the queue considered highly amusing and the aforementioned Wackarnagel who was furious about something — I heard words like cheat and traveller and scum being bandied around.

Before I could investigate the matter further I caught sight of Tanja, of all people, my Tanja, as invisible as always, sitting on a folding chair by the entrance to the chamber of horrors, as though she were on guard duty. It was a joy to observe that she had seen me first and now was waiting for *me* to notice her, and smile, which I assume I must have done because her eyes were downcast, with both pleasure and grace, of that there was little doubt.

This made it possible for me to continue gazing at her, from the front for a change. It was quite a sight: she was holding her knees together tightly beneath the hem of her red flowery dress, like Mother in shoe shop mode, and they were a bit pointed. *Too* pointed? Me, I've always had a soft spot for rounded knees. Moreover, she had such thin calves, from the knees down they went one way, inwards, until the skinny ankles passed into a pair of concertina'd stockings and large old-lady shoes, the type Gran wore in her rocking chair. Not forgetting her hair, that wonderful cascade of shiny ink that was now divided into two and ran down each side of the magical Modigliani face she, as I have said before, was making a half-hearted attempt to hide; it never occurred to me that it was not for my sake it hung there, it would always be there for me, whether I observed her from the front or the back, it was *my* hair, shaped and washed and combed for my sake, then I felt a blast of moist breath inside my ear.

'Your turn, Finn, but actually I think you should give this shithead a miss, there's somethin' dodgy goin' on here.'

Wackarnagel is a man whose advice one ought to heed, but I had set something in motion here, and it had to be finished, so I put fifty øre on the counter, and the great hulk shoved a zinc bowl towards me containing five darts of various colours plus a rifle way beyond well-used, which I weighed in my hands and studied: the scratches on the butt, the age, the wear and tear. I broke it open and loaded it, but as I was about to insert the first dart in the barrel, I started to quake, the dart fell out of my hands, and as I bent down to pick it up — to everyone's

amusement — again I caught the unmistakable aroma of flowers and petrol.

'The barrel's warped. Aim to the right.'

I straightened up, put the dart in the barrel
without looking around and took aim.

'No supporting,' the Swede said.

I sent him a questioning look. 'No
supporting!' he repeated even more vehe-
mently.

'He can barely reach up to the counter,'
Wackarnagel said.

The big man regarded me with dislike.

'O.K., then.'

I didn't even know what they were talking
about.

'Rest your elbows on the counter,'
Wackarnagel ordered.

I did as he said, that is, as I had already
done, supported the gun, squinted, aimed a
little to the right and hit the inner circle, a
nine, to the left of centre. I aimed the next
shot even further to the right and got even
closer to the centre. The third was a
bull's-eye, if that is what it is called, a ten,
and also the last two shots landed where they
should, all of this to mounting jubilation.

They were not all bull's-eyes, though, I was
informed, but forty-five points was enough
for a prize, Tarzan bathing trunks or bag of
Twist sweets.

'Take the sweets,' Wackarnagel said.

But there were tiger stripes on the trunks, so I took them, and at that moment my eyes met Tanja's, she was back on her chair with her irresistible knees.

'Are you gonna have another go?' Wackarnagel enquired.

'Haven't got any money.'

'Here. But this time take the Twist!'

Another fifty-øre coin landed on the counter, and the hulk pushed another bowl of darts towards me with a resigned sigh.

'No supporting!' he said again. And this time he meant it.

'Don't be an idiot!' Wackarnagel pitched in.

'Makes no odds,' I said.

Wackarnagel gave up and the crowd fell silent. I loaded, adopted a suitable stance, rested my left elbow on my hip bone and scored forty-five points again, to another round of cheering, and this time I chose the bag of Twist, which Wackarnagel seized and distributed its contents among deserving takers, and there was a surprisingly large number of them today, the atmosphere demanded it, I suppose.

'Christ, Finn beat the bugger, didn't 'e, lads. Here's another.'

Another fifty øre landed on the counter with a clink, such a smooth, shiny fifty øre it must have been at the zenith of its career as a coin, an unambiguous sign seen through the microscope of euphoria, every hair of the Norwegian buhund was visible, it barked. Now things had seriously begun to build up inside me, though, the ardent stares from between Tanja's two cascades over by the chamber of horrors, my laughable bid to escape, this autumn which had turned out no better than the spring, perhaps thanks to Kristian, and not least the fantastic birthday party which was taking place at this moment in our flat, *without* me.

But I couldn't tear my eyes away from the top shelf where there were no fewer than six enormous teddy bears — four pink, one light blue and one yellow — in a row constituting the shooting gallery's main attraction, above the sign with the unattainable '48–50 POINTS', which meant that if I managed to shoot three tens and a couple of nines I would be able to carry off the light-blue teddy bear and give it to Linda and solve all my problems, even if it did mean ignoring Wackarnagel's orders.

But that was a price I was prepared to pay.

Anyway, Tanja was calming my nerves, like the letter when it worked. And once the first ten in the third round was bagged, I felt even more confident. The next two were spot on as well. Then my feet turned to clay, unable to carry me, I had to relax my arms and put the gun on the counter and gasp for breath, I felt faint. Wackarnagel observed me with amazement.

'What is up, Finn?'

'Dunno,' I mumbled.

'Shut up!' he yelled to the assembled gathering. 'Finn's concentratin'!'

That was one way of looking at it, I suppose. The fact was, however, that I had to go down on my knees and lay my hands flat on the ground. But crouching in this impossible position restored my strength, I straightened up and loaded — slowly, in a trance, to respectful silence, I raised the gun and promptly scored another ten, this time not accompanied by an outburst of cheering but by a large collective gasp.

Where would I summon the strength for the last bull's-eye? From Tanja, again, and I already knew as I squeezed the trigger that it was on target. So did the Swede, who let out a booming, round curse as the dart struck the board.

'Five bags!' Wackarnagel cheered, and the unhappy stall owner was already counting the Twist bags when I received the signal from Tanja.

'No,' I declared with firmness. 'I want the

teddy bear. The blue one.'

Everything went quiet.

'Eh?' said Wackarnagel.

'Yes,' I said with equal firmness. 'The blue one.'

Wackarnagel looked around. But I felt I was on solid ground, and being the social genius he was, he switched on his fleshy smile and slapped me on the shoulder.

'Course you're gonna have the teddy, Finn.' Then added in a lower voice in my ear, 'You little shit, Finnikins,' and like the referee in a boxing ring, held up my right arm.

I grasped the bear, which was the same size as me, exchanged a final glance with Tanja, to receive the definitive nod of appreciation, but saw to my horror that instead she was rolling her eyes and looking away.

What?

I shouldered my way out of the laughing crowd and ran off, suddenly feeling decidedly stupid. As I passed No. 7 I found myself being watched again, by a gang of girls who were skipping, and being shouted at by name, and I was too old now, I knew that to the core of my being, to run around scot-free with a colossal teddy bear on my back, a synthetic monster which on the way down had become electric and was making my hair stand even more on end than usual. Beyond exhaustion,

I crawled up the stairs, slung down the monstrous animal and the Tarzan trunks in the hall and burst into my room to barricade myself behind a locked door.

'Are you there, Finn?' Linda called, rattling the door handle. 'Open up, come on.'

Easier said than done. For what on earth did Tanja mean by rolling her eyes?

I knew all too well what she meant. That was the problem. I had made the wrong choice, I had chosen Linda before her, it was unforgivable, childish, laughable — would anyone more accustomed to brothers and sisters have committed the same hideous blunder? Of course not. Brothers and sisters are people you hate and you do not weigh them down with gargantuan teddy bears; they deprive you of room and food, they are in the way and are too old or too young, too clever or too stupid, and I had opted for the sentimental rather than the magnificent path — I had had Tanja in the palm of my hand, not only that, I had stood up to Wackarnagel, no less, and converted his fifty øre into the dumbest bear on earth.

'Come on, Finn, open up!'

'No,' I said, not so loud, but it wasn't a bad attempt. And where was Mother?

'Open up,' Linda pestered. 'Are you hiding something?'

She even sounded curious. 'The bear's great.'

'It's a shit bear!'

'Eh?'

'It's a shit bear! I nicked it!'

Finally the sound of Mother's voice, unfamiliar and carefree:

'Don't mess about now, Finn, otherwise Kristian will have to break down the door.'

'What did you get from Freddy 1?' I summoned the strength to ask. And even more laughter was heard from the other side of the door, thereafter the noise of movement, a chair, the knob on the cooker, the left hob at the back, there was no mistaking it, the coffee pot hob, chatting and sugar bowls and teaspoons — I was simply being drowned out by everyday life and all I could do was turn the key in the lock. Linda opened the door, came in and thanked me for the bear.

'Thank you very much.'

It had been quite a party. For once Freddy 1 had not made a fool of himself with all the young girls, but he had eaten well, Kristian's conjuring tricks had gone down a bomb, so had Marlene's singing and the games, Kristian, the contented post-party family man with rolled-up shirtsleeves, on his home ground, he was no better than the blue teddy bear, he was on the same miserable level as the fact that my escape had gone unre-marked. Linda had not even noticed my absence until I returned, and Mother was intending to overlook it, I realised, as we sat round the supper table eating leftovers, cakes and sweets. Friendly comments on the guests were exchanged, a sport in which I could participate, as though I had not done a bunk at all but had performed my duty as the elder brother.

'Yes, now you two will be able to sleep well,' Mother said, stroking our cheeks when at last we were in our beds, first Linda, then me, then Linda, then me . . . for after such a wonderful day she could not decide who to stroke last, that is the way it should be in a nuclear family where symmetry prevails, I thought I had grown up, but in fact I was the child I had always been, the only difference was that now it seemed like a nightmare.

23

Things were not going too well for Linda in the new class, presumably because she could no longer stick up a hand and reel off the first thing that came into her mind in order to be praised and have her cheek stroked. I have a vague notion there was a pedagogic strategy behind all of this, don't mollycoddle Linda any more, she had been mollycoddled enough.

But she was not so lost any more either, and in the middle of a religion lesson in late October Flintstone made an unannounced appearance in our classroom beside frøken Henriksen, beckoned to me with a long, yellow finger, bent upwards to indicate that I should follow him into the corridor, and left.

Outside, he didn't say a word, he strode ahead at such a pace that I had to run to keep up with him, past all the doors and coats and down a staircase until we were by the canteen where Linda and her old teacher, Samuelsen the cleric, were involved in what looked like a bitter family row.

'I want Mamma!' she howled and threw herself around my neck.

It was the first time I had heard her use. that word. And there was no doubting who she meant.

'This has been going on for close on an hour,' Flintstone declared, looking reproachfully in my direction, as though to indicate that now I could see the upshot of my idiotic bid to save her. However, since I did not understand where he was going with this, he added with irritation: 'So I think you should take her to your mother.'

'What?'

'You heard what I said.'

Right, but there were loads of kids here who went nutty and wanted Mamma, and they were silenced, simply and brutally, so why give in to Linda of all children?

Flintstone made a wheel sign with his yellow finger to encourage us on our way. We went through the gate and down Lørenveien, both without our satchels, Linda clinging to my arm with such desperation that it was beginning to get on my nerves, especially since she would not say what was tormenting her, or what had put her in this state.

'Just tell me what this is all about!' I shouted.

We reached the terminal beside the corn silo where a tram was waiting for its next trip through the town, and we hopped onto the outside platform of the rear carriage, and stood there. As we rumbled down Trondhjemsveien at least we had something else to occupy our minds, what with the traffic and the noise, Torshovdalen Park and Sinsen Cinema where I had once seen a film, in colour, which inspired me to tell Linda about a fair with African medicine men and guns and teddy bears the size of Christmas trees, the type of story that made Linda laugh, when we were interrupted by the conductor rapping his ticket clippers against the little brass hatch in the door.

I was about to put sixty øre in the bowl when, lo and behold, there was Kristian on the other side of the glass door, just as surprised as I was, it seemed, and embarrassed? He shouted something, through the glass, and repeated it when he saw I couldn't hear, then gave up and came out onto the platform, closing the door behind him, and asked very sternly what we were doing here.

'We're going to see Mother.'

'During school hours?'

Yes, well, that was the way it was. But what concern was that of his?

Linda had hidden behind me and peeped out with a wary smile, for there was no doubt this was our lodger, completely out of context and wearing a uniform that made him look like King Håkon VII, the way we knew him from fru Syversen's jubilee plates.

'Don't you want any money?' I asked.

Kristian leaned back so far his cap slipped down the back of his neck, and he stared up at the sky.

'I'm having a think,' he said cryptically.

'Huh?'

'I'm wondering what to do, Finn! Do you understand? About you and this bloody sister of yours.'

'Here's the money, anyway,' I said, giving him the sixty øre. 'Two children.'

'Don't be so daft,' he retorted, snatching open the door and going back inside to the other passengers.

★　★　★

We didn't fare a great deal better in the shoe shop. We were not allowed to be there, so Mother used to hide us in the rear fitting room on the rare occasions we turned up, where we had to sit as quiet as mice and read. This time we didn't even have our school bags with us. And appearing without an explanation did nothing to improve matters, because Linda would still not say what this was all about. But she had at least calmed down, and Mother kept bundling some shoes

278

into the cubicle for her to try on, with me sitting on a small stool enjoying the shoe shop smell that has been an integral part of our family life since the dawn of time, and reflecting on what Flintstone had in mind, sending us here like this.

It was also strange that Mother didn't put the thumbscrews on Linda, although every time she popped by she asked what had happened, without once getting an answer.

On the way home it was the same old rigmarole. And now I was beginning to sense it again, Mother who could not take it any longer, Mother who turned her back on it all and didn't want to see or hear anything, and after we had eaten and Linda was despatched to her room to do her homework on a piece of art paper, she said tearfully that she couldn't face any more crises, please no more.

'Right,' I said.

She looked at me, dumbfounded.

'What do you mean *right*.'

'I don't know.'

She looked as if she were ready to lash out, but I wasn't even afraid, just cold, at which she blurted out that there was no end to these wretched adoption papers, we were being scrutinised from top to toe, the school and the doctors and every conceivable public body had to give its opinion on how far we were capable of taking care of Linda.

'Are we going to adopt her?'

'Yes, don't you want to?'

Of course I did, I had adopted her the day she arrived, but what was it with Mother, there she was, looking as if she wasn't going to adopt anybody at all, and in a rambling attempt to get the matter clarified I happened to mention that we had seen Kristian on the tram today.

'On the tram?'

'Yes, in uniform. We were about to pay for our tickets, and there he was.'

'On the *tram*?'

This was beyond the bounds of comprehension, and in my eyes, too, he was strangely out of place, but I had seen him and knew that this was no mirage, I repeated that three times. Whereupon she sat shaking her head and looking as if she didn't know whether to laugh or cry. But then she perked up again.

'Next time you make sure you bring your satchels back with you,' she said.

'What do you mean, next time?'

'Next time, that's what I mean. This will happen again, believe you me.'

I didn't understand. 'Look at me, Finn,' she said, grabbing me by the shoulders and staring deep into my inner soul. 'If anything should happen, you two have to be model pupils, no matter what, both of you, do you understand! Now go in and teach her some arithmetic.'

'She hasn't got any sums to do yet . . . '

'*Go in and teach her some arithmetic, I said!*'

★ ★ ★

Sad to say, Mother was proved to be right. Flintstone was there again the very next day, his yellow finger plucked me out of the classroom, down the corridor and stairs we went, to where Linda was howling for Mamma. But this time we didn't take the tram, we walked home, on foot, with our school bags, and did our homework as though we had become addicted to it.

The day after, it happened again, for the third time. And now the whole school knew what was going on, Tanja too, who in a spare minute came over to me and said she thought someone was picking on Linda.

'How do you know?'

She shrugged and tried to wriggle out of it. But for once her overwhelming beauty did not help her, besides the embarrassing bear was still fresh in my memory. 'How do you know that?' I repeated with undisguisable irritation, but I was simply sent one of her many watery smiles and I watched her go back to the girls in whose gang she would never be accepted, in a way that betokened she knew she would never be accepted anywhere, and had recognised her own image in Linda.

★ ★ ★

Today Linda would not say anything, either. We walked home again and did our homework. I threatened and cajoled and scolded her, even explained that unless she told me what was going on, Mother would throw in the towel and leave us, for good!

Nothing was of any use. Linda would only hold a pencil and write letters and draw, the tip of her tongue sticking out of the left corner of her mouth and her cheek pressed against the paper, so concentrated that there could be no doubt that she was on a journey into a realm where neither a Norwegian primary school nor bewildered half-brothers or step-mothers could pursue her. Linda was not of this world, one day I would come to understand this — she was a Martian come down to earth to speak in tongues to heathens, to speak French to Norwegians and Russian to Americans. She was fate, beauty and a catastrophe. A bit of everything. Mother's mirror and Mother's childhood. All over again. The last remaining fragment of that which will never vanish. God must have had a purpose with her, a secret plan — but what was the plan?

'What's that?' I ask.

'A giraffe,' Linda says, sending me the smile that means she knows bloody well it is neither a giraffe nor a dung beetle, but what does it matter, what the hell are we supposed to do with giraffes that look like giraffes? Put them in our piggy banks?

At last the moment had come.

I fetch the key from the jewellery box and unlock the dressing-table drawer that has been locked for two hundred years, and take out a pile of battered, sand-coloured, envelopes, an old album too, of photographs, which I spread over the kitchen table.

'Linda,' says Linda, placing her forefinger on a photo of me as a baby.

'No,' I say. 'That's me.'

She won't have that, and we squabble until I give in, when my eye is caught by Mother and the man who must be our father, with Uncle Oskar and Gran and Tor and the rest of the family. They look normal. They are on the beach, in the forest, sitting outside an old-fashioned white tent each holding a coffee cup with no handle. In one photograph Mother and the stranger beside her are standing by a statue in Frogner Park which I know is called The Wheel of Life. In another, the same man is standing on a newly mown meadow with a young Uncle Bjarne, they each have a pitchfork in one hand and one arm around the other's shoulders, like brothers. Nothing abnormal about any of that.

In other words, I see nothing at all. I see that by and large Mother is as good-looking as Marlene, in fact better-looking, and that our idiot of a father does not resemble us *that* much, neither me nor Linda, in short there is nothing of interest here.

If I had ever believed that we were afflicted by some illness, and indeed I have, and that the cause of it would be revealed by these photographs, like X-rays, then I was entirely mistaken. But does that mean that we are sound in mind and body now?

I sit with one photograph that will stay with me for the rest of my life and mean something through all its extraordinary phases, a picture of Tonsen estate while it was being developed, an estate under construction, with a crane in the midst of a sea of mud, swinging a concrete section into position in No. 4. Our father is in the cab of the crane, one hot summer's day in 1953, he is doing voluntary community work, like the swarm of other men to be seen in the photograph, men with wheelbarrows and cement-mixers, men in checked shirts with braces and rolled-up shirtsleeves and cloth caps, earning us the right to live here. It is essentially a proud picture, at any rate it is not an embarrassing secret. But he is invisible here too, an invisible man operating a crane looking like an iron heron or a gallows, at work lifting numbered concrete panels into precisely designated slots, so that for several decades to come people will be able to live their lives there, have dinner and sleep and raise children who grow up and confront mysteries and harbour secrets that threaten to explode inside them.

This photograph that has always been under lock and key in a drawer puts me in a solemn mood, I sit with it in my lap and place it on the table and tap it against the salt cellar, almost shamefaced, I look out through our new pastel-coloured blinds that only Mother knows how to operate, with cords Linda and I tangle and tie knots in, looking across to Freddy 1's mountain top, and down again at the picture, a black and white photograph of an invisible man at work.

My picture.

Linda has also found hers, a photograph of Mother sitting on the bumper of a black Ford which I immediately recognise as a 1936 model. She is wearing sandals and a white dress, with daisies in her hair, and seems to be smiling in response to a quip from someone like me, or Linda, someone she loves, at any rate. The most vibrant picture in the whole pile, a snapshot of a carefree moment in Mother's life. Could *that* be what she doesn't want to see again, or show us, a moment when she is smiling and happy?

Because it is a thing of the past?

I also find photographs of myself from a time that is past, alone in almost all of them, because Mother held the camera, and the rest are of her and me. Apart from the ones Marlene took this summer, where I am with Linda and Boris, and we don't have a problem looking at them, do we? That is what we have got them for. We pick up and put down photos at will, feeling that something is right, we sit quietly, private, letting our memories speak to us in friendly tones. Furthermore, we are as normal as the crowd pictured in the pile on the table.

'I want *that* one,' Linda says, pointing to the photograph of Mother, goes to the kitchen unit, pulls out the drawer of things that neither belong together nor anywhere else, takes out a roll of tape and scissors and goes into her room while I gather up all the pictures and eventually follow her.

Linda has stuck Mother on the wall above her bed.

Now she is lying back with her arms behind her head gazing at Mother. I replace the envelopes and the album in the drawer, put the key in the jewellery box and sit down on the chair where we lay our clothes and look at the photograph. We are lying and sitting like this — and I think it is quite nice but also strange to see how little Mother has changed since then, and wonder what is so special about it that it needs to be hidden — when in she walks.

I can see from her tired eyes that she has recieved another call at work today and is prepared for yet another futile bout with Linda, for even more of all the things she cannot face. Instead, however, she notices the photograph and pauses and considers how to react, and says:

'You've looked at the photographs then, I see.'

She goes to hang up her coat in the hall and comes back and sits down beside Linda. We look at the picture together. Mother on a car bumper. It is on the wall between us. She behaves the same way I behave when looking at photographs, and I sense that we are all thinking in silent unison: My God, how wonderful it is to be normal.

24

Then, luckily, it was the weekend. Linda and I got up before Mother, boiled some eggs and set the table. We all had breakfast, dressed and caught the bus to Fornebu Airport where we went up and down the escalator twenty-six times and inserted fifty øre in a machine that admitted us to a long roof terrace where we could admire the aeroplanes, the frightening iron insects bound for Anchorage and Rumania, and which strangely enough had people sitting inside, normal people, like us who, according to Mother, might not even be afraid — they had their hats and gloves in small pockets on the back of the seat in front, on the carpeted floor there were shoes and boots with tied laces; a girl of Linda's age had her budgerigar in a golden cage, for almost nothing of what is in an aeroplane is visible from the outside.

It took me no more than three or four take-offs to realise that with all this noise around you could yell as loud as you liked and you would not be heard. Then Linda started shouting as well. We couldn't hear a bloody thing. We stood there screaming our heads off and still you couldn't hear a solitary sound.

Then Mother began to bawl as well, a bit timid at first, she must have been out of training, but gradually she improved, and we couldn't hear her, either — we screeched at the top of our voices and laughed until our sides ached. Then we went into the restaurant and ate waffles and whispered to each other and we couldn't hear that, either — it was one of those days that could have lasted for ever.

On the bus home we sat right at the back, Linda slept with her head on Mother's lap, and Mother asked in a whisper if I had noticed anyone bothering Linda in the playground. I said no, and made the point that I had been on my guard, that is, in the few breaks we had been permitted last week.

'And what about at home, on the street?'

I hadn't seen anything there, either. But . . .

'But what?'

'She calls you Mamma.'

Mother lost her thread for a moment and stared out at Wessels plass where we had once been, in our childhood, with a formidable kitbag, before she asked:

'And did she really learn to swim this summer?'

'Yes, she did.'

'Properly?'

'All round the bay. Up and down.'

Mother nodded and mumbled that Marlene had said the same, and the bus set off and it was empty, it was three o'clock on a Sunday afternoon at the end of October, and the bus was empty, it hisses and groans and stops and opens its concertina doors and no-one gets off and no-one gets on and it proceeds as though nothing has happened, still it was one of the days that, as far as I was concerned, could have gone on for ever.

'Have you told anyone she's scared of watching T.V.?' Mother whispers.

'No,' I answer and point out she wasn't any more, that was why.

'Have you told anyone she wets the bed at night?'

'No. And she doesn't do that any more, either.'

'But did you tell anyone when she *did?*'

'No . . . '

'Are you sure you're telling me everything, Finn?!'

'Well, Anne-Berit did once say our room smelled of pee.'

'What! When?'

'Oh, it's a long time ago . . . '

Mother gives that some thought, I suppose she is counting and calculates that it is more than six months since she stopped putting a plastic cover on Linda's mattress, and four months since Linda was bought a new one, which does not smell of anything at all.

She asks even more questions, about what I might or might not have told others, until it dawns on me that this conversation is about me, that Mother is trying to eliminate the perils that might befall us, and that in my frenzied thoughtlessness I may constitute one of them, a mere few months ago this would have made me furious, but now it just wearies me, we are wriggling about under the microscope, we are under surveillance, by the authorities.

I notice that Linda has opened her eyes and tell Mother. Mother breaks off and strokes Linda's hair while staring at the sad facades of buildings in the Rosenhoff and Sinsen neighbourhoods and registers that it has started raining, the rain is getting heavier and heavier, as if we are hurtling into a waterfall, Linda asks:

'What *does* die mean?'

'What?'

'What does die mean?' she repeats, and Mother and I exchange glances.

'Why do you ask?'

292

But that is not the way to talk to Linda.

'*Who* said that?' I ask unflustered, looking out between the grey curtains.

'Dundas,' Linda says, as though talking to herself.

'Dundas?'

'Nickname, *ad undas*, a boy in her class, meaning drowning, failing,' I say, feeling a sudden rage I know will be hard to dispel, and perhaps this day should not last for ever, after all.

'What else has he said?'

But here we have to state an irrefutable fact:

'Dundas is a little shit,' I say. 'He's got so many poisonous green bogeys up his snitch that every time he breathes a load come flying out and you have to run for cover and that's how the bogeyman got his name . . . '

'That's enough of that, Finn.'

But Linda laughs and Mother smirks, her face averted in the hope she won't encourage me, then I continue to elaborate on the rottenness of Dundas, drawing on my whole repertoire, the full range of Traverveien's tribal code of invective, we laugh and shout, and when we start arguing about who was going to ring the bell for the bus to stop and have almost returned to normal, Mother says aloud:

'Did she really say our bedroom smelled of pee?'

* * *

As Mother gets down to preparing dinner I take my rage and the pouch of ball bearings, the hardest currency I have ever owned, and go up to Freddy 1's and present the matter to him, Freddy 1, who I suppose would have joined in anyway, without the offer of two more ball bearings, to rough up Dundas, Freddy 1 who is usually the one on the receiving end.

We walk over to No. 7 and press Dundas' bell, which is rung so seldom his mother feels obliged to study us with the utmost scepticism as we ask if Dundas can come out.

'That's not his name.'

But Dundas does not suspect a thing and can hardly pull on his sweater quick enough before flying down the steps like a shuttle-cock, with us hard on his heels, and when we confront him with what has happened to Linda, he gets the wrong end of the stick and takes this as a direct invitation:

'She's gonna die! She's gonna die! . . . '

He jigs around and puts on a show on the barren grass, which makes things even easier, we pounce on the little shrimp, each with our own designs, we knee him, we slap him, we punch him, first in improvised, uncoordinated fashion — Dundas hasn't a bloody clue what is going on — then gradually with more purpose until he is knocked flat and starts babbling, by now semi-conscious. The rage inside me subsides as I feel our bodies approach irrevocable ruin, the explosive moment when someone has to intervene before reality takes over. But I can still see Linda bawling her head off and Flintstone's yellow finger, I can see her bed and an idiotic teddy bear and the sketch pads with animals from an alien planet, all of this cycle is so out of control that it cannot be broken unless I do it myself. But at the sound of a crack somewhere beneath me, I come to my senses nonetheless and start shaking, screaming that I heard something snap, and lay off, but Freddy 1 just looks at me through his new-found savagery and yells:

'He's not even bleeding!'

He smacks a fist into the snotty nose making it crack once again. And again. Shouting has no effect. The silence is a wall, a mountain between the houses. I have to drag him off and roll over in the mud with him, I fight my way onto his back, Freddy 1, who with all his strength has no idea of restraint, staggers up and swings around with me still on his back, yelling:

'Lemme go, you shithead, I'm gonna kill 'im!'

But I do not let go, and Freddy 1 sinks to his knees gasping for breath, I am holding his life in my hands, he senses that, and perhaps he senses something else as well, because Dundas is lying on his back, motionless, he is unrecognisable, a hollow wail resonates between the blocks of flats. I release my grip and survey a deserted and dinner-eating estate one cold Sunday afternoon in October, the trumpeting sound fills my ears, my body and blood, I see Dundas move an arm and a knee and open an eye. But then the rage is back, and Linda's voice echoing around an empty bus. I stoop over the bulging eye and see it is brimful with terror, pure and unadulterated, it occurs to me then that if at that moment I had felt an ounce more defiance, he would never have stood up again.

So I do have it in me.

I get up and go, with this new, heavy burden. Freddy 1 goes too, with odd, unsteady steps, our legs are like rubber and we cast glances at each other, ensure that we are leaving the battlefield at the same time, look over our shoulders before clambering up our respective staircases and see that Dundas is still lying on the ground and making some terrifying attempts to get to his feet, Dundas who has never had a friend, but who is soon to have one.

25

The many phases and hues of punishment, I thought I knew them all by heart, the guilt and the abyss, Mother who doesn't ask as I come indoors, although she can see it on my face, Mother who doesn't want to know, and me who says nothing, but munches his supper with a different body because she doesn't want to know — besides, I don't understand her.

I go to bed before the others and watch Linda climbing up the little ladder to peer at me from over the edge of the bed.

'Are you frightened of going to school tomorrow?' I ask.

'No,' she says, and crawls right up and wants to wrestle with me, but instead sits on top of me, serious. 'Are you?'

'No.'

So I say: 'Dundas is dead.'

'No,' she laughs, as if this topic had already been exhausted on the bus from the airport, and she shows me a finger game which Jenny taught her.

Oh, the time it takes for it to happen, half of Monday has gone before we are summoned from the classroom and hauled before

Flintstone, where admonitions and grave solemnity hang in a thick smoky fug from cigarettes and radiators on far too high a setting. But the standard procedure has already been upset, perhaps because we don't look as petrified as we should, even though for once this is serious.

We are led out again and back to our classroom, without exchanging a word. We sit at our desks waiting and our minds are blank. Then I am called back to the headmaster's office, alone, and this time Mother is there too, sitting on a chair in a coat I have never seen before, expensive, as far as I can judge, with a hat on her head and a small bag on her lap which I haven't seen before either, her knees tightly pressed together and her back as stiff as a poker, Mother in an official capacity, the shoe shop assistant who can cash up the day's takings with pinpoint accuracy. She does not see me now, either. However, I am still her son, I soon realise, for the enemy is divided, Mother and the headmaster are not a united front.

'The boy has broken several ribs,' Flintstone says grimly, referring to Dundas. 'He has injuries to one arm, bruising all over his body, two teeth . . . '

Mother still does not look in my direction, but waits until Flintstone has finished, and into his fog she says undeterred:

'This will not happen again. I'll make sure of that.'

'Oh yes?' comes the sceptical response.

'Yes,' she persists. 'So now we'd better find out why no-one knew that Linda was being bullied . . . '

'There is absolutely no comparison.'

'Day after day she was forced to leave school while you did nothing. You teachers sent her home . . . '

'Heavens above!'

'Was anything ever done at all?'

'What are you insinuating?'

There is a lengthy silence. It is Flintstone's, the silence of the authority and judiciary. I glance over at her and see she has run out of steam, I turn and shout across the desk:

'You've had it if you tell tales!'

'What?'

'She didn't tell tales.'

Flintstone strangulates his cigarette and leans back.

'I see, young man. And what is that supposed to mean?'

Mother is back:

'He means that if she'd said anything she would have been . . . '

She leaves the sentence hanging in the air and looks suitably drawn by her visions of horror, which I cannot fail to notice makes a certain impression on Flintstone. He shakes his slate-grey head, and Mother drones on until she finishes with the incontrovertible conclusion: 'This kind of thing is the school's responsibility.'

Afterwards she needs another rest. And this time I can't come up with anything on the spot, but at least I stand erect, so no criticism can be made of my posture. Flintstone is the one to change tack.

'Are things so bad here?' he says in my direction, now on the defensive.

'No,' I say without hesitation. 'I mean, yes, they are.'

The most honest answer I have ever delivered. Then Mother wants an end to all of this:

'How long will he be expelled for?'

Flintstone has to take recourse to another cigarette and winds up proceedings with a flat:

'You will be informed.'

Mother rises to her feet.

'Right. Was there anything else?'

There wasn't anything else.

We emerge into the corridor, which providentially is free of eye-witnesses, and I have some insight into what this performance must have cost her as she staggers to the nearest wall and supports herself on a windowsill, her body taut and bent, I don't dare to say anything, just brace myself to catch her in case she should fall.

Nevertheless, I have a feeling that this drama is no longer my own, if indeed it ever had been, it is hers and Flintstone's, a public matter.

'Thank you,' she says and walks towards the teachers' exit with her heels click-clacking, leaving me behind in the desolate corridor.

But is this the same as standing on a quay one summer's day watching her boat recede into the distance? No, it is not, it is quite, quite different, it doesn't even hurt, because I can see from her back as she glides through the slamming glass doors that she is neither afraid nor unhappy, she might not even have immediate plans to leave us, on the contrary she is relieved as she struts down Lørenveien and disappears from sight behind the leafless scrub.

In a *green* coat?

I am caught between feeling guilty, reprieved and beaten black and blue: catharsis, I think this terrain is called. I stand there until the sounds in the building tell me the bell will be ringing soon, this inaudible rustling in the cement, a kind of latency, the noise that is there before it is there itself and every school child feels it like the rhythm of their own pulse.

Then I walk back to the classroom, knock and enter without waiting for frøken Henriksen's 'Come in', meet the enquiring gaze of Freddy 1 with a reassuring nod of the head, take my seat and look straight ahead — as though I have carried out an order — at frøken Henriksen of the refined voice, who wonders if she should take the matter into *her* hands too, deal with it in the context of the Second World War perhaps, a moment later we are saved by the bell.

26

We heard that Dundas had been taken to casualty and was maimed, crippled and dead, and that it was a police and a prison matter. But by Thursday he was back at school, his face swollen, his eyes bloodshot, one arm in a sling and a slowness about the normally-so-fidgety body that enabled him to stand still in the throng and answer searching questions.

There was an aura about him of brimstone, hornets' nest and sudden death. But I also noticed he was holding something in his hand, an object he rolled in and out of the sling, to and fro, there was an automatic feel about the movements, as though he had been practising, or as if the ball bearing had taken control of him.

I went over and asked:

'Where did you get that from?'

'Freddy 1,' he said without hesitation.

I looked down at the serene little fist holding the ball bearing, and almost flaunting it. Dundas was also two people in one, the poor soul for whom you could feel sympathy and the irritating sod with the howls and the screams and the stream of evergreen snot,

someone you just wanted to hurl into the sea.
And I knew that Freddy 1 was a repenter.
Freddy 1 was a good boy. I was a repenter
myself, but I was also a brooder and new to
this game and unable to atone for our crime
by forgiving Dundas for his, never. Instead I
tilted my head, accomplished a kind of nod,
turned and left.

★ ★ ★

That same day Freddy 1 and I had our letters
formally handed over in the classroom. We
were to pack our things and leave the school
forthwith and not show our faces before
Monday: a very mild punishment, the
typewritten text said in reproving tones, due
to the fact that 'the incident had taken place
outside school limits'.

We walked home, I was relieved, Freddy 1
had concerns of his own.

'I'm in for it now.'

'Is your Dad at home?'

'No, my mother, she's got a hell of a slap
on her.'

'Haven't you told her?'

'Nope . . . '

Freddy 1's family did not possess a
telephone, either, and he chucked away the
letter we were given on Monday, so the only

305

people left in the dark were Freddy 1's mother and his sisters who went to Framhald School.

Freddy 1 didn't go out that night, he was sitting in his window and flashing signals to me with his torch, I didn't go out either because I was not sure how I would be received.

At home the Dundas Affair had been a non-topic from the Monday onwards, even though it lay there like a rotting carcass at the kitchen table and represented another stage in the mother-son relationship. Not to mention in the son-lodger relationship.

Kristian had, in fact, been made party to the affair and refrained from talking about it so hard you could hear him straining at the seams, as though at long last we were allies and conspirators and could immerse ourselves in the question of how to convert Fahrenheit into Celsius, while I was just thinking about the coin he had once described to me, the history and the wear and tear, now I also knew what inexpiable meant, it was a sin for which there was no atonement nor redemption, an unpardonable crime that is lodged within you and remains there, like a scar.

There was more style about Mother.

'I've drawn a line under this business,' she

said when I came home on Monday afternoon. 'What do you want on your bread?'

'Where did you get that coat?'

'What?'

'The coat you were wearing today.'

'Don't you dare.'

And that was that.

'I want one slice with ham, one with salami and one with Banos honey.'

'That's not what you say, Finn, you know that.'

'Then *may* I have . . . ?'

'That's better.'

'Did you borrow it?'

'Borrow what?'

'The coat.'

'Are you at it again?'

I had a think.

'It looked lovely.'

'*Finn!*'

' . . . '

I raised my hands in the air, and even though I trusted the shoulders I had seen leaving the school building earlier in the day, I felt I could no longer wind her up to a point where she would melt into a resigned, liberating burst of laughter, like before. Instead I peered into the darkness outside the window where my reflection in the glass reminded me that autumn was turning into winter. Mother tidied away the margarine, the bread and the rest, poured a cup of coffee, sat down and looked across the table at me, only now seeming to discover that I was glowering:

'What's on your mind?'

It might have sounded like an invitation, indeed it did, but I could not bring myself to utter the words: 'That coat . . . '

We did not know what to say, either of us.

* * *

That was Monday. Now it was Thursday, the jury had reached its verdict, and I had been out on the streets and had noticed a new attitude, I would not call it respect, not because that was not what this was all about, bearing in mind the extreme nature of the incident, although all we had done was make an offender a victim — we were forced at length to concede this — and Dundas did not deserve it, or perhaps it was what he did deserve? This balance sheet was a mess, it was in perpetual flux.

Also Freddy 1 was ill-at-ease and restless in his new role as a figure of respect, he had assumed a somewhat *braggadoccio* gait and a hollow laugh, he even intervened in a scrap between two little kids rowing over some film star photographs, probably thought he should be dispensing the law of the land, something greater than himself. But by Friday he had managed to ruin everything by setting a new belching record, a trick for which he was legendary, by going all the way down to 'o' in the alphabet in one belch, and was so impressive that the girls screamed uugh, as they always had, and the boys were reassured he was still the same old Freddy 1, the man with scores and P.B.s in sports no-one else played.

Moreover, Dundas was now at his side and the most ardent fan of the belching, Dundas the victim; he would be rid of the sling some time next week. Six or seven days after that his bruises would also be gone. The best solution is a good beating, in Freddy 1's opinion, but then it is also his opinion that crime pays.

And Linda?

She sat indoors doing her homework and had begun to reason and speak in whole sentences.

'Can I borrow your coloured crayons, Finn, if I promise to give them back on Tuesday?'

'That's three days away, you know.'

'Yes, that's how long it takes.'

'What does?'

'A drawing I'm going to do — and give away.'

'Who to?'

'I'm not telling you.'

'You've got your own crayons, haven't you?'

'I haven't got orange.'

'Can't you just borrow an orange one then?'

'No.'

For a few days she walked to school with Freddy 1 and me. Then she walked with the twins again and soldier girl, Jenny. A letter arrived saying she might be dyslexic, and Mother had to summon all her strength. But there is something odd about those parts of hell labelled in Greek: Linda was given special lessons by the school's nicest teacher, Gillebo, and sat looking at watercolours of badgers and cranes, which he had painted himself, and listened to his hypnotic voice for three hours, then she was back in the classroom, beside the twins and Dundas, who had never ever learned to read. She was where she should be. So perhaps it wasn't dyslexia after all, the next letter said, a clean bill of health, as Mother called it, before it was filed away with all the other correspondence which had accrued in the course of this year, the longest year ever, but there was something else about it, for of course there had to be something else. Then the snow came.

27

It came to stay. With ski slopes and toboggan slides, snowballs and frostbitten fingertips and thick milky-white ice. This was the way winter should be. With a roar and a crash and enduring silence. Christmas was approaching. I gave Freddy 1 another ball bearing, and he gave me one, it was impossible to tell them apart, but mine was wrapped. Linda would get skis, there was so much secrecy surrounding this that Kristian had to spend his evenings in the basement hobby room mounting the bindings and impregnating the skis and then carrying them up to the store room in the loft and hiding them behind the suitcase that had been to Dombås.

A Christmas tree was bought and stood in the swirling snow on the balcony from the 19th onwards, to be admired every evening by Mother and Linda, with me in the background. The annual debate about where we would spend Christmas Eve had also to be resolved, but under different circumstances this time.

After all, we had not seen much of the family over the past year, and rumours were flying around that Uncle Tor had been given the boot from the restaurant where he was working, because he had been drunk, Mother said without beating around the bush. But then he had enrolled at the Seamen's School to become a ship's engineer on the seven seas, he had started a new and better life, Uncle Tor had, a Romeo and a dandy, as Uncle Bjarne called him. Gran wasn't getting any younger, either, sitting in her chair, stoking her glowing wood burner and playing patience and winning.

But once again I had something on my mind.

'I want to stay at home,' I said.

I said it quietly, I had no intention of causing a row, it was simply a sentence that had to be expressed for unclear reasons, the same vagueness that had steered me all through the autumn, as though I had *seen* something again.

What's more, we had enjoyed some peaceful weeks, since the Dundas business, a cosy family life of the kind that proceeded as it *should* on an estate, the rhythmic round-the-clock routine that at its best is redolent of soft music on tiny radios very late at night, without Kristian, and how was Mother?

Well, she was fine, relaxed, sitting and

glancing at me from over the top edge of *Rain Follows The Dew*, a story we had heard two or three times, about two people who, like Tanja and me, didn't find each other, albeit for more prosaic reasons, but I knew she liked to read it alone, so that she could have a sniffle whenever she felt like it, and since I could not give an answer as to why I wanted to keep away from the family, I directed my gaze at Linda, who was lying on her tummy in front of the T.V. with her chin in her hands and swinging her thin legs back and forth, and Mother took that as a hint.

'What do you say, Linda, shall we visit the family on Christmas Eve?'

'Yes,' said Linda to the screen, without hesitation.

We filled the old rucksack with presents and off we went, at twelve o'clock on the 24th, me with the carefully wrapped skis over my shoulder, Linda at my side with her satchel and expectant smiles, stealing furtive upward glances, while making stupid little hops and skips. Mother was out of breath and red-cheeked from all the carrying well before we arrived, and armed herself straightaway with her family voice as she got down to cooking the food, with which there was quite a bit to find fault, not to mention the shopping which a neighbour, following

Gran's senile instructions, had attended to.

Linda and I were sent down to the cellar, to Uncle Oskar, who was his usual old self, in overalls and a peaked cap with an axe in his hand, nice and cosy. But the store room had shrunk since the last time and the ceiling was lower — it was the first sign that something was wrong. Had I grown *too* much? Or was Linda taking up too much room in her new, white dress with the red ribbons and her trilled chuckles that made Uncle Oskar roar out loud with laughter, looking as though he had just been cured of cancer?

'Well I never,' he kept saying in response to her stream of chatter, and Uncle Oskar was not the type to overdo the smiles, we were serious folk down here, we worked with firewood, we concentrated. But the axe had become lighter, I didn't need to hold it with both hands any more, the piles had shrunk, and Linda stacked the logs according to our instructions and was black with dust and coke by the time we surfaced to the smell of pork ribs, each carrying an armful of kindling, we could show her off to the newly arrived pushy cousins who always managed to give the impression that there were twice as many of them as there really were.

Now they took it upon themselves to spruce up the new member of the family in the minuscule bathroom, where there was a miniature tub on lion's feet, stained brown and green from the brass taps right down to the plughole which resembled a pig's snout. We heard giggles and shouts from inside, a dialect which became even more remote through the locked door, while Mother paced to and fro like a nervous gatekeeper and kept knocking on the door and asking just how long they were going to be inside there and if they had the light on, and saying it was time they came out, no-one else seemed to notice her bizarre behaviour, I had seen it before, but it was only now I was fully aware of it.

'Is the light on?' she screeched.

'Pick a card,' Gran said.

I picked an eight of spades. And not even that was how it should be.

The candles on the Christmas tree were electric this year, there were Smarties and hazelnuts and sand cake and the aromas of lard and caraway and hair lacquer and cigarettes, the fireguard quivered in the heat as always, and Uncle Tor sat on the windowsill drinking shorts and chain-smoking and said I had grown enormously since last time, which at least was a polite exaggeration, while Uncle Bjarne didn't think I had grown a single millimetre, which was a rude under-exaggeration.

'Look at Marit,' Uncle Bjarne said. 'If she carries on like this she'll end up being a glamour model, I reckon.'

'Ha ha, the fat tub,' Uncle Tor laughed in the middle of a deep drag and had to cough and clear his throat to stifle his laughter, and Uncle Bjarne told him to keep his trap shut, 'she can hear you, you bonehead'. Aunty Marit brushed nut shells off her dress, stood up and said:

'My God, I'm damned if I'm going to sit here and listen to this.'

She went into the kitchen where Mother had succeeded in recovering her composure, since the girls were out of the bathroom, and she was hard at work cooking and didn't want any help, not at all, she hadn't come here to be helped, and Uncle Bjarne, in the ladies' absence, saw his chance to be dismissive about Uncle Tor's new career, the engineering course at the Seamen's School, which I assumed must have been a kind of special education class for adults.

I tried to behave as if nothing had happened, but there was no mistaking the atmosphere: Uncle Bjarne was in a blue suit and a navy blue tie, with a crease in his trousers, clean-shaven, groomed, smelling of aftershave, with polished black shoes. And Uncle Tor was the complete opposite in every detail, though there was something eye-catching and self-assured about his brown shoes, bootlace tie, Teddy boy hairstyle and devil-may-care knees in his unpressed trousers, as though he represented a counterpart to his elder brother, they were not just two incongruent worlds but two different eras, sitting here and jousting with little jibes and smirks that were more like unhealable surface wounds than jolly banter, and perhaps they had been there since they were boys, I just hadn't noticed before, like Uncle Oskar's laughter — had that been there all along, too?

Or was it something Linda had brought out in them?

I could also see that Gran was perhaps not as senile as officially pronounced and approved, perhaps she had just drawn the blinds for the evening and the occasion, and was not sitting in her rocking chair counting cards but the minutes, waiting for it all to be over and done with, as Mother used to say as we walked home after these dramas, it was an ongoing countdown.

And me?

I could be seen in a narrow black-framed mirror that had always hung on the wall behind Gran, usually covered with a hand-woven tapestry, and perhaps in truth I had grown, as if it had been four years since I was last here, I was a head taller, there was no room for my shoulders, my chest and arms had disappeared, I couldn't see my hands even though I held them in front of my face and pressed them against the flaking glass, there was no room for my eyes either, there was no room for anything at all, nothing that had anything to do with me at any rate, but there still was no need to be frightened, because it was the same as with Mother, the others didn't notice.

'Well?' Gran said. 'Stick or twist?'

I looked down at the little table that Uncle Oskar had made for her, at a card placed face down, and pretended I was considering whether to turn it over or not, but I was also aware of the teasing smile at the wrinkled corners of her mouth, and slowly shook my head.

'I daren't,' I said with the broadest smile I could manage.

'Wise move,' she said, putting the card back in the pack, and began to shuffle and deal again, shuffle and deal . . .

At length Linda was dolled up and led round like a princess and had her ears stuffed with how elegant she was, and small and pretty and clever, and she could curtsey, too, then I saw there was something in all of this drivel, it had just taken us a year to find out, the others were watching her, and now you could even read it on Aunty Marit's crabby face, Linda was not only like everyone else, she even threatened to outclass her daughters.

That was the fourth danger signal. Or the fifth . . .

It turned out that the girls had been given a pre-Christmas present on the train here — so that they would be able to keep the peace until we had got the food down us and the decent-sized parcels could be opened — a game of Mikado, which was strewn over the kitchen table and which Linda won again and again: her little hand was as steady as a rock and plucked out all the sticks every time without touching any of the others, of course this was tempting fate, Marit had to resort to one of her tricks.

'You touched one! I saw you!'

Linda, however, preferred to trust her own large, puzzled eyes, which were far more reliable than Marit's exotically-inflected claim.

'You can't bear to lose, can you, Marit,' Uncle Tor laughed on his way to the kitchen to fetch more soda water and in passing gave Linda a pat on the head by way of acknowledgement.

'Are you calling me a liar?'

'Oh, put a sock in it.'

'Don't you dare talk to her like that, Tor,' said Uncle Bjarne, who had followed him.

'I'll talk in any bloody way I want, she's a bad loser.'

'Take it easy now, bruv, or else I'll give you a taste of this,' Uncle Bjarne said, holding up a fist with a jovial expression in an attempt to lighten the atmosphere that had been becoming increasingly tense as the afternoon had progressed, as though we were on an accelerating carousel. Uncle Tor planted his unpolished shoes a couple of feet apart, adopted a professional boxer's stance and began to jig around like a second Ingemar Johansson, throwing jabs at bags of sugar, tins of coffee and a begonia that trembled on the windowsill and Mother's pan of simmering sauerkraut, then grabbed her firmly by the waist and swung her round in a sweeping waltz, singing the theme from *The Third Man* as he did so, and for some reason the fury in the face of the successful paper-factory engineer became more and more obvious, we all saw it, something was going to happen now, but it was Aunty Marit who managed to whisper loud enough for us all to be able to hear:

'I told you we shouldn't have come this year.'

'No, you bloody well did not!'

'Oh, didn't I indeed?'

'No, you did not indeed, you were going to see the screwy girl, come hell or high water.'

'Bjarne, please.'

With that, the dance was over. Mother shook herself free from Uncle Tor's arms, took three purposeful strides across the floor and, with every last drop of her strength, whacked brother number two's face so hard he was sent reeling, and slumped down on the bench where he was wont to spend the latter part of the evening finishing off the two books he knew he would be given.

'What the bloody hell do you think you're . . . ?'

He tried to struggle to his feet, but he was halted by a further slap and remained seated, for good. A semi-stifled howl emanated from Aunty Marit. Mother's neck and arms were ablaze and she looked as if she were preparing to launch another onslaught, which Uncle Oskar must have noticed as well because he tried to wrap himself around her, with the result that he, too, copped one in the mush.

'Oh, now you want to intervene, do you,' she yelled. 'Where were you when I needed you?!'

'What are you doing out there?' Gran called from the living room.

'Look at her!' Mother shrieked with a voice like steel, pointing to Linda who was sitting clutching a Mikado stick in one hand and me in the other, unless it was vice versa. 'Can't you see the similarity?! *Can't you see?!*'

Uncle Oskar collapsed in abject shame. 'You were an adult and you saw what was going on,' Mother ploughed on. 'You and that old cow in there!'

'Ouch, that hurt,' Marit said, and the other girls burst into tears one after the other, Mother now appeared to be allowing some data to percolate through, Uncle Bjarne's incomprehensible words perhaps:

'Do you imagine it was just you he abused, you dope?'

Then there was something about the darkness in the bathroom, which I gathered involved their father, my grandfather, of whom even less was said than of my father — we hadn't even been to his grave, it was Uncle Oskar who tended it; I had been there once, one frosty morning, Christmas Eve four years ago, to light a candle and lay a wreath among millions of others, at the time I asked if Grandad was in heaven, and Uncle Oskar mumbled quietly into his frozen breath: 'No, he's in hell.'

This was not part of Uncle Oskar's everyday vocabulary, so I stood poking around in the snow with the tip of my shoe, but the way he expressed himself made it sound a bit like, well, we all have to live somewhere, so I forgot it again, until I saw that Uncle Tor had also been struck by some mysterious affliction and was standing with his forehead against the ice cold windowpane, crying like a baby.

'There's obviously been a lot of fun and games in this family,' Mother snorted and announced that the party was, as far as we were concerned, over, dragged us into the hall and started dressing Linda, who stood like a candle in the dark, still holding the Mikado stick which Mother had to snap to put on her gloves, while I gathered up all our presents and tucked them into the rucksack.

'What are you doing out there?' Gran called.

'Nothing,' Mother said. 'As always.'

28

It can't have been more than four o'clock. All the streets were silent, and all the houses, and the heavens too, and we did not say a word either, as we trudged off in the powdery snow until we found ourselves under the railway bridge by the timber yard, where Mother came to a sudden halt and looked down at me:

'Did you know this was going to happen?'

'Not sure.' I shrank under her gaze. But she crouched down and would not let the matter rest, grabbed me by the shoulders, shook me and stared into the depths of what was left of me. 'Did you know this was going to happen, Finn?'

'Not sure,' I said. 'But I think I can see . . . something.'

'What? What can you see?'

Perhaps I had a chance here to find her again, but that would have required more from me than I was capable of, I was on the verge of tears.

'Don't you start as well,' she said, straightening up and looking around at the snowy railway bridge and the carless road that forked here, the glistening snow-covered ground that lay ahead of us, a good kilometre's walk home in the cold early Christmas darkness, as though again she was wondering where on earth she was when she tore off one of Linda's mittens and saw blood on her hand.

'My God, what's this?'

Linda looked crestfallen. 'What *is* it? Answer me, girl!'

'I stabbed her in the thigh.'

'What?'

Linda repeated the sentence, abashed.

'*Who* did you stab in the thigh?'

'Marit. With the stick.'

Mother and I exchanged glances, me desperately hoping that we might be able to laugh together again, at long last, the laughter of ours which had vanished. But she was lost to me, and remained so.

'God Almighty. Unwrap them.'

'Unwrap what?'

'These,' she repeated with resolve, grabbing the skis I was carrying on my shoulder and passed them to Linda, who was watching her, wide-eyed.

'*Here?*'

'Yes, here, missie, come on now.'

Linda stood still, smiled, opened the gift tag and read — To Linda from Mamma and

Finn — and began to remove the paper, with infinite care so as not to ruin it, folded it up and put it in her school bag while Mother and I looked on.

A pair of Splitkein skis, one metre forty long, which Kristian had impregnated and strapped together with a small wooden block in the middle to retain the elasticity, with Kandahar bindings that can be adjusted on both sides using small brass screws; there is something dependable and cultivated about a pair of Splitkeins that speaks to your heart of snowy landscapes, the glossy, mahogany-brown surface with light-coloured inlays oozing chocolate and time-honoured solidity, libraries and violins.

'She hasn't got any boots, has she?'

'Yes, she has. Here.'

Mother unhitched her rucksack, pulled out Linda's pitch-seam skiing boots, ordered her to sit down and changed her footwear while I loosened the straps and realised there was no wax under the skis, just a black impregnate which still stank of tar. Linda carefully placed her boots in the bindings so that I could fasten and adjust them. Mother said:

'Off you go now.'

Linda took two steps and fell, I got her on her feet, and she fell again. Mother removed the rope from the rucksack and tied a loop at one end. 'Hold onto this and we'll pull you.'

Linda grabbed the rope and we dragged her up through Muselunden Park and Disen estate, it was like a Nativity scene depicting life's most fundamental relationship. I caught Mother smiling once, and then a second time. She slipped on the ice beneath the snow, went flying and sat eating snow from her gloves, laughing and commenting on Linda's skiing style, Linda lost her temper and tried to dunk Mother in the snow, and they began to wrestle while I looked on, a spectator, because — in front of my very eyes — yet another chapter had opened in Mother's unfathomable nature.

It started snowing again, white ash fluttering down from a black void and turning yellow in the street lights from Trondhjemsveien before settling on skin and clothes and ground. They sat beside each other like two young schoolgirls, and it is thanks to this image that I always think of childhood as yellow, these lights that, for once, shone for no purpose, there was not a car to be seen, my heart was ticking in a bell of matt glass — when Mother began to speak in the same earnest manner that she had used when leaving us on the island in the summer, about this hospital she had been to, which was no ordinary hospital like Aker, for example, which we could just see through the falling snow, where you had your tonsils or appendix removed, but a hospital that worked to eradicate bad memories, such as being locked up and knocked senseless in your childhood, by your own father, memories that remained and bled like a burst appendix in your mind, no matter how old you became, and threatened to poison even the smallest thought, so even though we might have considered this to have been a difficult year it had been good for her, when all was said and done, she just hadn't realised it until now, this very minute, thanks to the mysterious hospital the gift of Linda, who had given her fresh courage and taught her something she believed she would never unlearn, and also you, she added, fortunately, I was still there and was not exhibiting any signs of going mad, not just yet.

'Do you understand what I'm telling you, Finn?' she said in much too loud a voice, but with a broad smile, for it was meant in jest, she sat there so in control and unvanquished and secure.

'Yes,' I said, compliant rather than enlightened. Linda said yes as well and nodded a couple of times because it was important here to have agreement, we perceived it that way at least, and for Mother to be at ease with herself, and that was more than enough.

★   ★   ★

It had just turned six when we clattered into the flat where Mother went into action frying the chops and rissoles which had been intended for Christmas Day. I wrapped Linda up in a duvet and sat her in front of the Christmas tree which this year not only had egg-carton decorations but proper red-and-white hearts, woven by Linda and me and Freddy 1, who created the biggest of them all, a yellow one. We devoured home-made marzipan and pepper nuts for all we were worth until dinner was on the table. And then at last we were ready for some hearty laughter, what an evening, tomorrow we would have to make do with sauerkraut and gravy!

After the food, there were even more presents. Clothes and an autograph album for Linda, a watch for Mother from Kristian, who this year was also celebrating with his family, plus a pile of books for me.

But, when Linda had fallen asleep and we were listening to carols on the radio and I was reading *Five Go To Smugglers' Top* and Mother was drinking red wine, three glasses

330

already, and was snugly ensconced in her armchair gawping at the Christmas tree, unhappily there came a devastating postscript to the relief I had felt out in the snow.

'Do you think I should marry Kristian?'

She was winding the wrist watch that she had unpacked with a much more practised air than when the gold hare first made its appearance.

'He's asked me. What do you think?'

I said no without a moment's hesitation. Repeated it, too, quite loud.

'Why not?'

'Why?'

Because men were just comic characters, I had a dead father, a grandfather in hell, I knew Frank from over the way, who whistled and smelled of horses, Freddy 1's father who was never there, Jan with the dry ice and the high-pitched voice, who had the same ill-fated profession as Uncle Tor; Uncle Oskar was the only one I got along with, in my own way, but he, too, was guilty of something I dare not even imagine. And the very thought of Mother going to bed with the lodger in the temporary digs made my spine run cold.

'I know, I know, he's a deceitful devil,' she mumbled unprompted, but with a strange laugh.

'I don't want to be adopted by Kristian,' I said.

'Yes, there is that,' she said with the same casual intonation, letting the watch dangle from around her wrist like a noose. But then something occurred to her. 'But then we won't be able to sort out Linda's papers.'

'What do you mean?'

'I'm a single mother, Finn. Only married women are allowed to adopt. And all this mess we've made . . . '

This was a reference to everything from Linda's being given medicines, which was tantamount to child abuse, to the row at school, to Linda's possible dyslexia or whatever the thing was bloody called and to this thing that wasn't there but nonetheless would not go away. And, as I had nothing to add, because I had no brain left to think with, that was when it came:

'Someone is ruining everything for us, but I'm not allowed to see the papers, all they tell me is that it could take a bit more time, a bit longer . . . And . . . '

'Yes?' I said as she paused.

'And then they come up with this business about me having been unwell . . . '

'But there's nothing wrong with you!'

'No, of course not . . . '

I wanted to scream, the evening was being

blown sky-high after all, I would have jumped up and run away, had it not been for the fact that I had already done so, I wanted to see black and white pictures of people sitting by a tent holding a cup of coffee, standing in a field with pitchforks over their shoulders and looking as if they were enjoying themselves, I wanted to see an invisible crane driver and Mother on the bumper of a Ford, above all I wanted to see her as she had been only a few hours ago, sitting beside Linda, eating snow and saying, in an almost credible way, it had been a great year.

'But we have a triumph card,' she said, interrupting my thoughts.

'It's called a *trump!*' I shouted angrily.

She laughed and took a swig of wine.

'You're unbelievable.'

'What is it then?' I yelled. 'The trump?'

She looked straight at me and said, coolly:

'It's *you*. You're related to her. It's a blood . . . '

'Blood tie?'

'Yes, you're her only relative, apart from the mother. Neither her nor . . . your father have any surviving . . . '

'So you don't need to marry Kristian after all,' I exclaimed, and she stared dreamily at the Christmas tree, at Freddy 1's Christmas heart, or so I reckoned, it distinguished itself by being the biggest, the clumsiest and by some distance the yellowest that has ever been hung on a Christmas tree. But then she spotted something which I had hoped she would not, and which, in the light of the latest phase of the conversation, I had made up my mind to hide away, so long as she didn't notice it, that is, a final present concealed behind the base of the tree, a small cylinder in green paper with a home-made tag.

'What's this?' she asked, getting to her feet and picking it up.

Linda had read out the names on the presents this year, but she had forgotten this one or intentionally ignored it, and now Mother was studying the tag. To Kristian from Linda.

She searched my face, of course Mother and I hadn't bought anything for Kristian, as far as I was aware, for all the good reasons in existence for not giving someone a present, it means altogether too much in a situation like ours.

'What's this?'

'I don't know,' I said. But those days were gone, for ever, she only needed to look at me. 'A drawing,' I was forced to admit. 'I think it's a horse.'

'A horse?'

'Yes, a *horse!*'

★   ★   ★

And so ends the evening, Christmas Eve, with Mother clutching a rolled-up drawing of an unrecognisable horse which she cannot decide whether to open or hide or hand over to the rightful owner, and I look down at the faded letters in the book I have been given and make myself more comfortable on the sofa, so that the last thing she said will not vanish into the night, the bit about the trump, 'hope it will work', hear the patter of feet in the flats all around us, voices and muffled laughter, a door slamming and a tap being turned on, the sounds of the building, the murmuring bloodflow of the radiators, and also the rubbish chute — the hatch and the fall and the clatter in the cellar — and the footsteps that fade away before the world awakens to the smell of candle wax, gravy and spruce twigs. It is night time on the estate. The night of the year. I see Linda running towards me, see her dissolving into thin air and slipping between my fingers as I awake in a sea of sweat to the sound of thunder.

But it is the sound of sleep.

A faraway island in the dark. *Two* islands, Linda and Mother, breathing, and I lie listening to the turbulent sky that only a mother can create and also only a mother can destroy, until the sweat on my body dries, for everything becomes clearer from a vantage point such as this, looking down from the pinnacle of night, all I have to do is get up and fetch the watch from her bedside table and take it to the kitchen and retrieve the hammer from the shoe box where we keep the tools high in a cupboard above the sink, and with one well-aimed blow smash the bloody watch to pieces on the formica table.

I sweep up the bits, the cogwheels and hands and slivers of glass, and put them in a pile beside the hammer, like one of Freddy 1's Christmas decorations, and go back to the bedroom.

'What was that?' she mumbles.

'Just me,' I whisper, climbing onto the top bunk and going to sleep.

★ ★ ★

Next day the weather is clear and bright. Uncle Oskar drops by, with a pork joint under one arm and a bottle of aquavit under the other, Uncle Oskar who never touches a drop and will not do so now, neither he nor Mother. They are sitting at the kitchen table, each with a cup of coffee, and finishing a serious conversation when Linda and I come in after a hard session on the ski slopes, where Linda has made great progress, depending on how you see that, but she has not attracted as much attention as Freddy 1, who was given jumping skis for Christmas.

'Ah, here come the young 'uns,' Uncle Oskar chuckles, and Mother looks at us as though she is of like mind, *my* young 'uns, the trump card and his sister, she can't even be bothered to help us off with our boots and clothes, we have to do that ourselves. But she sits there watching, with the same smile that had been on Uncle Oskar's face in the gleam from the paraffin lamp in Gran's wood cellar when he discovered that Linda was no different from everyone else, the man who had never seen her before, as though fresh eyes were needed.

The aroma of roast pork in the flat, warmth, a glass of Solo, Christmas all over again, Mother and Uncle Oskar are talking about snow, it is a winter made for young people, and not a word is said about the catastrophic Christmas Eve, nor about the marriage. And when the smashed watch is not brought up either, I realise it must have been a dream.

As we take our places for dinner Jan and Marlene also drop by and Mother says they

337

may as well stay. Marlene, with her new engagement ring, bought on the Swedish border, who drinks aquavit at the same speed as Uncle Tor, without looking any the worse for wear. Stories are told about the summer, about dry ice and the potato race and a shop that is open and closed at the same time, stories that share common ground with photographs in that they can be listened to without your feeling any desire to cry. We sit around the kitchen table talking and chomping on skull-crunching cold crackling and then play Crazy Eights and whist, which Linda wins once, with me as a partner, easy as wink. I meet Mother's gaze across the table, and we agree — I feel — that now life is bloody well beginning! Now things are beginning to go the way they should, in our family too. And that is how they will continue through the winter and spring, touch wood, and summer and autumn and through the rest of the Sixties, this incredible decade when men became boys and housewives women, which started with some pointless decorating and being hard-up, and especially when the poor mite got off the Grorud bus one dark November day with a bombshell in a small, light-blue suitcase and turned our lives upside down.

29

They came for Linda on 8th January, at school. In other words, they knew what they were doing. The same afternoon we were visited by a man in a hat and coat who handed over a document and said they had found her some good foster parents somewhere, who already had a son of my age, so the transition would not be so difficult, she would be fine.

Since Mother could not bring herself to sign the paper, he said it didn't matter, the formalities were in place anyway, approved by the hairdresser woman and the authorities. So the only question left was whether Linda would be allowed to take any more than her school bag and the clothes she was standing up in, things she was fond of, games, a doll?

Neither Mother nor I had much to say in this regard either.

We sat in our chairs in the sitting room and had stopped living. The man who was here in the name of charity and justice had not. He could understand us, he said, but experience told him things like this were done in the child's best interests.

Then he left.

Mother and I said nothing to each other that day, as far as I can remember. The morning after we got up as usual, we sat without looking at each other across the breakfast table, and we didn't eat much either. Afterwards we went our different ways, a mother to work in a shop selling dresses and shoes to whoever might be interested, and a son to school to sit behind Tanja and stare at her black hair, not hearing a word that was said.

We met again at the dinner table and still had nothing to say. But in the middle of the night Mother broke down while I lay motionless, listening to sounds from the time Linda stopped taking her medicine. And when I returned from school the next afternoon her things had gone, clothes, games, books. Amalie. The following day her bed was gone, too, I suppose it must have ended up back in the loft, without any help from me this time. We were paralysed victims of natural forces and sat as still as mice waiting for things to get even worse.

Two weeks later Kristian moved out, he didn't wear a hat and coat any more but a jumper covered in snowflakes and reindeer. He had bought himself an old Chevrolet which he filled with all his worldly goods. He left behind the microscope and the chess board. He also wanted to leave us the T.V. set.

'Take it with you,' Mother said in a tone that made him take it with him.

There must have been a winter and spring that year as well, a summer too, for all I know, but we stayed indoors, under cover, me back in my old room, the lodger's room, with a view over to Essi. And Mother in her old room, with a view of nothing. I could not bring myself to look at her any more, we lived our own lives, at the bottom of an ocean of silence, and did not resurface until some time in September. Then we started to do the place up again, at long last we bought a bookcase and adorned the whole flat in an even more discreet wallpaper, costly.

'Can we afford this?' I asked.

'What do *you* think?' Mother said, and cut the wallpaper and stirred the paste at night and went to work during the day, she was working overtime, she went to evening classes and studied book-keeping and checked the accounts for fru Haraldsen, from whom Linda and I had had to hide in a fitting room on one occasion. Then she took over accounts, was put in charge of buying and worked longer hours. We were what everyone else in this country was, we were better off.

'It's as if it never happened,' Mother said

341

one evening at the end of October, coming down from the step-ladder and casting an eye over our new world, mumbling, in complete seriousness, that Linda had just been an angel that Our Lord had sent down to patch up her life, we had only had her on loan and should be grateful for the time we had spent together.

I looked at her and knew this was something I would never be able to forgive.

I plastered the walls of my room with pictures of English pop stars and spectacular planets, an unrecognisable orange horse and a blown-up aerial photo of Tonsen estate, the way it looked before we moved there, in the Fifties. The crane driver in the middle of the picture was my father doing his bit for the local community, invisible in the photograph and invisible in life, locked in a drawer with his daughter, now as invisible as he, standing on a beach with Boris and me and *without* a swimming belt.

I started Ungdomsskole the year The Doors sang 'When the Music's Over'. And Gymnas to the tones of Led Zeppelin. Where I met Boris again. We were in the same class doing maths and science and were still like two peas in a pod. But we didn't have quiffs any longer. We had shoulder-length hair, we wore battered military jackets, talked in code and were preparing for the revolution. We were what everyone else in this country was, we were better off.

30

The summer I was due to finish school, a letter arrived which I happened to get my mitts on before Mother. I sat looking at it for a while. Typed address and sender, whatever that was supposed to mean. Oslo post mark. An envelope which gave nothing away.

So why didn't I open it?

Because I was unable to decide which would be worse, terrible handwriting informing us about a tragedy, or a firm, steady hand telling us how everything had worked out fine. Either Linda had landed in a temple of horrors inhabited by idiots who abused and destroyed her. And that scenario tortures my soul. Or she emerged from a car to be welcomed by her new parents, a well-balanced mother and a perfect father, and of course, a boy of my age. She tightens her grasp around the mother's two fingers, the grasp that her new brother, let's call him Knut, immediately recognises as a grasp for life, one of the grasps that locks itself around your heart and holds it in a vice until you die and is still there as you lie rotting in your grave.

From then on everything goes the way it

should; the family lives on the first floor of a duplex, and Linda starts at a venerable old school in surroundings with more chestnut trees than people; she meets teachers who teach her what she needs to know and makes friends who don't have to look at her twice to see which frequency to communicate on. In the summer she goes on holiday with Knut and the parents, not in a fire-damaged tent but in a chalet out somewhere where there are lots of interesting activities with which Knut can give her a patient, helping hand. Knut turns out to be a great guy. He turns out to be better than me. So stealing her from us might have been the right option.

This scenario tortures my soul too.

There is nothing in between.

★ ★ ★

I left the letter unopened and went to see Freddy 1 who, after his parents had separated, lived more or less on his own in the old flat which we called the Eyrie, where I knew he and Dundas would be sniffing his solvent, Dundas with hair down to his waist and well set for a blossoming criminal career that would have been legendary but for the fact that his little body still survived on short-term tactics and had no long-term strategy. As usual, Freddy 1 was happy to see me, and said what he usually said on the rare occasions we met, that he would soon stop sniffing and would start at Gymnas as well.

'Or do you think I'm too stupid, Finn?'

'I don't think you're too stupid, Numero Uno,' I say to his broad grin and sit down and tell them I have received a letter from Linda.

'Do you remember Linda?'

'No,' Dundas says.

'Certainly do,' Freddy 1 says, and even brightens up.

'I need some advice,' I say, but I beat about the bush a fair bit before mentioning that I am wondering whether I should show the letter to my mother.

'Have you read it?' asks Freddy 1.

'No.'

We sit recalling this and that about Linda, trying also perhaps to revive those things that on the face of it do not seem open to being revived, until I get a kind of yes from Freddy 1, since Mother is the only cool woman in Traverveien, and a definitive no from Dundas who shivers narcotically and says that everything that has anything to do with childhood should remain buried.

'Tear it to pieces.'

★ ★ ★

It was hot that day. It would soon be the summer holidays, the beginning of another silence. I went out again, up Hagan to view the blocks of flats, my mountain range, to see if I could see anything. And I saw a childhood which had gone, and a childhood which would always be there, two worlds which had nothing to do with each other. Satisfied with that, I walked back home, to the letter which reminded me of all the other letters that had been received and read with so much fear and trembling in this flat.

* * *

Her handwriting was rounded and girlish and flawless and as steady as a rock, formed by a hand that at one time could lift not one but all the Mikado sticks from a kitchen table ablaze with hysteria. And she was fine. Yes, there was quite a bit to say about how fine she was.

But she pointed a kind of accusatory finger at us, in the shape of a concluding question, the same question I had asked myself several thousand times, but had never dared to ask Mother: why did we just let her go like that?

So, she hadn't suffered in any way — but how on earth could we be at peace with ourselves knowing someone had broken into our lives and stolen a childhood?

Then I remembered the time I was about to leave school in Sinsen, when Flintstone caught sight of me and called me one final time into that smoke-filled temple of his because, as he put it, he wished to share an observation with me.

'I have worked in this school since it was built,' he said with that yellow smile I still couldn't work out. 'And in the course of all these years I have never experienced anything like what you and that strange classmate of yours did when your sister was being bullied. Never.'

I had no idea where he was heading.

'It was quite unforgivable,' he said. 'You two almost killed the fellow.' After a short pause, he went on, 'Children don't do that kind of thing.'

'Eh?'

'Children don't stick up for each other in that way, not even siblings.'

He looked as if he had said something of great import. All the same, I was only able to repeat my perpetual 'eh?' And now he was beginning to become impatient.

'So perhaps that was not how it happened?'

'How what happened?'

'How you two set about him in order to stick up for your sister. *Could there have been something else at play?'*

At last I saw the light.

'You mean we just *felt* like beating him up?'

'For example.'

He had risen to his feet and stood waving a cigarette about.

'Yes, well, maybe,' I said obligingly, but with an old feeling I thought Linda had taken with her for good, because if Freddy 1 had not been wilder than me that evening, if he had not gone completely berserk, *I* would have done, and Dundas would have never got to his feet again. But this was not what Flintstone wanted to hear. And I was no longer sure of my motivation, that I had had it in me.

'Mhm, alright,' he said. 'Let's leave it at that then.'

★   ★   ★

I stayed on the balcony until I saw Mother rounding the corner of No. 2 in her new summer outfit, skirt and blouse and a short, light-coloured jacket — past the drying frame and up the flagstones to the front entrance, an elegant walk, purposeful and precise. There was still time to rush in and remove the letter. But I stayed put until I heard the key in the door, and, soon after, her voice inside the flat:

'Haven't you put on the potatoes?'

'No,' I called back. 'We've got a letter. It's on the kitchen table.'

There was a long silence. Eventually she came out onto the balcony with the letter in one hand and a cup of coffee in the other and sat down on the camp chair, resting her feet on the stool I used to stand on when I washed up as a child. She had been to the bathroom and had removed her makeup, and perhaps not just that, for she had long since stopped hiding her tears — she was an attractive, successful woman with a patched-up childhood, the branch manager with her books balanced, all her life balanced, seen from the distant perspective of a lodger.

'Thank goodness,' she said with her eyes on the letter.

'Are you going to answer it?' I asked when nothing else was forthcoming.

'Of course.'

'I mean — are you going to answer her question?'

'Of course,' she repeated. And read the letter once more.

'And what are you going to say?'

She looked up, but not at me.

'She would have been alright here, too,' she said thoughtfully. 'But I didn't know that at the time. I suppose, maybe, that's why I didn't do anything . . . '

'So it was *alright* that they came and took her?'

'I didn't say that,' she answered as I got up and clenched my fists around the balcony railing and stared over to Essi's mountain. 'Our case simply wasn't good enough, you see.'

I turned. And now she did look at me. 'They knew everything about us.'

'Eh?'

Again this expression she adopts when I don't understand the obvious.

'The lodger?' I asked. I did understand after all. 'Because you refused to marry him?'

She nodded evasively.

'I don't know for sure, but . . . '

She paused. 'I tried to find her once.'

'Without telling me?'

'You were just a child, Finn.'

I considered whether I had ever been a child and noted that neither of us had called the lodger by his right name since he left us, and in fact I had known all along. Kristian, the tram conductor and seaman, toolmaker, construction worker and trade union man, tent owner and wear-and-tear philosopher in a poplin mac, was so full of tales I should never have been in any doubt.

'You liked him, didn't you?' Mother asked.

351

'I don't know.'

'You tried anyway.'

I suppose I did do my best, yes, for her sake. And now I felt I could either do the same as she did, nod with a kind of satisfaction that everything had gone well for Linda and leave it at that, or I could go into my room and smash the microscope and chop up the chess board. But I couldn't do either.

'I think *you* should write,' she said. 'You're the clever one after all.'

'And tell her it didn't matter that they took her away?' I sniped and regretted it instantly. 'Of course,' I corrected myself. 'Of course I'll write.'

'Let's do it right now,' she said and got up to fetch a pen and paper.

For a while I stood looking down at her coffee cup which she had placed like a paperweight on Linda's letter, so that the wind wouldn't catch it, the final acquittal, I suppose that was how Mother viewed it, then I stared into Essi's mountain, without averting my eyes, wondering if I was really ready to find out whether I had it in me, whether I had ever had it in me.

80003512406

SPECIAL ██████████████████████ EADERS

THE ULVERSCROFT FOUNDATION
(registered UK charity number 264873)
was established in 1972 to provide funds for
research, diagnosis and treatment of eye diseases.
Examples of major projects funded by
the Ulverscroft Foundation are:-

- The Children's Eye Unit at Moorfields Eye Hospital, London
- The Ulverscroft Children's Eye Unit at Great Ormond Street Hospital for Sick Children
- Funding research into eye diseases and treatment at the Department of Ophthalmology, University of Leicester
- The Ulverscroft Vision Research Group, Institute of Child Health
- Twin operating theatres at the Western Ophthalmic Hospital, London
- The Chair of Ophthalmology at the Royal Australian College of Ophthalmologists

You can help further the work of the Foundation
by making a donation or leaving a legacy.
Every contribution is gratefully received. If you
would like to help support the Foundation or
require further information, please contact:

THE ULVERSCROFT FOUNDATION
The Green, Bradgate Road, Anstey
Leicester LE7 7FU, England
Tel: (0116) 236 4325

DISCARDED

website: www.foundation.ulverscroft.com

Roy Jacobsen is a Norwegian novelist and short-story writer. Born in Oslo, he made his publishing debut in 1982 with the short story collection *Fangeliv* (Prison Life). He is a winner of the prestigious Norwegian Critics Prize for Literature.